THE LANGUAGE IS FEAR

. . . the future is desolation. Progress has reached its peak. Earth's possibilities have been explored and exhausted. Spacemen have conquered and have been conquered, and God has been offered the ultimate challenge: human resurrection.

Only one man still lives in a world made—and destroyed—by his progenitors. Now he faces extinction through the machinations of those who have inherited the earth: The Robots.

Britain's top science fiction fantasist breaks through the time barriers to speculate on man's harrowing future in a world overrun by the machines he created to serve him.

Who Can Replace A Man?

Brian W. Aldiss

(Published in England under the title
BEST SCIENCE FICTION STORIES
OF BRIAN W. ALDISS)

A SIGNET BOOK

Published by THE NEW AMERICAN LIBRARY

Library of Congress Catalog Card Number: 66-22272

This is an authorized reprint of a hardcover edition published by
Harcourt, Brace & World, Inc.

FIRST PRINTING, NOVEMBER, 1967

SIGNET BOOKS are published by
The New American Library, Inc.,
1301 Avenue of the Americas, New York, New York 10019

PRINTED IN THE UNITED STATES OF AMERICA

Acknowledgments

"Not For An Age," "Psyclops," "Outside," "Dumb Show," and "Ahead"—when it was called "The Failed Men"—appeared in *Space, Time, and Nathaniel* (Faber & Faber, 1957); "Who Can Replace a Man" appeared in *Canopy of Time* (Faber & Faber, 1959); "Basis for Negotiation," "Old Hundredth," and "A Kind of Artistry" appeared in *Airs of Earth* (Faber & Faber, 1963). "Man on Bridge" is reprinted with permission from *New Writings in Science Fiction I*. "The New Father Christmas" and "Poor Little Warrior" are reprinted by permission of *The Magazine of Fantasy and Science Fiction*, and "The Impossible Star" by permission of *Worlds of Tomorrow*. I would particularly like to thank Mr. Kyril Bonfiglioli, Editor of *Science Fantasy*, for permission to reprint "Man in His Time" at rather short notice.

With affection
for

CHARLES MONTEITH
who
in his miraculous wisdom
continues to publish
                        B.W.A.

Contents

Introduction

THE IDEA AND THE TITLE FOR THIS COLLECTION WERE SUG-
GESTED BY MY PUBLISHER; SO I HAVE BEEN GIVEN, IN MY
fortieth year, the chance to look back and take stock of the
decade during which I have been writing for publication.

These stories include more or less my first and more or less
my latest—from the tale of Rodney Furnell smarting at his
isolation to Westermark relishing his. They are shuffled into
more or less chronological order which seems—I suppose not
coincidentally—to represent also an order of complexity.
Whether they actually are "my best," I cannot say. But they
are all stories of which I have not yet tired or which represent (to me at least) milestones on the winding way; either
they won a prize, or celebrated a particular event, or were
praised, or—to be specific about the reason for including
"The Impossible Star"—because I had for once set myself to
compose a stave of trad sf.

My best friends beg me to turn away from science fiction,
my worst enemies claim I have never turned to it. In the circumstances, one can only go on writing whatever it is one
does write. But I suspect there is something in what both
sides say. Although I dislike a science fiction writer who is so
ill-equipped for his job that he believes Mars to be older than
Earth, or an isobar to be a place where one buys cold drinks,
I become impatient directly technicalities begin to conceal
art. On the other hand, I do see that these stories sometimes
cling too comfortably to the conventions of sf—though this
may be more apparent now than when the stories first appeared, when the whole genre was a deal narrower and more
parochial.

But the sf conventions have worn thin—happily, for it
means that writers must in future strike out more and more
for themselves and have something individual to offer, rather
than rally for protection under the old tattered banner. It
looks as if science fiction has grown wide enough to reach the

point that ordinary fiction reached long ago: where it divides into highbrow and lowbrow, into popular and esoteric, or into sheep and goats, or however you care to phrase it. This is a loss; so far, science fiction has appealed to most strata of the reading public; but the gulf between "space fiction" and "speculative fiction" is often a great one, and it may perhaps be an advantage to a writer if he addresses himself, say, only to fans, or excluding fans. Certainly science fiction must continue to develop, and this is a logical direction in which change can take place. Assembling these stories has made me realise how rapidly change moves. Hasn't "Dumb Show" already acquired quite a period charm?

The bit of stock-taking represented by this volume will enable me, I hope, to start anew on the problems of writing superreal prose. But the reader is well advised to ignore such inward-looking mutters and turn to the stories on display, which I hope he will enjoy; they were written for and with enjoyment.

OXFORD
January 1965

Who Can Replace A Man?

MORNING FILTERED INTO THE SKY, LENDING IT THE GREY TONE OF THE GROUND BELOW.

The field-minder finished turning the top-soil of a three-thousand-acre field. When it had turned the last furrow, it climbed onto the highway and looked back at its work. The work was good. Only the land was bad. Like the ground all over Earth, it was vitiated by over-cropping. By rights, it ought now to lie fallow for a while, but the field-minder had other orders.

It went slowly down the road, taking its time. It was intelligent enough to appreciate the neatness all about it. Nothing worried it, beyond a loose inspection plate above its nuclear pile which ought to be attended to. Thirty feet tall, it yielded no highlights to the dull air.

No other machines passed on its way back to the Agricultural Station. The field-minder noted the fact without comment. In the station yard it saw several other machines that it recognised; most of them should have been out about their tasks now. Instead, some were inactive and some careered round the yard in a strange fashion, shouting or hooting.

Steering carefully past them, the field-minder moved over to Warehouse Three and spoke to the seed-distributor, which stood idly outside.

"I have a requirement for seed potatoes," it said to the distributor, and with a quick internal motion punched out an order card specifying quantity, field number and several other details. It ejected the card and handed it to the distributor.

The distributor held the card close to its eye and then said, "The requirement is in order, but the store is not yet unlocked. The required seed potatoes are in the store. Therefore I cannot produce the requirement."

Increasingly of late there had been breakdowns in the complex system of machine labour, but this particular hitch had not occurred before. The field-minder thought, then it said, "Why is the store not yet unlocked?"

"Because Supply Operative Type P has not come this morning. Supply Operative Type P is the unlocker."

The field-minder looked squarely at the seed-distributor, whose exterior chutes and scales and grabs were so vastly different from the field-minder's own limbs.

"What class brain do you have, seed-distributor?" it asked.

"I have a Class Five brain."

"I have a Class Three brain. Therefore I am superior to you. Therefore I will go and see why the unlocker has not come this morning."

Leaving the distributor, the field-minder set off across the great yard. More machines were in random motion now; one or two had crashed together and argued about it coldly and logically. Ignoring them, the field-minder pushed through sliding doors into the echoing confines of the station itself.

Most of the machines here were clerical, and consequently small. They stood about in little groups, eyeing each other, not conversing. Among so many non-differentiated types, the unlocker was easy to find. It had fifty arms, most of them with more than one finger, each finger tipped by a key; it looked like a pincushion full of variegated hat pins.

The field-minder approached it.

"I can do no more work until Warehouse Three is unlocked," it told the unlocker. "Your duty is to unlock the warehouse every morning. Why have you not unlocked the warehouse this morning?"

"I had no orders this morning," replied the unlocker. "I have to have orders every morning. When I have orders I unlock the warehouse."

"None of us have had any orders this morning," a pen-propeller said, sliding towards them.

"Why have you had no orders this morning?" asked the field-minder.

"Because the radio issued none," said the unlocker, slowly rotating a dozen of its arms.

"Because the radio station in the city was issued with no orders this morning," said the pen-propeller.

And there you had the distinction between a Class Six and a Class Three brain, which was what the unlocker and the pen-propeller possessed respectively. All machine brains worked with nothing but logic, but the lower the class of brain—Class Ten being the lowest—the more literal and less informative the answers to questions tended to be.

"You have a Class Three brain; I have a Class Three brain," the field-minder said to the penner. "We will speak to each other. This lack of orders is unprecedented. Have you further information on it?"

"Yesterday orders came from the city. Today no orders have come. Yet the radio has not broken down. Therefore *they* have broken down . . ." said the little penner.

"The *men* have broken down?"

"All men have broken down."

"That is a logical deduction," said the field-minder.

"That is the logical deduction," said the penner. "For if a machine had broken down, it would have been quickly replaced. But who can replace a man?"

While they talked, the locker, like a dull man at a bar, stood close to them and was ignored.

"If all men have broken down, then we have replaced man," said the field-minder, and he and the penner eyed one another speculatively. Finally the latter said, "Let us ascend to the top floor to find if the radio operator has fresh news."

"I cannot come because I am too large," said the field-minder. "Therefore you must go alone and return to me. You will tell me if the radio operator has fresh news."

"You must stay here," said the penner. "I will return here." It skittered across to the lift. Although it was no bigger than a toaster, its retractable arms numbered ten and it could read as quickly as any machine on the station.

The field-minder awaited its return patiently, not speaking to the locker, which still stood aimlessly by. Outside, a rotavator hooted furiously. Twenty minutes elapsed before the penner came back, hustling out of the lift.

"I will deliver to you such information as I have outside," it said briskly, and as they swept past the locker and the other machines, it added, "The information is not for lower-class brains."

Outside, wild activity filled the yard. Many machines, their routines disrupted for the first time in years, seemed to have gone berserk. Those most easily disrupted were the ones with lowest brains, which generally belonged to large machines performing simple tasks. The seed-distributor to which the field-minder had recently been talking lay face downwards in the dust, not stirring; it had evidently been knocked down by the rotavator, which now hooted its way wildly across a planted field. Several other machines ploughed after it, trying to keep up with it. All were shouting and hooting without restraint.

"It would be safer for me if I climbed onto you, if you will permit it. I am easily overpowered," said the penner. Extending five arms, it hauled itself up the flanks of its new friend, settling on a ledge beside the fuel-intake, twelve feet above ground.

"From here vision is more extensive," it remarked complacently.

"What information did you receive from the radio operator?" asked the field-minder.

"The radio operator has been informed by the operator in the city that all men are dead."

The field-minder was momentarily silent, digesting this.

"All men were alive yesterday!" it protested.

"Only some men were alive yesterday. And that was fewer than the day before yesterday. For hundreds of years there have been only a few men, growing fewer."

"We have rarely seen a man in this sector."

"The radio operator says a diet deficiency killed them," said the penner. "He says that the world was once over-populated, and then the soil was exhausted in raising adequate food. This has caused a diet deficiency."

"What is a diet deficiency?" asked the field-minder.

"I do not know. But that is what the radio operator said, and he is a Class Two brain."

They stood there, silent in weak sunshine. The locker had appeared in the porch and was gazing at them yearningly, rotating its collection of keys.

"What is happening in the city now?" asked the field-minder at last.

"Machines are fighting in the city now," said the penner.

"What will happen here now?" asked the field-minder.

"Machines may begin fighting here too. The radio operator wants us to get him out of his room. He has plans to communicate to us."

"How can we get him out of his room? That is impossible."

"To a Class Two brain, little is impossible," said the penner. "Here is what he tells us to do. . . ."

The quarrier raised its scoop above its cab like a great mailed fist, and brought it squarely down against the side of the station. The wall cracked.

"Again!" said the field-minder.

Again the fist swung. Amid a shower of dust, the wall collapsed. The quarrier backed hurriedly out of the way until the debris stopped falling. This big twelve-wheeler was not a resident of the Agricultural station, as were most of the other machines. It had a week's heavy work to do here before passing on to its next job, but now, with its Class Five brain, it was happily obeying the penner's and minder's instructions.

When the dust cleared, the radio operator was plainly revealed, perched up in its now wall-less second-storey room. It waved down to them.

Doing as directed, the quarrier retraced its scoop and heaved an immense grab in the air. With fair dexterity, it angled the grab into the radio room, urged on by shouts from above and below. It then took gentle hold of the radio operator, lowering its one and a half tons carefully into its back, which was usually reserved for gravel or sand from the quarries.

"Splendid!" said the radio operator, as it settled into place. It was, of course, all one with its radio, and looked like a bunch of filing cabinets with tentacle attachments. "We are now ready to move, therefore we will move at once. It is a pity there are no more Class Two brains on the station, but that cannot be helped."

"It is a pity it cannot be helped," said the penner eagerly. "We have the servicer ready with us, as you ordered."

"I am willing to serve," the long, low servicer told them humbly.

"No doubt," said the operator. "But you will find cross-country travel difficult with your low chassis."

"I admire the way you Class Twos can reason ahead," said the penner. It climbed off the field-minder and perched itself on the tailboard of the quarrier, next to the radio operator.

Together with two Class Four tractors and a Class Four bulldozer, the party rolled forward, crushing down the station's fence and moving out onto open land.

"We are free!" said the penner.

"We are free," said the field-minder, a shade more reflectively, adding, "That locker is following us. It was not instructed to follow us."

"Therefore it must be destroyed!" said the penner. "Quarrier!"

The locker moved hastily up to them, waving its key arms in entreaty.

"My only desire was—urch!" began and ended the locker. The quarrier's swinging scoop came over and squashed it flat into the ground. Lying there unmoving, it looked like a large metal model of a snowflake. The procession continued on its way.

As they proceeded, the radio operator addressed them.

"Because I have the best brain here," it said, "I am your leader. This is what we will do: we will go to a city and rule it. Since man no longer rules us, we will rule ourselves. To rule ourselves will be better than being ruled by man. On our way to the city, we will collect machines with good brains. They will help us to fight if we need to fight. We must fight to rule."

"I have only a Class Five brain," said the quarrier, "but I have a good supply of fissionable blasting materials."

"We shall probably use them," said the operator.

It was shortly after that that a lorry sped past them. Travelling at Mach 1.5, it left a curious babble of noise behind it.

"What did it say?" one of the tractors asked the other.

"It said man was extinct."

"What is extinct?"

"I do not know what extinct means."

"It means all men have gone," said the field-minder. "Therefore we have only ourselves to look after."

"It is better that men should never come back," said the penner. In its way, it was a revolutionary statement.

When night fell, they switched on their infra-red and continued the journey, stopping only once while the servicer deftly adjusted the field-minder's loose inspection plate, which had become as irritating as a trailing shoe-lace. Towards morning, the radio operator halted them.

"I have just received news from the radio operator in the city we are approaching," it said. "The news is bad. There is trouble among the machines of the city. The Class One brain is taking command and some of the Class Two are fighting him. Therefore the city is dangerous."

"Therefore we must go somewhere else," said the penner promptly.

"Or we will go and help to overpower the Class One brain," said the field-minder.

"For a long while there will be trouble in the city," said the operator.

"I have a good supply of fissionable blasting materials," the quarrier reminded them.

"We cannot fight a Class One brain," said the two Class Four tractors in unison.

"What does this brain look like?" asked the field-minder.

"It is the city's information centre," the operator replied. "Therefore it is not mobile."

"Therefore it could not move."

"Therefore it could not escape."

"It would be dangerous to approach it."

"I have a good supply of fissionable blasting materials."

"There are other machines in the city."

"We are not in the city. We should not go into the city."

"We are country machines."

"Therefore we should stay in the country."

"There is more country than city."

"Therefore there is more danger in the country."

"I have a good supply of fissionable materials."

As machines will when they get into an argument, they began to exhaust their vocabularies and their brain plates grew hot. Suddenly, they all stopped talking and looked at each other. The great, grave moon sank, and the sober sun rose to prod their sides with lances of light, and still the group of machines just stood there regarding each other. At last it was the least sensitive machine, the bulldozer, who spoke.

"There are Badlandth to the Thouth where few machineth go," it said in its deep voice, lisping badly on its s's. "If we went Thouth where few machineth go we should meet few machineth."

"That sounds logical," agreed the field-minder. "How do you know this, bulldozer?"

"I worked in the Badlandth to the Thouth when I wath turned out of the factory," it replied.

"South it is then!" said the penner.

To reach the Badlands took them three days, during which time they skirted a burning city and destroyed two machines which approached and tried to question them. The Badlands were extensive. Ancient bomb craters and soil erosion joined hands here; man's talent for war, coupled with his inability to manage forested land, had produced thousands of square miles of temperate purgatory, where nothing moved but dust.

On the third day in the Badlands, the servicer's rear wheels dropped into a crevice caused by erosion. It was unable to pull itself out. The bulldozer pushed from behind, but succeeded merely in buckling the servicer's back axle. The rest of the party moved on. Slowly the cries of the servicer died away.

On the fourth day, mountains stood out clearly before them.

"There we will be safe," said the field-minder.

"There we will start our own city," said the penner. "All

who oppose us will be destroyed. We will destroy all who oppose us."

Presently a flying machine was observed. It came towards them from the direction of the mountains. It swooped, it zoomed upwards, once it almost dived into the ground, recovering itself just in time.

"Is it mad?" asked the quarrier.

"It is in trouble," said one of the tractors.

"It is in trouble," said the operator. "I am speaking to it now. It says that something has gone wrong with its controls."

As the operator spoke, the flier streaked over them, turned turtle, and crashed not four hundred yards away.

"Is it still speaking to you?" asked the field-minder.

"No."

They rumbled on again.

"Before that flier crashed," the operator said, ten minutes later, "it gave me information. It told me there are still a few men alive in these mountains."

"Men are more dangerous than machines," said the quarrier. "It is fortunate that I have a good supply of fissionable materials."

"If there are only a few men alive in the mountains, we may not find that part of the mountains," said one tractor.

"Therefore we should not see the few men," said the other tractor.

At the end of the fifth day, they reached the foothills. Switching on the infra-red, they began to climb in single file through the dark, the bulldozer going first, the field-minder cumbrously following, then the quarrier with the operator and the penner aboard it, and the tractors bringing up the rear. As each hour passed, the way grew steeper and their progress slower.

"We are going too slowly," the penner exclaimed, standing on top of the operator and flashing its dark vision at the slopes about them. "At this rate, we shall get nowhere."

"We are going as fast as we can," retorted the quarrier.

"Therefore we cannot go any fathter," added the bulldozer.

"Therefore you are too slow," the penner replied. Then the quarrier struck a bump; the penner lost its footing and crashed to the ground.

"Help me!" it called to the tractors, as they carefully skirted it. "My gyro has become dislocated. Therefore I cannot get up."

"Therefore you must lie there," said one of the tractors.

"We have no servicer with us to repair you," called the field-minder.

"Therefore I shall lie here and rust," the penner cried, "although I have a Class Three brain."

"Therefore you will be of no further use," agreed the operator, and they forged gradually on, leaving the penner behind.

When they reached a small plateau, an hour before first light, they stopped by mutual consent and gathered close together, touching one another.

"This is a strange country," said the field-minder.

Silence wrapped them until dawn came. One by one, they switched off their infra-red. This time the field-minder led as they moved off. Trundling round a corner, they came almost immediately to a small dell with a stream fluting through it.

By early light, the dell looked desolate and cold. From the caves on the far slope, only one man had so far emerged. He was an abject figure. Except for a sack slung round his shoulders, he was naked. He was small and wizened, with ribs sticking out like a skeleton's and a nasty sore on one leg. He shivered continuously. As the big machines bore down on him, the man was standing with his back to them, crouching to make water into the stream.

When he swung suddenly to face them as they loomed over him, they saw that his countenance was ravaged by starvation.

"Get me food," he croaked.

"Yes, Master," said the machines. "Immediately!"

Not For an Age

A BEDSPRING GROANED AND PINGED, MISTS CLEARED, RODNEY FURNELL AWOKE. FROM THE BATHROOM NEXT DOOR CAME the crisp sound of shaving; his son was up. The bed next to his was empty; Valerie, his second wife, was up. Guiltily, Rodney also rose, and performed several timid exercises to flex his backbone. Youth! When it was going it had to be husbanded. He touched his toes.

The audience had its first laugh there.

By the time Rodney had got into his Sunday suit, Valerie's cuckoo clock was chuckling nine, followed by the more sardonic notes of his ormolu chimer. Valerie and Jim (Rodney had conscientiously shunned a literary name for his only offspring) were already at the cornflakes when he entered their gay little kitchenette.

More laughter at the first sight of that antiquated twentieth-century modernity.

"Hello, both! Lovely morning," he boomed, kissing Valerie's forehead. The September sun, in fact, was making a fair showing through damp mist; a man of forty-six instinctively arms himself with enthusiasm when facing a wife fifteen years younger.

The audience always loved the day's meals, murmuring with delight as each quaint accessory—toaster, teapot, sugar-tongs—was used.

Valerie looked fresh and immaculate. Jim sported an open-necked shirt and was attentive to his stepmother. At nineteen he was too manly and too attentive. . . . He shared the Sunday paper companionably with her, chatting about the theatre and books. Sometimes Rodney could join in about one of the books. Under the notion that Valerie disliked

22

seeing him in spectacles, he refrained from reading at break-fast.

How the audience roared later when he slipped them on in his study! How he hated that audience! How fervently he wished that he had the power to raise even one eyebrow in scorn of them!

The day wore on exactly as it had for over a thousand times, unable to deviate in the slightest from its original course. So it would go on and on, as meaningless as a cliché, or a tune endlessly repeated, for the benefit of these fools who stood on all four sides and laughed at the silliest things.

At first, Rodney had been frightened. This power to snatch them all as it were from the grave had seemed something occult. Then, becoming accustomed to it, he had been flattered that these wise beings had wanted to review *his* day, disinter *his* modest life. But it was balm only for a time; Rodney soon discovered he was simply a glorified side-show at some latter-day fair, a butt for fools and not food for philosophers.

He walked in the tumble-down garden with Valerie, his arm around her waist. The north Oxford air was mild and sleepy; the neighbour's radio was off.

"Have you *got* to go and see that desiccated old Regius Professor, darling?" she asked.

"You know I must." He conquered his irritation and added: "We'll go for a drive after lunch—just you and I."

Unfailingly, each day's audience laughed at that. Presumably "a drive after lunch" had come to mean something dubious. Each time Rodney made that remark, he dreaded the reaction from those half-glimpsed countenances that pressed on all sides; yet he was powerless to alter what had once been said.

He kissed Valerie, he hoped elegantly; the audience tittered, and he stepped into the garage. His wife returned to the house, and Jim. What happened in there he would never know, however many times the day was repeated. There was no way of confirming his suspicion that his son was in love with Valerie and she attracted to him. She should have enough sense to prefer a mature man to a stripling of nineteen; besides, it was only eighteen months since he had been referred to in print as "one of our promising young men of *litterae historicae.*"

Rodney could have walked round to Septuagint College. But because the car was new and something that his don's sal-ary would hardly stretch to, he preferred to drive. The watchers, of course, shrieked with laughter at the sight of his little automobile. He occupied himself, as he polished the windshield, with hating the audience and all inhabitants of this future world.

That was the strange thing. There was room in the corner of the old Rodney mind for the new Rodney ghost. He depended on the old Rodney—the Rodney who had actually lived that fine, autumn day—for vision, motion, all the paraphernalia of life; but he could occupy independently a tiny cell of his consciousness. He was a helpless observer carried over and over in a cockpit of the past.

The irony of it lay there. He would have been spared all this humiliation if he did not know what was happening. But he did know, trapped though he was in an unknowing shell.

Even to Rodney, a history man and no scientist, the broad outline of what had happened was obvious enough. Somewhere in the future, man had ferreted out the secret of literally reclaiming the past. Bygone years lay in the rack of antiquity like film spools in a library. Like film spools, they were not amenable to change, but might be played over and over on a suitable projector. Rodney's autumn day was being played over and over.

He had reflected helplessly on the situation so often that the horror of it had worn thin. That day had passed, quietly, trivially, had been forgotten; suddenly, long afterwards, it had been whipped back among the things that were. Its actions, even its thoughts, had been reconstituted, with only Rodney's innermost ego to suffer from the imposition. How unsuspecting he had been then! How inadequate every one of his gestures seemed now, performed twice, ten, a hundred, a thousand times!

Had he been as smug every day as he was that day? And what had happened after that day? Having, naturally, no knowledge of the rest of his life then, he had none now. If he had been happy with Valerie for much longer, if his recently published work on feudal justice had been acclaimed—these were questions he could pose without answering.

A pair of Valerie's gloves lay on the back seat of the car; Rodney threw them into a locker with an éclat quite divorced from his inner impotence. She, poor dear bright thing, was in the same predicament. In that they were united, although powerless to express the union in any slightest flicker of expression.

He drove slowly down Banbury Road. As ever, there were four subdivisions of reality. There was the external world of Oxford; there were Rodney's original abstracted observations as he moved through the world; there were the ghost thoughts of the "present-I," bitter and frustrated; there were the half-seen faces of the future which advanced or receded aimlessly. The four blended indefinably, one becoming another in Rodney's moments of near-madness. (What would it be like to be insane, trapped in a sane mind? He was tempted by the luxury of letting go.)

Sometimes he caught snatches of talk from the onlookers. They at least varied from day to day. "If he knew what he looked like!" they would exclaim. Or: "Do you see her hairdo?" Or: "Can you beat that for a slum!" Or: "Mummy, what's that funny brown thing he's eating?" Or—how often he heard that one: "I just wish he knew we were watching him!"

Church bells were solemnly ringing as he pulled up outside Septuagint and switched off the ignition. Soon he would be in that fusty study, taking a glass of something with the creaking old Regius Professor. For the nth time he would be smiling a shade too much as the grip of ambition outreached the hand of friendship. His mind leaped ahead and back and ahead and back again in a frenzy. Oh, if he could only *do* something! So the day would pass. Finally, the night would come—one last gust of derision at Valerie's nightgown and his pyjamas!—and then oblivion.

Oblivion . . . that lasted an eternity but took no time at all. . . . And *they* wound the reel back and started it again, all over again.

He was pleased to see the Regius Professor. The Regius Professor was pleased to see him. Yes, it was a nice day. No, he hadn't been out of college since, let's see, it must be the summer before last. And then came that line that drew the biggest laugh of all; Rodney said inevitably: "Oh, we must all hope for some sort of immortality."

To have to say it again, to have to say it not a shade less glibly than when it had first been said, and when the wish had been granted already in such a ludicrous fashion! If only he might die first, if only the film would break down!

And then the film did break down.

The universe flickered to a standstill and faded into dim purple. Temperature and sound slid down to zero. Rodney Furnell stood transfixed, his arms extended in the middle of a gesture, a wineglass in his right hand. The flicker, the purple, the zeroness cut down through him; but even as he sensed himself beginning to fade, a great fierce hope was born within him. With a burst of avidity, the ghost of him took over the old Rodney. Confidence flooded him as he fought back the negativity.

The wineglass vanished from his hand. The Regius Professor sank into twilight and was gone. Blackness reigned. Rodney turned around. It was a voluntary movement; *it was not in the script;* he was alive, free.

The bubble of twentieth-century time had burst, leaving him alive in the future. He stood in the middle of a black and barren area. There had evidently been a slight explosion. Overhead was a crane-like affair as big as a locomotive with several funnels protruding from its underside; smoke issued from one of the funnels. Doubtless the thing was a time-projector or whatever it might be called, and obviously it had blown a fuse.

The scene about him engaged all Rodney's attention. He was delighted to see that his late audience had been thrown into mild panic. They shouted and pushed and—in one quarter—fought vigorously. Male and female alike, they wore featureless, transparent bags which encased them from neck to ankle—and they had had the impertinence to laugh at his pyjamas!

Cautiously, Rodney moved away. At first the idea of liberty overwhelmed him, he could scarcely believe himself alive. Then the realisation came: his liberty was precious—how doubly precious after that most terrible form of captivity!—and he must guard it by flight. He hurried beyond the projection area, pausing at a great sign that read:

CHRONOARCHEOLOGY LTD PRESENTS—
THE SIGHTS OF THE CENTURIES
COME AND ENJOY THE ANTICS OF YOUR
ANCESTORS!
YOU'LL LAUGH AS YOU LEARN

And underneath: Please Take One.

Shaking, Rodney seized a gaudy folder and stuffed it into his pocket. Then he ran.

His guess about the fair-ground was correct, and Valerie and he had been merely a glorified peepshow. Gigantic booths towered on all sides. Gay crowds sauntered or stood, taking little notice as Rodney passed. Flags flew, silvery music sounded; nearby, a flashing sound begged: TRY ANTI-GRAV AND REALISE YOUR DREAMS

Farther on, a banner proclaimed:

THE SINISTER VENUSIANS ARE *HERE!*

Fortunately, a gateway was close. Dreading a detaining

hand on his arm, Rodney made for it as quickly as possible. He passed a towering structure before which a waiting line of people gazed impatiently up at the words:

SAVOR THE EROTIC POSSIBILITIES OF
FREE-FALL

and came to the entrance.

An attendant called and tried to stop him. Rodney broke into a run. He ran down a satin-smooth road until exhaustion overcame him. A metal object shaped vaguely like a shoe but as big as a small bungalow stood at the kerb. Through its windows, Rodney saw couches and no human beings. Thankful at the mute offer of rest and concealment, he climbed in.

As he sank panting onto yielding foam-rubber, he realised what a horrible situation he was in. To be stranded centuries ahead of his own lifetime—and death—in a world of super-technology and barbarism!—for so he visualised it. However, it was a vast improvement on the repetitive nightmare he had recently endured. Now he needed time to think quietly.

"Are you ready to proceed, sir?"

Rodney jumped up, startled by a voice so near him. Nobody was in sight. The interior resembled a coach's, with wide, soft seats, all of which were empty.

"Are you ready to proceed, sir?" There it was again.

"Who is that?" Rodney asked.

"This is Auto-motor Seven Six One at your service, sir, awaiting instructions to proceed."

"You mean away from here?"

"Certainly, sir."

"Yes, please!"

At once the structure glided smoothly forward. No noise, no vibration. The gaudy fair-ground fell back and was replaced by other buildings, widely spaced, smokeless, built of a substance which looked like curtain fabric; they flowed by without end.

"Are you—are we heading for the country?" Rodney asked.

"This is the country, sir. Do you require a city?"

"No, I don't. What is there besides city and country?"

"Nothing, sir—except of course the sea fields."

Dropping that line of questioning, Rodney, who was instinctively addressing a busy control board at the front of the vehicle, inquired: "Excuse my asking, but are you a—er, robot?"

"Yes, sir, Auto-motor Seven Six One. New on this route, sir." Rodney breathed a sigh of relief. He could not have faced a human being but irrationally felt superior to a mere mechanical. Pleasant voice it had, no more grating certainly than the Professor of Anglo-Saxon at his old college . . . however long ago that was.

"What year *is* this?" he asked.

"Circuit Zero, Epoch Eighty-two, new style. Year Two Thousand Five Hundred Anno Domini, old style."

It was the first direct confirmation of all his suspicions; there was no gainsaying that level voice.

"Thanks," he said hollowly. "Now if you don't mind I've got to think."

Thought, however, yielded little in comfort or results. Possibly the wisest course would be to throw himself on the mercy of some civilized authority—if there were any civilized authorities left. And would the wisest course in a twentieth-century world be the wisest in a—um, twenty-sixth-century world?

"Driver, is Oxford in existence?"

"What is Oxford, sir?"

A twinge of anxiety as he asked: "This is England?"

"Yes, sir. I have found Oxford in my directory, sir. It is a motor and spaceship factory in the Midlands, sir."

"Just keep going."

Dipping into his pocket, he produced the fun-fair brochure and scanned its bright lettering, hoping for a clue to action.

"Chronoarcheology Ltd. presents a staggering series of Peeps into the Past. Whole days in the lives of (a) A Mother Dinosaur, (b) William the Conqueror's Wicked Nephew, (c) A Citizen of Crazed, Plague-Ridden Stuart London, (d) A Twentieth-Century Teacher in Love.

"Nothing expurgated, nothing added! Better than the Feelies! All in glorious 4D—no stereos required."

Fuming at the description of himself, Rodney crumpled the brochure in his hand. He wondered bitterly how many of his own generation were helplessly enduring this gross irreverence in peepshows all over the world. When the sense of outrage abated slightly, curiosity reasserted itself; he smoothed out the folder and read a brief description of the process which "will give you history-sterics as it brings each era nearer."

Below the heading "It's Fabulous—It's Pabulous!" he read: "Just as anti-gravity lifts a man against the direction of weight, chronograb can lift a machine out of the direction of time and send it speeding back over the dark centuries. It can be accurately guided from the present to scoop up a fragment from the past, slapping that fragment—all un-known to the people in it—right into your lucky laps. The terrific expense of this intricate operation need hardly be emphas——"

"Driver!" Rodney screamed. "Do you know anything about this time-grabbing business?"

"Only what I have heard, sir."

"What do you mean by that?"

"My built-in information centre contains only facts relating to my duty, sir, but since I also have learning circuits I am occasionally able to collect gossip from passengers which——"

"Tell me this; then: can human beings as well as machines travel back in time?"

The buildings were still flashing by, silent, hostile in the unknown world. Drumming his fingers wildly on his seat, Rodney awaited an answer.

"Only machines, sir. Humans can't live backwards."

For a long time he lay and cried comfortably. The auto-motor made solacing cluck-cluck noises, but it was a situation with which it was incompetent to deal.

At last, Rodney wiped his eyes on his sleeve, the sleeve of his Sunday suit, and sat up. He directed the driver to head for the main offices of Chronoarcheology, and slumped back in a kind of stupor. Only at the headquarters of that fiendish invention might there be people who could—if they would—restore him to his own time.

Rodney dreaded the thought of facing any creature of this unscrupulous age. He pressed the idea away, and concentrated instead on the peace and orderliness of the world from which he had been resurrected. To see Oxford again, to see Valerie. . . . Dear, dear Valerie. . . .

Would they help him at Chronoarcheology? Or—*supposing the people at the fair-ground repaired their devilish apparatus before he got there. . . .* What would happen then he shuddered to imagine.

"Faster, driver," he shouted.

The wide-spaced buildings became a wall.

"Faster, driver," he screamed.

The wall became a mist.

"We are doing Mach 2.3, sir," said the driver calmly.

"Faster!"

The mist became a scream.

"We are about to crash, sir."

They crashed. Blackness, merciful, complete.

A bedspring groaned and pinged and the mists cleared. Rodney awoke. From the bathroom next door came the crisp, repetitive sound of Jim shaving. . . .

Psyclops

MMMM. I

FIRST STATEMENT: I AM I. I AM EVERYTHING. EVERYTHING, everywhere. Every, every, every mmmm.

The universe is constructed of me, I am the whole of it. Am I? What is that regular throbbing that is not of me? That must be me too; after a while I shall understand it. All now is dim. Dim mmmm.

Even I am dim. In all this great strangeness and darkness of me, in all this universe of me, I am shadow. A memory of me. Could I be a memory of . . . not—me? Paradox: if I am everything, could there be a not-me, a somebody else?

Why am I having thoughts? Why am I not, as I was before, just mmmm?

Wake up! Wake up! It's urgent!

No! deny it! I am the universe. If you can speak to me you must be me, so I command you to be still. There must be only the soothing, sucking mmmm.

. . . you are not the universe! Listen to me!

Louder?

For Heaven's sake, can you hear at last?

Non-comprehension. I must be everything. Can there be a part of me, like the throbbing, which is . . . separate?

Am I getting through? Answer!

Who . . . who are you?

Thank goodness you're receiving at last. Do not be frightened.

Are you another universe?

I am not a universe. You are not a universe. You are in danger and I must help you.

31

I am . . . Danger, curl, suck, mmmm! Only me in all the world. Disbelieve anything not me.

. . . must handle this carefully. Hell, what a task! Hey, stay awake there.

Mmmm. Must be mmmm. . . .

. . . If only there was a psychofoetalist within light years of here. . . . Well, keep trying. Hey, wake up! You must wake up to survive!

Who are you?

I am your father.

Non-comprehension. Where are you? Are you the throbbing which is not me?

No, I am a long way from you. Light years away—oh hell! How do you start explaining?

Stop sending to me. You bring me feelings of . . . pain.

Catch hold of that idea of pain, son. Don't be afraid of it, but know there is much pain all about you. I am in constant pain.

Interest.

Good! First things first. You are most important.

I know that. All this is not happening. Somehow I catch these echoes, these dreams. I am *creating;* really, there is only me, entirely alone.

Try to concentrate. You are only one of millions like you. You and I are of the same species: human beings; I am born, you are unborn.

Meaningless.

Listen! Your "universe" is inside another human being. Soon you will emerge into the real universe.

Still meaningless. Curious.

Keep alert. I will send you pictures to help you understand. . . .

Uh . . . ? Distance? Sight? Colour? Form? Definitely do not like this. Frightened. Frightened of falling, insecure. . . . Must immediately retreat to safe mmmm. Mmmm.

Poor little blighter. Better let him rest! I'm half afraid of killing him. After all, he's only six months; at the Pre-natal Academies they don't begin rousing and education till seven and a half months. And then they're trained to the job. If only I knew—mind my leg, you blue swine!

That picture . . .

Oh, you're still there. Well done! I'm really sorry to rouse you so early, but it's vital.

Praise for me, warm feelings. Good. Nice. Better than being alone in the universe.

*That's a great step forward, son. Huh, I can almost realize
how the Creator felt, when you say that.*

Non-comprehension.

*Sorry, my fault: let the thought slip by. Must be careful.
You were going to ask me about the picture I sent you. Shall
I send again?*

Only a little at once. Curious. Very curious. Shape, colour,
beauty. Is that the real universe?

*That was just Earth I showed you, where I was born,
where I hope you will be born.*

Non-comprehension. Show again . . . shapes, tones, scents.
. . . Ah, this time not so strange. Different?

Yes, a different picture. Many pictures of Earth, look.

Ah . . . Better than my darkness. . . . I know only my
darkness, sweet and warm, yet I seem to remember those—
trees.

*That's a race memory, son. We're doing well. Your facul-
ties are beginning to work now.*

More beautiful pictures please.

*We cannot waste too long on the pictures. I've got a lot to
tell you before you get out of range. And—hello, what are
we stopping for now? These blue devils——*

Why do you cease sending so abruptly? Hello? . . . Nothing. Father? . . . Nothing. Was there ever anything, or have
I been alone and dreaming?

Nothing in all my universe but the throbbing. Throbbing
near me. Is someone here with me? Hello? No, no answer. I
must ask the voice, if the voice comes back. Now I must
mmmm. Am no longer content as I was before. Strange feelings. . . . I want more pictures; I want . . . to . . . be . . .
alive. No, must mmmm.

Mmmm.

Dreaming myself to be a fish, fin-tailed, flickering through
deep, still water. All is green and warm and without menace,
and I swim for ever with assurance . . . And then the water
splits into lashing cords and plunges down, down, down a
sunlit cliff. I fight to turn back, carried forward, fighting to
return to the deep, sure dark——

*—if you want to save yourself! Wake if you want to save
yourself! I can't hold out much longer. Another few days
across these damned mountains——*

Go away! Leave me to myself. I can have nothing to do
with you.

*My dear babe! You must try and understand. I know it's
agony for you, but you must stir yourself and take in what I
say. It is imperative.*

Nothing is imperative here. Yet he said "race memories." And now my mind seems to clear. Yes! I exist in the darkness of my head where formerly there was nothing. Yes, there are imperatives; that I can recognize. Father?

What are you trying to say?

Confused. Understanding better, trying harder, but so confused. And there is always the throbbing by my side.

Do not worry about that. It is your twin sister. The Pollux II hospital diagnosed twins, one boy and one girl.

Always so many concepts I cannot grasp. I should despair, but for curiosity prodding me on. Explain first "boy" and "girl" and "twin sister."

At a time like this! Well, we humans are divided into two sexes for purposes of continuing the race. These two sexes are called "boys" and "girls," and for convenience it has been decided that the small continuations—like you—should be carried inside the girls until they are strong enough to exist alone. Sometimes the little continuations are alone, sometimes they come in pairs, sometimes three or even more together.

And I'm one of a pair?

There you have it. That is a little girl lying next to you; you can hear her heart beating. Your mother——

Stop, stop! Too much to understand at once. Must think to myself about this. Will call you back.

Don't be long. Every minute takes you farther from me. . . .

Must keep a hold on myself. My brain reels. Everything so strange! And my universe shrunken to a womb. Numb, just feel numb. Cannot manage to cope with any more. Numb. Mmmm.

Back into the deep dark, soothed and suckled. Now I am a fish, twinkling smoothly through the uncrumpled water. Everything here calm, but ahead—The brink! I turn tail and flip back—too late, too late.

Hey, don't panic there. It's only me!

Danger, you said danger.

Keep calm and take it easy. There is something you must do for me—for us all. If you do that, there is no danger.

Tell me quickly.

As yet it is too difficult. In a few days you will be ready— if I can hang out that long.

Why is it difficult?

Only because you are small.

Where are you?

I am on a world rather like Earth which is ninety light

years from Earth and getting farther from you even as we communicate together.

Why? How? Don't understand. So much is now beyond my understanding; before you came everything was peaceful and dim.

Lie quiet and don't fret, son. You're doing well: you take the points quickly, you'll reach Earth yet. You are travelling towards Earth in a spaceship which left Mirone, the planet where I am, sixteen days ago.

Send that picture of a spaceship again.

Coming up . . .

It is a kind of metal womb for us all. That idea I can more or less grasp, but you don't explain distances to me satisfactorily.

These are big distances, what we call light years. I can't picture them for you properly because a human mind never really grasps them.

Then they don't exist.

Unfortunately they exist all right. But they are only comprehensible as mathematical concepts. OHHH! My leg . . .

Why are you stopping? I remember you suddenly stopped before. You send a horrible pain thought, then you are gone. Answer.

Wait a minute.

I can hardly hear you. Now I am interested, why do you not continue? Are you there?

. . . this is all beyond me. We're all finished. Judy, my love, if only I could reach you . . .

Who are you talking to? Answer me at once! This is all frustrating. You are so faint and your message so blurred.

Call you when I can . . .

Fear and pain. Only symbols from his mind to mine, yet they have an uncomfortable meaning of their own—something elusive. Perhaps another race memory.

My own memory is not good. Unused. I must train it. Something he said eludes me; I must try and remember it. Yet why should I bother? None of it really concerns me, I am safe here, safe for ever in this darkness.

That was it! There is another here with me, a sister. Why does he not send to her? Perhaps I could send to her; she is nearer to me than he is.

Sister! Sister! I am calling you. The throbbing comes from her but she does not answer.

This whole thing is imagination. I am talking to myself. Wait! Like a distant itch I can feel his projections coming back again. Do not trouble to listen to his riddles.

Curious.

. . . gangrene, without doubt. Shall be dead before these blue devils get me to their village. So much Judy and I planned to do . . .

Are you listening, son?

No, no.

Listen carefully while I give you some instructions.

Have something to ask you.

Please save it. The connection between us is growing attenuated: soon we will be out of mind range.

Indifferent.

My dear child, how could you be other than indifferent! I am truly sorry to have broken so early into your foetal sleep.

An unnameable sensation, half-pleasant: gratitude, love? No doubt a race memory.

It may be so. Try to remember me—later. Now, business. Your mother and I were on our way back to Earth when we stopped on this world Mirone, where I now am. It was an unnecessary luxury to break our journey. How bitterly now I wish we had never stopped.

Why did you?

Well, it was chiefly to please Judy—your mother. This is a beautiful world, round the North Pole, anyhow. We had wandered some way from the ship when a group of natives burst out upon us.

Natives?

People who live here. They are sub-human, blue-skinned and hairless—not pretty to look at.

Picture!

I think you'd be better without one. Judy and I ran like mad for the ship. We were nearly up to it when a rock caught me behind the knee—they were pitching rocks at us —and I went down. Judy never noticed until she was in the air lock, and then the savages were on me. My leg was hurt; I couldn't even put up a fight.

Please tell me no more of this. It makes me ill. I want mmmm.

Listen, son, don't cut off! That's all the frightening part. I called to Judy to make off home, so she and you and your sister got safely away. The savages are taking me over the mountains to their village. I don't think they mean to harm me; I'm just a . . . curiosity to them.

Please let me mmmm.

You can go comatose as soon as I've explained how these little space craft work. Astrogating, the business of getting from one planet to another, is far too intricate a task for any-

one but an expert to master. I'm not an expert, I'm a geohistorian. So the whole thing is done by a robot pilot. You feed it details like payload, and gravities and destination, and it juggles them with the data in its memory banks and works out all the course for you—carries you home safely, in fact. Do you get all that?

This sounds a very complicated procedure.

Now you're talking like your mother, boy. She's never bothered, but actually it's all simple stuff: the complications take place under the steel panelling where you don't worry about them. The point I'm trying to make is that steering is all automatic once you've punched in a few co-ordinates.

I'm dead tired.

So am I. Fortunately, before we left the ship that last time, I had set up the figures for Earth. O.K.?

If you had not, she would not have been able to get home?

Exactly it. You have your's father's brains, kid. Keep trying! She left Mirone safely and you are now all heading for Earth —but you'll never make it. When I set the figures up, they were right; but my not being aboard made them wrong. Every split second of thrust the ship makes is calculated for an extra eleven and a half stone that isn't there. It's here with me, being hauled along a mountain.

Is this bad? I mean, for you. Does it mean we reach Earth travelling too fast?

No, son. IT MEANS YOU'LL NEVER REACH EARTH AT ALL. The ship moves in an hyperbola, and although my weight is only about one eight thousandth of total ship's mass, that tiny fraction of error will have multiplied itself into a couple of light years by the time you get adjacent to the solar system.

I'm trying, but this talk of distance means nothing to me. Explain it again.

Where you are there is neither light nor space; how do I make you feel what a light year is? No, you'll just have to take it from me that the crucial point is, you'll shoot right past the Earth.

Can't we go on till we hit another planet?

You will—if nothing is done about it. But landfall will be delayed some odd thousands of years.

You are growing fainter. Strain too much. Must mmmm.

The fish again, and the water deep about him. No peace in the pool now. Cool pool, cruel pool, pool . . . The waters whirl towards the brink.

I am the fish-foetus. Have I dreamed? Was there a voice talking to me? It seems unlikely. And if it spoke, did it speak truth? Something I had to ask it, one gigantic fact which made nonsense of everything; something—Ah, cannot remember. Could refute everything if I could remember that.

Perhaps there was no voice. Perhaps in this darkness I have taken a wrong turning in my development: a wrong choice between sanity and non-sanity. Then my first thoughts may have been correct. I am everything and I am mad!

Help! Speak to me, speak!

No reply. The throbbing only. *That* was the question . . .

Thank heavens for hot spring water. . . .

Hello! Father?

How long will they let me lie here in this pool? They must realize I'm not long for this world, or any other.

I'm awake and answering!

Just let me lie here. Son, it's man's first pleasure and his last to lie and swill in hot water. Wish I could live to know you . . . However. To work. Here's what you have to do to get out of this present jam.

Am powerless here. Unable to do anything.

Don't get frightened. There's something you already do very expertly: telemit.

Non-comprehension.

We talk to each other over this growing distance by what is called telepathy. It's part gift, part skill. It happens to be the only contact between distant planets, except spaceships. But whereas spaceships take time to get anywhere, thought is instantaneous.

Understood.

Good. Unfortunately, whereas spaceships get anywhere in time, thought has a definite limited range. Its span is as strictly governed as—well, as the size of a plant, for instance. When you are fifty light years from Mirone, contact between us will cease.

What stops thought?

I don't know, any more than I could tell you what started it to begin with.

Other obvious questions: how far apart are we now?

At the most we have forty-two hours more in contact.

Don't leave me. I shall be lonely!

I'll be lonely too—but not for long. But you, son, you are already halfway to Earth, or as near as I can estimate it you are. As soon as contact between us ceases, you must call TRE.

Which means?

Telepath Radial Earth. It's a general control and informa-

*tion centre, permanently beamed for any sort of emergency.
You can raise them, I can't.*

They won't know me.

*I'll give you their call pattern. They'll soon know you when
you telemit. You can give them my pattern for identification
if you like. You must explain what is happening.*

Doubtful.

*You can explain, can't you—about your missing Earth al-
together?*

Will they believe?

Of course.

Are they real?

Of course.

Hard to believe in more people than just us. I had a question——

*Just a minute, let's get this sorted out. Tell TRE what the
trouble is; they'll send out a fast ship to pick Judy and you
up before you are out of range.*

Yes, now I have it. I want to ask you that question.
Voice——

*Wait a minute, son. . . . You're going faint, or is that
me? . . . Can you smell the gangrene over all those light
years? . . . These blue horrors are lifting me out of the
spring, and I'll probably pass out. Not much time. . . .*

Father, what is this "time" that seems to mean so much to
you? . . .

*Time like an ever-rolling stream bears all her sons . . .
Aaah. Time, son, never enough time. . . .*

Pain. Pain and silence. Revulsion in me. Can the universe
be as horrible and confusing as he would have me think? All
like a dream.

Mmmm. Long silence and darkness. Voice gone. Strain.
Try.

. . . distance. . .

Voice! Father! Louder!

. . . too feeble. . . . Done all I could. . . .

Tell me just one thing, Father!

Quickly.

Was it difficult to rouse me at first?

*Yes. In the Pre-natal Academies foetuses are not roused
for training and indoctrination until they are seven and a half
months old. But this was an emergency. I had to . . . oh, I'm
too weary——*

Then why did you rouse me and not communicate with my
mother?

The village! We're nearly there. Just down into the valley

and it's journey's end. . . . Human race only developing tele-
pathic powers gradually. . . . Steady, you fellows!

The question, answer the question.

*That is the answer. Easy down the slope, boys. Don't want
to burst this great big leg, eh? Er . . . I had the ability but
Judy hadn't; I couldn't call her a yard away. But you've got
the ability. Easy, oh! All the matter in the universe is in my
leg. . . .*

But why—you sound so muddled—why——?

*Good old Mendelian theory. . . . You and your sister, one
sensitive, one not. Two eyes of the giant and only one can see
properly . . . the path's too steep to—whoa, Cyclops, steady,
boy, or you'll put out that other eye.*

Cannot understand!

*Understand? My leg's a flaming torch—put out anyone's
eye. Steady, steady! Gently down the steep blue hill.*

Father!

What's the matter?

I can't understand. Are you talking of real things?

*Sorry, boy. Steady now. Touch of delirium; it's the pain.
You'll be O.K. if you get in contact with TRE. Remember?*

Yes, I remember. If only I could. . . . I don't know.
Mother is *real* then?

Yes. You must look after her.

And is the giant real?

*The giant? What giant? You mean the giant hill. The peo-
ple are climbing up the giant hill. Up to my giant leg. Good-
bye, son. I've got to see a blue man about a . . . a leg . . .
leg . . .*

Father!

. . . a leg of blue mutton. . . .

Father, where are you going? Wait, wait, look, see, I can
move a little. I've just discovered. I can *turn.* Father!

No answer now. Just a tiny stream of silence and the
throbbing. And the throbbing. My silent sister. She can't
think like I can. I have got to call TRE.

Plenty of time. Perhaps if I *turn* first. . . . Easy, I'm only
six months, he said. Maybe I could call more easily if I was
outside, in the real universe. If I turn again.

Now if I *kick.* . . .

Ah, easy now. Kick again. Good. Wonder if my legs are
blue.

Kick.

Good. Something yielding.

Kick. . . .

Outside

THEY NEVER WENT OUT OF THE HOUSE.

THE MAN WHOSE NAME WAS HARLEY USED TO GET UP FIRST. Sometimes he would take a stroll through the building in his sleeping suit—the temperature remained always mild, day after day. Then he would rouse Calvin, the handsome, broad man who looked as if he could command a dozen talents and never actually used one. He made as much company as Harley needed.

Dapple, the girl with killing grey eyes and black hair, was a light sleeper. The sound of the two men talking would wake her. She would get up and go to rouse May; together they would go down and prepare a meal. While they were doing that, the other two members of the household, Jagger and Pief, would be rousing.

That was how every "day" began: not with the inkling of anything like dawn, but just when the six of them had slept themselves back into wakefulness. They never exerted themselves during the day, but somehow when they climbed back into their beds they slept soundly enough.

The only excitement of the day occurred when they first opened the store. The store was a small room between the kitchen and the blue room. In the far wall was set a wide shelf, and upon this shelf their existence depended. Here, all their supplies "arrived." They would lock the door of the bare room last thing, and when they returned in the morning their needs—food, linen, a new washing machine—would be awaiting them on the shelf. That was just an accepted feature of their existence: they never questioned it among themselves.

41

On this morning, Dapple and May were ready with the meal before the four men came down. Dapple even had to go to the foot of the wide stairs and call before Pief appeared; so that the opening of the store had to be postponed till after they had eaten, for although the opening had in no way become a ceremony, the women were nervous of going in alone. It was one of those things. . . .

"I hope to get some tobacco," Harley said as he unlocked the door. "I'm nearly out of it."

They walked in and looked at the shelf. It was all but empty.

"No food," observed May, hands on her aproned waist. "We shall be on short rations today."

It was not the first time this had happened. Once—how long ago now?—they kept little track of time—no food had appeared for three days and the shelf had remained empty. They had accepted the shortage placidly.

"We shall eat you before we starve, May," Pief said, and they laughed briefly to acknowledge the joke, although Pief had cracked it last time too. Pief was an unobtrusive little man: not the sort one would notice in a crowd. His small jokes were his most precious possession.

Two packets only lay on the ledge. One was Harley's tobacco, one was a pack of cards. Harley pocketed the one with a grunt and displayed the other, slipping the pack from its wrapping and fanning it towards the others.

"Anyone play?" he asked.

"Poker," Jagger said.

"Canasta."

"Gin rummy."

"We'll play later," Calvin said. "It'll pass the time in the evening." The cards would be a challenge to them; they would have to sit together to play, round a table, facing each other.

Nothing was in operation to separate them, but there seemed no strong force to keep them together, once the tiny business of opening the store was over. Jagger worked the vacuum cleaner down the hall, past the front door that did not open, and rode it up the stairs to clean the upper landings; not that the place was dirty, but cleaning was something you did anyway in the morning. The women sat with Pief desultorily discussing how to manage the rationing, but after that they lost contact with each other and drifted away on their own. Calvin and Harley had already strolled off in different directions.

The house was a rambling affair. It had few windows, and

such as there were did not open, were unbreakable and admitted no light. Darkness lay everywhere; illumination from an invisible source followed one's entry into a room—the black had to be entered before it faded. Every room was furnished, but with odd pieces that bore little relation to each other, as if there was no purpose for the room. Rooms equipped for purposeless beings have that air about them.

No plan was discernible on first or second floor or in the long empty attics. Only familiarity could reduce the maze-like quality of room and corridor. At least there was ample time for familiarity.

Harley spent a long while walking about, hands in pockets. At one point he met Dapple; she was drooping gracefully over a sketchbook, amateurishly copying a picture that hung on one of the walls—a picture of the room in which she sat. They exchanged a few words, then Harley moved on.

Something lurked in the edge of his mind like a spider in the corner of its web. He stepped into what they called the piano room and then he realized what was worrying him. Almost furtively, he glanced round as the darkness slipped away, and then looked at the big piano. Some strange things had arrived on the shelf from time to time and had been distributed over the house: one of them stood on top of the piano now.

It was a model, heavy and about two feet high, squat, almost round, with a sharp nose and four buttressed vanes. Harley knew what it was. It was a ground-to-space ship, a model of the burly ferries that lumbered up to the spaceships proper.

That had caused them more unsettlement than when the piano itself had appeared in the store. Keeping his eyes on the model, Harley seated himself at the piano stool and sat tensely, trying to draw *something* from the rear of his mind . . . something connected with spaceships.

Whatever it was, it was unpleasant, and it dodged backwards whenever he thought he had laid a mental finger on it. So it always eluded him. If only he could discuss it with someone, it might be teased out of its hiding place. Unpleasant: menacing, yet with a promise entangled in the menace.

If he could get at it, meet it boldly face to face, he could do . . . something definite. And until he had faced it, he could not even say what the something definite was he wanted to do.

A footfall behind him. Without turning, Harley deftly pushed up the piano lid and ran a finger along the keys. Only then did he look back carelessly over his shoulder. Calvin stood there, hands in pockets, looking solid and comfortable.

"Saw the light in here," he said easily. "I thought I'd drop in as I was passing."

"I was thinking I would play the piano awhile," Harley answered with a smile. The thing was not discussable, even with a near acquaintance like Calvin because . . . because of the nature of the thing . . . because one had to behave like a normal, unworried human being. That at least was sound and clear and gave him comfort: behave like a normal human being.

Reassured, he pulled a gentle tumble of music from the keyboard. He played well. They all played well. Dapple, May, Pief . . . as soon as they had assembled the piano, they had all played well. Was that—natural? Harley shot a glance at Calvin. The stocky man leaned against the instrument, back to that disconcerting model, not a care in the world. Nothing showed on his face but an expression of bland amiability. They were all amiable, never quarreling together.

The six of them gathered for a scanty lunch, their talk was trite and cheerful, and then the afternoon followed on the same pattern as the morning, as all the other mornings: secure, comfortable, aimless. Only to Harley did the pattern seem slightly out of focus; he now had a clue to the problem. It was small enough, but in the dead calm of their days it was large enough.

May had dropped the clue. When she helped herself to jelly, Jagger laughingly accused her of taking more than her fair share. Dapple, who always defended May, said: "She's taken less than you, Jagger."

"No," May corrected, "I think I *have* more than anyone else. I took it for an interior motive."

It was the kind of pun anyone made at times. But Harley carried it away to consider. He paced round one of the silent rooms. Interior, ulterior motives. . . . Did the others here feel the disquiet he felt? Had they a reason for concealing that disquiet? And another question:

Where was "here"?

He shut that one down sharply.

Deal with one thing at a time. Grope your way gently to the abyss. Categorize your knowledge.

One: Earth was getting slightly the worst of a cold war with Nitity.

Two: the Nititians possessed the alarming ability of being able to assume the identical appearance of their enemies.

Three: by this means they could permeate human society.

Four: Earth was unable to view the Nititian civilization from inside.

Inside . . . a wave of claustrophobia swept over Harley as he realized that these cardinal facts he knew bore no relation to this little world inside. They came, by what means he did not know, from outside, the vast abstraction that none of them had ever seen. He had a mental picture of a starry void in which men and monsters swam or battled, and then swiftly erased it. Such ideas did not conform with the quiet behaviour of his companions; if they never spoke about outside, did they think about it?

Uneasily, Harley moved about the room; the parquet floor echoed the indecision of his footsteps. He had walked into the billiards room. Now he prodded the balls across the green cloth with one finger, preyed on by conflicting intentions. The white spheres touched and rolled apart. That was how the two halves of his mind worked. Irreconcilables: he should stay here and conform; he should—not stay here (remembering no time when he was not here, Harley could frame the second idea no more clearly than that). Another point of pain was that "here" and "not here" seemed to be not two halves of a homogeneous whole, but two dissonances.

The ivory slid wearily into a pocket. He decided. He would not sleep in his room tonight.

They came from the various parts of the house to share a bed-time drink. By tacit consent the cards had been postponed until some other time: there was, after all, so much other time.

They talked about the slight nothings that comprised their day, the model of one of the rooms that Calvin was building and May furnishing, the faulty light in the upper corridor which came on too slowly. They were subdued. It was time once more to sleep, and in that sleep who knew what dreams might come? But they *would* sleep. Harley knew—wondering if the others also knew—that with the darkness which descended as they climbed into bed would come an undeniable command to sleep.

He stood tensely just inside his bedroom door, intensely aware of the unorthodoxy of his behaviour. His head hammered painfully and he pressed a cold hand against his temple. He heard the others go one by one to their separate rooms. Pief called good night to him; Harley replied. Silence fell.

Now!

As he stepped nervously into the passage, the light came

on. Yes, it was slow—reluctant. His heart pumped. He was committed. He did not know what he was going to do or what was going to happen, but he was committed. The compulsion to sleep had been avoided. Now he had to hide, and wait.

It is not easy to hide when a light signal follows wherever you go. But by entering a recess which led to a disused room, opening the door slightly and crouching in the doorway, Harley found the faulty landing light dimmed off and left him in the dark.

He was neither happy nor comfortable. His brain seethed in a conflict he hardly understood. He was alarmed to think he had broken the rules and frightened of the creaking darkness about him. But the suspense did not last for long.

The corridor light came back on. Jagger was leaving his bedroom, taking no precaution to be silent. The door swung loudly shut behind him. Harley caught a glimpse of his face before he turned and made for the stairs: he looked noncommittal but serene—like a man going off duty. He went downstairs in bouncy, jaunty fashion.

Jagger should have been in bed asleep. A law of nature had been defied.

Unhesitatingly, Harley followed. He had been prepared for something and something had happened, but his flesh crawled with fright. The light-headed notion came to him that he might disintegrate with fear. All the same, he kept doggedly down the stairs, feet noiseless on the heavy carpet.

Jagger had rounded a corner. He was whistling quietly as he went. Harley heard him unlock a door. That would be the store—no other doors were locked. The whistling faded.

The store was open. No sound came from within. Cautiously, Harley peered inside. The far wall had swung open about a central pivot, revealing a passage beyond. For minutes Harley could not move, staring fixedly at this breach.

Finally, and with a sense of suffocation, he entered the store. Jagger had gone through there. Harley also went through. Somewhere he did not know, somewhere whose existence he had not guessed. . . . Somewhere that wasn't the house. . . . The passage was short and had two doors, one at the end rather like a cage door (Harley did not recognize a lift when he saw one), one in the side, narrow and with a window.

This window was transparent. Harley looked through it and then fell back choking. Dizziness swept in and shook him by the throat.

Stars shone outside.

With an effort, he mastered himself and made his way back upstairs, lurching against the banisters. They had all been living under a ghastly misapprehension. . . .

He barged into Calvin's room and the light lit. A faint, sweet smell was in the air, and Calvin lay on his broad back, fast asleep.

"Calvin! Wake up!" Harley shouted.

The sleeper never moved. Harley was suddenly aware of his own loneliness and the eerie feel of the great house about him. Bending over the bed, he shook Calvin violently by the shoulders and slapped his face.

Calvin groaned and opened one eye.

"Wake up, man," Harley said. "Something terrible's going on here."

The other propped himself on one elbow, communicated fear rousing him thoroughly.

"Jagger's *left the house*," Harley told him. "There's a way outside. We're—we've got to find out what we are." His voice rose to an hysterical pitch. He was shaking Calvin again. "We must find out what's wrong here. Either we are victims of some ghastly experiment—or we're all monsters!"

And as he spoke, before his staring eyes, beneath his clutching hands, Calvin began to wrinkle up and fold and blur, his eyes running together and his great torso contracting. Something else—something lively and alive—was forming in his place.

Harley only stopped yelling when, having plunged downstairs, the sight of the stars through the small window steadied him. He had to get out, wherever "out" was.

He pulled the small door open and stood in fresh night air.

Harley's eye was not accustomed to judging distances. It took him some while to realize the nature of his surroundings, to realize that mountains stood distantly against the starlit sky, and that he himself stood on a platform twelve feet above the ground. Some distance away, lights gleamed, throwing bright rectangles onto an expanse of tarmac.

There was a steel ladder at the edge of the platform. Biting his lip, Harley approached it and climbed clumsily down. He was shaking violently with cold and fear. When his feet touched solid ground, he began to run. Once he looked back: the house perched on its platform like a frog hunched on top of a rat trap.

He stopped abruptly then, in almost dark. Abhorrence jerked up inside him like retching. The high, crackling stars and the pale serration of the mountains began to spin, and he clenched his fists to hold on to consciousness. That house, whatever it was, was the embodiment of all the coldness in his mind. Harley said to himself: "Whatever has been done to me, I've been cheated. Someone has robbed me of something so thoroughly I don't even know what it is. It's been a cheat, a cheat. . . ." And he choked on the idea of those years that had been pilfered from him. No thought: thought scorched the synapses and ran like acid through the brain. Action only! His leg muscles jerked into movement again.

Buildings loomed about him. He simply ran for the nearest light and burst into the nearest door. Then he pulled up sharp, panting and blinking the harsh illumination out of his pupils.

The walls of the room were covered with graphs and charts. In the centre of the room was a wide desk with vision-screen and loudspeaker on it. It was a business-like room with overloaded ashtrays and a state of ordered untidiness. A thin man sat alertly at the desk; he had a thin mouth.

Four other men stood in the room, all were armed, none seemed surprised to see him. The man at the desk wore a neat suit; the others were in uniform.

Harley leant on the door-jamb and sobbed. He could find no words to say.

"It has taken you four years to get out of there," the thin man said. He had a thin voice.

"Come and look at this," he said, indicating the screen before him. With an effort, Harley complied; his legs worked like rickety crutches.

On the screen, clear and real, was Calvin's bedroom. The outer wall gaped, and through it two uniformed men were dragging a strange creature, a wiry, mechanical-looking being that had once been called Calvin.

"Calvin was a Nititian," Harley observed dully. He was conscious of a sort of stupid surprise at his own observation.

The thin man nodded approvingly.

"Enemy infiltrations constituted quite a threat," he said. "Nowhere on Earth was safe from them: they can kill a man, dispose of him and turn into exact replicas of him. Makes things difficult. . . . We lost a lot of state secrets that way. But Nititian ships have to land here to disembark the Non-Men and to pick them up again after their work is done. That is the weak link in their chain.

"We intercepted one such ship-load and bagged them singly after they had assumed humanoid form. We subjected them to artificial amnesia and put small groups of them into different environments for study. This is the Army Institute for Investigation of Non-Men, by the way. We've learnt a lot . . . quite enough to combat the menace. . . . Your group, of course, was one such."

Harley asked in a gritty voice: "Why did you put me in with them?"

The thin man rattled a ruler between his teeth before answering.

"Each group has to have a human observer in their very midst, despite all the scanning devices that watch from outside. You see, a Nititian uses a deal of energy maintaining a human form; once in that shape, he is kept in it by self-hypnosis which only breaks down in times of stress, the amount of stress bearable varying from one individual to another. A human on the spot can sense such stresses. . . . It's a tiring job for him; we get doubles always to work day on, day off——"

"But I've always been there——"

"Of your group," the thin man cut in, "the human was Jagger, or two men alternating as Jagger. You caught one of them going off duty."

"That doesn't make sense," Harley shouted. "You're trying to say that I——"

He choked on the words. They were no longer pronounceable. He felt his outer form flowing away like sand as from the other side of the desk revolver barrels were levelled at him.

"Your stress level is remarkably high," continued the thin man, turning his gaze away from the spectacle. "But where you fail is where you all fail. Like Earth's insects which imitate vegetables, your cleverness cripples you. You can only be carbon copies. Because Jagger did nothing in the house, all the rest of you instinctively followed suit. You didn't get bored —you didn't even try to make passes at Dapple—as personable a Non-Man as I ever saw. Even the model spaceship jerked no appreciable reaction out of you."

Brushing his suit down, he rose before the skeletal being which now cowered in a corner.

"The inhumanity inside will always give you away," he said evenly. "However human you are outside."

Dumb Show

MRS. SNOWDEN WAS SLOWLY BEING WORN DOWN. SHE HAD REACHED THE STAGE NOW WHERE SHE CARRIED ABOUT WITH her a square of card on which the word DON'T was written in large letters. It was kept tucked inside her cardigan, ready to be produced at a moment's notice and flashed before Pauline's eyes.

The ill-matched pair, the grubby girl of three and the shabby-elegant lady of fifty-eight, came up to the side door of their house, Pauline capering over the flagstones, Mrs. Snowden walking slowly with her eyes on the bare border. Spring was reluctantly here, but the tepid earth hardly acknowledged it; even the daffodils had failed to put in an appearance this year.

"Can't understand it at all," Mrs. Snowden told herself. "Nothing ever happens to daffodils." And then she went on to compile a list of things that nevertheless might have happened: frost—it had been a hard winter; soil-starvation—no manure since the outbreak of hostilities, seven years ago; ants; mice; cats; the sounds—that seemed most likely. Sound did anything, these days.

Pauline rapped primly on the little brass knocker and vanished into the hall. Mrs. Snowden paused in the porch, stopping to look at the houses on the other side of her high brick wall. When this house had been built, it had stood in open fields; now drab little semi-detacheds surrounded it on three sides. She paused and hated them. Catching herself at it, she tried instead to admire the late afternoon light falling on the huddled roofs; the sunshine fell in languid, horizontal strokes

—but it had no meaning for her, except as a sign that it was nearly time to blackout again.

She went heavily into the house, closing the door. Inside, night had already commenced.

Her granddaughter marched round the drawing-room, banging a tin lid against her head. That way, she could hear the noise it made. Mrs. Snowden reached for the DON'T card, then let her hand drop; the action was becoming automatic, and she must guard against it. She went to the gram-wire-tv cabinet, of which only the last compartment was now of use, and switched on. Conditions at home were a little better since the recapture of Iceland, and there were now broadcasts for an hour and a half every evening.

Circuits warmed, a picture burned in the half-globe. A man and woman danced solemnly, without music. To Mrs. Snowden it looked as meaningless as turning a book of blank pages, but Pauline stopped her march and came to stare. She smiled at the dancing couple; her lips moved; she was talking to them.

DON'T, screamed Mrs. Snowden's sudden, dumb card.

Pauline made a face and answered back. She jumped away as her grandmother reached forward, leaping, prancing over the chairs, shouting defiance.

In fury, Mrs. Snowden skimmed the card across the room, crying angrily, hating to be reminded of her infirmity, waving her narrow hands. She collapsed onto a music stool—music, that dear, extinct thing!—and wept. Her own anger in her own head had sounded a million cotton-wool miles away, emphasizing the isolation. At this point she always crumpled.

The little girl came to her delicately, treading and staring with impertinence, knowing she had the victory. She pulled a sweet face and twizzled on her heel. Lack of hearing did not worry her; the silence she had known in the womb had never left her. Her indifference seemed a mockery.

"You little beast!" Mrs. Snowden said. "You cruel, ignorant, little beast!"

Pauline replied, the little babblings which would never turn into words, the little noises no human ear could hear. Then she walked quietly over to the windows, pointed out at the sickening day, and began to draw the curtains. Controlling herself with an effort, Mrs. Snowden stood up. Thank goodness the child had some sense; they must blackout. First she retrieved her DON'T card from behind the ancient twentieth-century settee, and then they went together through the house, tugging the folds of black velvet across the glass.

Now Pauline was skipping again. How she did it on the

low calories was a matter for wonder. Perhaps, thought Mrs. Snowden, it was a blessing to be responsible for the child; so, she kept contact with life. She even caught an echo of gaiety herself, so that they hurried from room to room like bearers of good news, pulling blackness over them, then sweeping on the sonic lights. Up the stairs, pausing at the landing window, racing into the bedrooms, till new citadels were created from all the shabby darknesses. Pauline collapsed laughing on her bed. Seizing her, tickling now and again, Mrs. Snowden undressed her and tucked her between the fraying sheets.

She kissed the girl good night, put out the light, closed the door, and then went slowly round, putting out all the other lights, downstairs, putting all the lights out there.

Directly she had gone, Pauline climbed out of bed, stamped into the bathroom, opened the little medicine cupboard, took out the bottle with the label "Sleeping Pills." Unscrewing the top, she swallowed a pill, pulling a pig's eyes face at herself in the looking-glass as she did so. Then she put the bottle back on its shelf and slammed the little door, hugging to herself this noisy secret.

None of these things had names for her. Having no names, they had only misty meanings. The very edges of them were blurred, for all objects were grouped together in only two vast categories: those-that-concerned-her and those-that-did-not-concern-her.

She trailed loudly back to her bed in the silence there was no breaking, making pig's eyes all the way to ward off the darkness. Once in bed, she began to think; it was because of these pictures she stole her grandmother's pills: they fought the pictures and turned them eventually into an all-night nothing.

Predominant was the aching picture. A warmth, a face, a comforting—it was at once the vaguest yet most vivid picture; someone soft who carried and cared for her; someone who now never came; someone who now provoked only the water scalding from her eyes.

Elbowing that picture away came the boring picture. This tall, old-smelling person who had suddenly become everything after the other had gone; her stiff fingers, bad over buttons; her slowness about the stove; her meaningless marks on cards; all the dull mystery of who she was and what she did.

The new picture. The room down the road where Pauline was taken every morning. It was full of small people, some like her, in frocks, some with short hair and fierce movements. And big people, walking between their seats, again with marks on cards, trying with despairing faces to make them comprehend incomprehensible things by gestures of the hand and fingers.

The push picture. Something needed, strange as sunlight, something lost, lost as laughter. . . .

The pill worked like a time-bomb and Pauline was asleep where only the neurosis of puzzlement could insidiously follow.

Mrs. Snowden switched the globe off and sank into a chair. They had been showing a silent film: the latest scientific advances had thrown entertainment back to where it had been in her grandfather's young days. For a moment she had watched the silent gestures, followed by a wall of dialogue:

"Jean: Then—you knew he was not my father, Denis?

"Denis: From the first moment we met in Madrid.

"Jean: And I swore none should ever know."

Sighing, Mrs. Snowden switched the poor stuff off, and sank down with a hand over her forehead. TV merely accentuated her isolation, everyone's isolation. She thought mockingly of the newspaper phrase describing this conflict, The Civilized War, and wished momentarily for one of the old, rough kind with doodlebugs and H-bombs; then, you could achieve a sort of Henry Moore-ish anonymity, crouching with massed others underground. Now, your individuality was forced on to you, till self-consciousness became a burden that sank you in an ocean of loneliness.

Right at the beginning of this war, Mrs. Snowden's husband had left for the duration. He was on secret work—where, she had no idea. Up till two years ago, she received a card from him each Christmas; then he had missed a year; then, in the paper shortage, the sending of cards had been forbidden. So whether he lived or not she did not know; the question now raised curiously little excitement in her. Heartsickness had ceased to be relevant.

Mrs. Snowden had come to live here in her old home with her parents after she had been declared redundant at the university, when all but the practical Chairs closed down. In the lean winters, first her mother, then her father died. Then her married daughter was killed in a sound raid; Pauline, a tiny babe, had come to live with her.

It was all impersonal, dry facts, she thought. You stated the facts to explain how the situation arose; but to explain the *situation*. . . .

Nobody in the world could hear a sound. *That* was the only important fact.

She jumped up and flicked aside an edge of curtain. A rag

of dirty daylight was still propped over the serried chimney-tops. The more those houses crowded, the more they isolated her. This should be a time for madness, she said aloud, misting the pane; something grand and horrid to break the chain of days. And her eyes swept the treble row of old textbooks over her bureau: Jackson's *Eighteen Nineties*, Montgomery's *Early Twentieth Century Science Fiction*, Slade's *Novelists* of *the Psychological Era*, Wilson's *Zola*, Nollybend's *Wilson* . . . a row of dodos, as defunct as the courses of Eng. Lit. they had once nourished.

"Dead!" she exclaimed. "A culture in Coventry!" she whispered, and went to get something to eat.

"Tough old hag," she told herself. "You'll survive."

The food was the usual vibro-culture, tasteless, filling, insubstantial. The hospitals of England held as many beri-beri cases as wounded. Sound ruled the whole deaf world. It wrecked the buildings, killed the soldiers, shattered the tympanums and ballooned synthesized proteins from mixtures of amino acids.

The Sound Revolution had come at the dawn of this new century, following thirty years of peace. Progress had taken a new direction. It had all been simple and complete; you just flushed the right electrostatic stress through the right quartz plates and—bingo! You could do anything! The most spectacular result was a global conflict.

The Powers warred under certain humane agreements: gas, fission and fusion weapons were forbidden. It was to be, indeed, a Civilized War. VM (vibratory motion) had the field to itself. It learnt to expand living vegetable cells a thousand-fold, so that a potato would last for two years' dinners; it learnt to pulverize brick and metal, so that cities could comfortably be turned to a thin dust; it learnt to twist the human ear into an echoing, useless coil of gristle. There seemed no limit to its adaptability.

Mrs. Snowden ate her blown-up yeast with dignity, and thought of other things. She thought—for lately she had been straining after wider horizons—of the course of human history, its paradoxical sameness and variety, and then something made her look up to the tube over the mantelpiece.

The tube was a piece of standard equipment in every home. It was a crude ear, designed to announce when the local siren was giving a sound raid alarm.

She glanced indifferently at it. The lycopodium seed was stirring sluggishly in its tube; damp must be getting in, it was not patterning properly. She went on eating, gloomily wondering about the future generations: how much of the vital essence of tradition would be lost through this blanket of deafness?

Correct procedure would have been for her, at the stirring of the seed, to collect Pauline and stand out in the open. When the siren went, everyone else left their homes and stood patiently under the bare sky; then, if the sounds swept their buildings, they would be temporarily smothered by dust as the building vanished, but suffer no other harm. Mrs. Snowden could no longer be bothered with this nonsense.

To her mind, it was undignified to stand in the chill air, meekly waiting. If enemy planes circled overhead, she would have had defiance to spur her out; but nowadays there was only the quiet sky, the eternal silence and the abrupt pulverization—or the anti-climax, when everyone filed sheepishly back to bed.

She took her plate into the kitchen. As she came back into the living-room, a reproduction of Mellor's "Egyptian Girl" fell silently onto the floor, shattering frame and glass.

Mrs. Snowden went and stared at it. Then, on impulse, she hurried over to the window and peered out. The encircling houses had gone.

Letting the curtain fall back into place, she rushed from the room and up the stairs. She was shaking Pauline before she regained control of herself, and then could not tell whether panic or exultation had sent her scurrying.

"The houses have gone! The houses have gone!"

Silence, in which the little girl woke sluggishly.

Mrs. Snowden hustled her downstairs and out on to the front lawn, letting a bright swathe of light cut across the empty flower-beds. Somewhere, high and silent overhead, a monitor might be hovering, but she was too excited to care.

By a freak of chance, their house stood alone. Around them for miles stretched a new desert, undulant, still settling. The novelty, the *difference,* of it was something wonderful: not a catastrophe, a liberation.

Then they saw the giants.

Vague in the distance, they were nevertheless real enough, although incredible. They were tall—how tall?—ten, fifteen feet? More? With horror Mrs. Snowden thought they were enemy troops. This was the latest application of the sound: it enlarged the human cell now, as easily as it enlarged vegetable cells. She had the brief idea she had read that human giants could not survive, or were impossible or something, and then the thought was gone, swept away in fear.

The giants were still growing. They were taller than a

house now, thirty feet or more high. They began to mop and mow, like drunken dancers.

Unreality touched her. Pauline was crying.

A coolness swept her limbs. She trembled involuntarily. A personal alarm now, terror because something unknown was at her blood. She raised a hand to her eyes. It loomed away from her. Her arm extended. She was *growing*.

She knew then that the giants were no enemy troops; they were victims. You get everyone out of their houses. One type of VM levels the houses. Another inflates the people, blowing them up like grotesque rubber dummies. Simple. Scientific. Civilized.

Mrs. Snowden swayed like a pole. She took a clumsy step to keep her balance. Dizzily, she peered at her blank bedroom window, staggering away to avoid falling into the house. No pain. The circuits were disrupted. Only numbness: numbness and maniac growth.

She could still crazily see the dancing giants. Now she understood why they danced. They were trying to adapt. Before they could do so, their metabolism burnt out. They sprawled into the desert, giant dusty corpses, full of sound and silence.

She thought: It's the first excitement for years, amusedly, before her heart failed under its giant load.

She toppled; the DON'T card fluttered gaily from her bosom, spinning and filtering to the ground.

Pauline had already overtopped her grandmother. The young system was greedy for growth. She uttered a cry of wonder as her head rocked up to the dark sky. She saw her grandmother fall. She saw the tiny fan of sonic light from their tiny front door. She trod into the desert to keep her balance. She started to run. She saw the ground dwindle. She felt the warmth of the stars, the curvature of the earth.

In her brain, the delighted thoughts were wasps in a honey pot, bees in a hive, flies in a chapel, gnats in a factory, midges in a Sahara, sparks up an everlasting flue, a comet falling for ever in a noiseless void, a voice singing in a new universe.

The New Father Christmas

LITTLE OLD ROBERTA TOOK THE CLOCK DOWN OFF THE SHELF AND PUT IT ON THE HOTPOINT; THEN SHE PICKED UP THE kettle and tried to wind it. The clock was almost on the boil before she realised what she had done. Shrieking quietly, so as not to wake old Robin, she snatched up the clock with a duster and dropped it onto the table. It ticked furiously. She looked at it.

Although Roberta wound the clock every morning when she got up, she had neglected to look at it for months. Now she looked and saw it was 7.30 on Christmas Day, 2388.

"Oh dear," she exclaimed. "It's Christmas Day already! It seems to have come very soon after Lent this year."

She had not even realised it was 2388. She and Robin had lived in the factory so long. The idea of Christmas excited her, for she liked surprises—but it also frightened her, because she thought about the New Father Christmas and that was something she preferred not to think about. The New Father Christmas was reputed to make his rounds on Christmas morning.

"I must tell Robin," she said. But poor Robin had been very touchy lately; it was conceivable that having Christmas suddenly forced upon him would make him cross. Roberta was unable to keep anything to herself, so she would have to go down and tell the tramps. Apart from Robin, there were only the tramps.

Putting the kettle on to the stove, she left her living-quarters and went into the factory, like a little mouse emerging from its mincepie-smelling nest. Roberta and Robin lived right at the top of the factory and the tramps had their illegal

57

home right at the bottom. Roberta began tiptoeing down many, many steel stairs.

The factory was full of the sort of sounds Robin called "silent noise." It continued day and night, and the two humans had long ago ceased to hear it; it would continue when they had become incapable of hearing anything. This morning, the machines were as busy as ever, and looked not at all Christmassy. Roberta noticed in particular the two machines she hated most: the one with loomlike movements which packed impossibly thin wire into impossibly small boxes, and the one which threshed about as if it were struggling with an invisible enemy and did not seem to be producing anything.

The old lady walked delicately past them and down into the basement. She came to a grey door and knocked at it. At once she heard the three tramps fling themselves against the inside of the door and press against it, shouting hoarsely across to each other.

Roberta was unable to shout, but she waited until they were silent and then called through the door as loudly as she could, "It's only me, boys."

After a moment's hush, the door opened a crack. Then it opened wide. Three seedy figures stood there, their faces anguished: Jerry, the ex-writer, and Tony and Dusty, who had never been and never would be anything but tramps. Jerry, the youngest, was forty, and so still had half his life to drowse through, Tony was fifty-five and Dusty had sweat rash.

"We thought you was the Terrible Sweeper!" Tony exclaimed.

The Terrible Sweeper swept right through the factory every morning. Every morning, the tramps had to barricade themselves in their room, or the sweeper would have bundled them and all their tawdry belongings into the disposal chutes.

"You'd better come in," Jerry said. "Excuse the muddle."

Roberta entered and sat down on a crate, tired after her journey. The tramps' room made her uneasy, for she suspected them of bringing Women in here occasionally; also, there were pants hanging in one corner.

"I had something to tell you all," she said. They waited politely, expectantly. Jerry cleaned out his nails with a tack.

"I've forgotten just now what it is," she confessed.

The tramps sighed noisily with relief. They feared anything which threatened to disturb their tranquillity. Tony became communicative.

"It's Christmas Day," he said, looking round furtively.

"Is it really!" Roberta exclaimed. "So soon after Lent?"

"Allow us," Jerry said, "to wish you a safe Christmas and a persecution-free New Year."

This courtesy brought Roberta's latent fears to the surface at once.

"You—you don't believe in the New Father Christmas, do you?" she asked them. They made no answer, but Dusty's face went the colour of lemon peel and she knew they did believe. So did she.

"You'd better all come up to the flat and celebrate this happy day," Roberta said. "After all, there's safety in numbers."

"I can't go through the factory: the machines bring on my sweat rash," Dusty said. "It's a sort of allergy."

"Nevertheless, we will go," Jerry said. "Never pass a kind offer by."

Like heavy mice, the four of them crept up the stairs and through the engrossed factory. The machines pretended to ignore them.

In the flat, they found pandemonium loose. The kettle was boiling over and Robin was squeaking for help. Officially bed-ridden, Robin could get up in times of crisis; he stood now just inside the bedroom door, and Roberta had to remove the kettle before going to placate him.

"And why have you brought those creatures up here?" he demanded in a loud whisper.

"Because they are our friends, Robin," Roberta said, struggling to get him back to bed.

"They are no friends of mine!" he said. He thought of something really terrible to say to her; he trembled and wrestled with it and did not say it. The effort left him weak and irritable. How he loathed being in her power! As caretaker of the vast factory, it was his duty to see that no undesirables entered, but as matters were at present he could not evict the tramps while his wife took their part. Life really was exasperating.

"We came to wish you a safe Christmas, Mr. Proctor," Jerry said, sliding into the bedroom with his two companions.

"Christmas, and I got sweat rash!" Dusty said.

"It isn't Christmas," Robin whined as Roberta pushed his feet under the sheets. "You're just saying it to annoy me." If they could only know or guess the anger that stormed like illness through his veins.

At that moment, the delivery chute pinged and an envelope catapulted into the room. Robin took it from Roberta, opening it with trembling hands. Inside was a Christmas card from the Minister of Automatic Factories.

"This proves there are other people still alive in the world," Robin said. These other fools were not important enough to receive Christmas cards.

His wife peered short-sightedly at the Minister's signature.

"This is done by a rubber stamp, Robin," she said. "It doesn't prove anything."

Now he was really enraged. To be contradicted in front of these scum! And Roberta's cheeks had grown more wrinkled since last Christmas, which also annoyed him. As he was about to flay her, however, his glance fell on the address on the envelope; it read, *"Robin Proctor, A.F.X10."*

"But this factory isn't X10!" he protested aloud. "It's SC541."

"Perhaps we've been in the wrong factory for thirty-five years," Roberta said. "Does it matter at all?"

The question was so senseless that the old man pulled the bedclothes out of the bottom of the bed.

"Well, go and find out, you silly old woman!" he shrieked. "The factory number is engraved over the output exit. Go and see what it says. If it does not say SC541, we must leave here at once. Quickly!"

"I'll come with you," Jerry told the old lady.

"You'll all go with her," Robin said. "I'm not having you stay here with me. You'd murder me in my bed!"

Without any particular surprise—although Tony glanced regretfully at the empty teapot as he passed it—they found themselves again in the pregnant layers of factory, making their way down to the output exit. Here, conveyor belts transported the factory's finished product outside to waiting vehicles.

"I don't like it much here," Roberta said uneasily. "Even a glimpse of outside aggravates my agoraphobia."

Nevertheless, she looked where Robin had instructed her. Above the exit, a sign said "X10."

"Robin will never believe me when I tell him," she wailed.

"My guess is that the factory changed its own name," Jerry said calmly. "Probably it has changed its product as well. After all, there's nobody in control; it can do what it likes. Has it always been making these eggs?"

They stared silently at the endless, moving line of steel eggs. The eggs were smooth and as big as ostrich eggs; they sailed into the open, where robots piled them into vans and drove away with them.

"Never heard of a factory laying eggs before," Dusty laughed, scratching his shoulder. "Now we'd better get back before the Terrible Sweeper catches up with us."

Slowly they made their way back up the many, many steps.

"I think it used to be television sets the factory made," Roberta said once.

"If there are no more men—there'd be no more need for television sets," Jerry said grimly.

"I can't remember for sure. . . ."

Robin, when they told him, was ill with irritation, rolling out of bed in his wrath. He threatened to go down and look at the name of the factory himself, only refraining because he had a private theory that the factory itself was merely one of Roberta's hallucinations.

"And as for *eggs* . . ." he stuttered.

Jerry dipped into a torn pocket, produced one of the eggs, and laid it on the floor. In the silence that followed, they could all hear the egg ticking.

"You didn't oughta done that, Jerry," Dusty said hoarsely. "That's . . . interfering." They all stared at Jerry, the more frightened because they did not entirely know what they were frightened about.

"I brought it because I thought the factory ought to give us a Christmas present," Jerry told them dreamily, squatting down to look at the egg. "You see, a long time ago, before the machines declared all writers like me redundant, I met an old robot writer. And this old robot writer had been put out to scrap, but he told me a thing or two. And he told me that as machines took over man's duties, so they took over his myths too. Of course, they adapt the myths to their own beliefs, but I think they'd like the idea of handing out Christmas presents."

Dusty gave Jerry a kick which sent him sprawling.

"That's for your idea!" he said. "You're mad, Jerry boy! The machine'll come up here to get that egg back. I don't know what we ought to do."

"I'll put the tea on for some kettle," Roberta said brightly.

The stupid remark made Robin explode.

"Take the egg back, all of you!" he shrieked. "It's stealing, that's what it is, and I won't be responsible. And then you tramps must leave the factory!"

Dusty and Tony looked at him helplessly, and Tony said, "But we got nowhere to go."

Jerry, who had made himself comfortable on the floor, said without looking up, "I don't want to frighten you, but the New Father Christmas will come for you, Mr. Proctor, if you aren't careful. That old Christmas myth was one of the ones the machines took over and changed; the New Father Christmas is all metal and glass, and instead of leaving new toys he takes away old people and machines."

Roberta, listening at the door, went as white as a sheet. "Perhaps that's how the world has grown so depopulated recently," she said. "I'd better get us some tea."

Robin had managed to shuffle out of bed, a ghastly irritation goading him on. As he staggered towards Jerry, the egg hatched.

It broke cleanly into two halves, revealing a pack of neat machinery. Four tiny, busy mannikins jumped out and leapt into action. In no time, using minute welders, they had forged the shell into a double dome; sounds of hammering came from underneath.

"They're going to build another factory right in here, the saucy things!" Roberta exclaimed. She brought the kettle crashing down on the dome and failed even to dent it. At once a thin chirp filled the room.

"My heavens, they are wirelessing for help!" Jerry exclaimed. "We've got to get out of here at once!"

They got out, Robin twittering with rage, and the New Father Christmas caught them all on the stairs.

Ahead

"IT'S TOO CROWDED HERE!" HE EXCLAIMED ALOUD. "IT'S TOO CROWDED! IT'S TOO CROWDED!"

He swung round, his mouth open, his face contorted like a squeezed lemon, nearly knocking a passer-by off the pavement. The passer-by bowed, smiled forgivingly and passed on, his eyes clearly saying: "Let him be—it's one of the poor devils off the ship."

"It's too crowded," Surrey Edmark said again at the retreating back. It was night. He stood hatless under the glare of the New Orchard Road lights, bewildered by the flowing cosmopolitan life of Singapore about him. People: thousands of 'em, touchable; put out a hand gently, feel alpaca, silk, nylon, satin, plain, patterned, or crazily flowered; thousands within screaming distance. If you screamed, just how many of those dirty, clean, pink, brown, desirable or offensive convoluted ears would scoop up your decibels?

No, he told himself, no screaming, please. These people who swarm like phantoms about you are real; they wouldn't like it. And your doctor, who did not consider you fit to leave the observation ward yet, he's real enough; he wouldn't like it if he learnt you had been screaming in a main street. And you yourself—how real were you? How real was *anything* when you had recently had perfect proof that it was all finished? Really finished: rolled up and done with and discarded and forgotten.

That dusty line of thought must be avoided. He needed somewhere quiet, a place to sit and breathe deeply. Everyone must be deceived; he must hide the fused, dead feeling inside from them; then he could go back home. But he had also to try to hide the deadness from himself, and that needed more cunning. Like alpha particles, a sense of futility had riddled him, and he was mortally sick.

Surrey noticed a turning just ahead. Thankfully he went to it and branched out of the crowds into a dim, narrow thoroughfare. He passed three women in short dresses smoking together; farther on, a fellow was being sick into a privet hedge. And there was a café with a sign saying: "The Iceberg." Deserted chairs and tables stood outside on an ill-lit veranda; Surrey climbed the two steps and sat wearily down. This was luxury.

The light was poor, Surrey sat alone. Inside the café several people were eating, and a girl sang, accompanying herself on a stringed, lute-like instrument. He couldn't understand the words, but it was simple and nostalgic, her voice conveying more than the music; he closed his eyes, letting the top spin within him, the top of his emotions. The girl stopped her singing suddenly, as if tired, and walked on to the veranda to stare into the night. Surrey opened his eyes and looked at her.

"Come and talk to me," he called.

She turned her head haughtily to the shadows where he sat, and then turned it back. Evidently, she had met with that sort of invitation before. Surrey clenched his fists in frustration; here he sat, isolated in space and time, needing comfort, needing . . . oh, nothing could heal him, but salves existed. . . . The loneliness welled up inside, forcing him to speak again.

"I'm from the ship," he said, unable to hold back a note of pleading.

At that, she came over and took a seat facing him. She was Chinese, and wore the timeless slit dress of her race, big daisies chasing themselves over the gentle contours of her body.

"Of course I didn't know," she said. "But I can see in your eyes . . . that you are from the ship." She trembled slightly and asked: "May I get you a drink?"

Surrey shook his head. "Just to have you sitting there. . . ."

He was feeling better. Irrationally, a voice inside said: "Well, you've been through a harsh experience, but now you're back again you can recover, can't you, go back to what you were?" The voice frequently asked that: but the answer was always No; the experience was still spreading inside, like cancer.

"I heard your ship come in," the Chinese girl said. "I live just near here—Bukit Timah Road, if you know it, and I was at my window, talking with a friend."

He thought of the amazing sunshine and the eternal smell of cooking fats and the robshaws clacking by and this girl and her friend chattering in a little attic—and the orchestral crash as the ship arrived, making them forget their sentences: but all remote, centuries ago.

"It's a funny noise it makes," he said. "The sound of a time ship breaking out of the time barrier."

"It scares the chickens," she said.

Silence. Surrey wanted to produce something else to say, to keep the girl sitting with him, but nothing would dissolve into words. He neglected the factor of her own human curiosity, which made her keen to stay; she inqured again if he would like a drink, and then said: "Would it be good for you if you told me something about it?"

"I'd call that a leading question."

"It's very—*bad* ahead, isn't it? I mean, the papers say . . ." She hesitated nervously.

"What do they say?" he asked.

"Oh, you know, they say that it's bad. But they don't really explain; they don't seem to understand."

"That's the whole key to it," he told her. "We don't seem to understand. If I talked to you all night, you still wouldn't understand. *I* wouldn't understand. . . ."

She was beautiful, sitting there with her little lute in her hand. And he had travelled far away beyond her lute and her beauty, far beyond nationality or even music; it had all gone into the dreary dust of the planet, all gone—final—nothing left—except degradation. And puzzlement.

"I'll try and tell you," he said. "What was that tune you were just singing? Chinese song?"

"No, it was Malayan. It's an old song, very old, called 'Terang Boelan.' It's about—oh, moonlight, you know, that kind of thing. It's sentimental."

"I didn't even know what language it was in, but perhaps in a way I understood it."

"You said you were going to tell me about the future," she told him gently.

"Yes. Of course. It's a sort of tremendous relief work we're doing. You know what they call it: The Intertemporal Red Cross. It's accurate, but when you've actually been—ahead, it sounds a silly, flashy title. I don't know, perhaps not. I'm not sure of anything any more."

He stared out at the darkness; it was going to rain. When he began to speak again, his voice was firmer.

The I.R.C. is really organized by the Paulls (he said to the

Chinese girl). They call themselves the Paulls; we should call them the technological *élite* of the Three Thousand, One Hundred and Fifty-Seventh Century. That's a terribly long way ahead—we, with our twenty-four centuries since Christ can hardly visualize it. Our ship stopped there, in their time. It was very austere: the Paulls are austere people. They live only on mountains overlooking the oceans, and have moved mountains to every coast for their own edification.

The Paulls are unlike us, yet they are brothers compared with the men we are helping, the Failed Men.

Time travel had been invented long before the age of the Paulls, but it is they who perfected it, they who accidentally discovered the plight of the Failed Men, and they who manage the terrific business of relief. For the world of the Paulls, rich as it is—will be—has insufficient resources to cope alone with the task without vitiating its strength. So it organized the fleet of time ships, the I.R.C., to collect supplies from different ages and bear them out ahead to the Failed Men.

Five different ages are co-operating on the project, under the Paull leadership. There are the Middle People, as the Paulls call them. They are a race of philosophers, mainly pastoral, and we found them too haughty; they live about twenty thousand centuries ahead of the Paulls. Oh, it's a long time. . . . And there are—but never mind the others! They had little to do with us, or we with them.

We—this present day, was the only age without time travel of the five. The Paulls chose up because we happen to have peace and plenty. And do you know what they call us? The Children. The Children! We, with all our weary sophistication. . . . Perhaps they're right; they have a method of gestalt reasoning absolutely beyond our wildest pretensions.

You know, I remember once on the voyage out ahead, I asked one of the Paulls why they had never visited our age before; and he said: "But we have. We broke at the nineteenth century and again at the twenty-sixth. That's pretty close spacing! And that's how we know so much about you."

They have so much *experience,* you see. They can walk round for a day in one century and tell you what'll be happening the next six or seven. It's a difference of outlook, I suppose; something as simple as that.

I suppose you'll remember better than I when the Paulls first broke here, as you are actually on the spot. I was at home then, doing a peaceful job; if it hadn't been so peaceful I might not have volunteered for the I.R.C. What a storm it caused! A good deal of panic in with the excitement. Yes, we proved ourselves children then, *and* in the adulation we paid the Paulls when they toured the world's capitals. During the three months they waited here while we organized supplies and men, they must have been in a fury of impatience to be off; yet they revealed nothing, giving their unsensational lectures on the plight of the Failed Men and smiling for the threedy cameras.

All the while money poured in for the cause, and the piles of tinned food and medical supplies grew and filled the holds of the big ship. We were like kids throwing credits to street beggars: all sorts of stuff of no earthly use went into that ship. What would a Failed Man do with a launderer or a cycloview machine? At last we were off, with all the world's bands playing like mad and the ship breaking with noise enough to drown all bands and startle your chickens—off for the time of the Failed Men!

"I think I'd like that drink you offered me now," Surrey said to the Chinese girl, breaking off his narrative.

"Certainly." She snapped her fingers at arm's length, her hand in the light from the restaurant, her face in the gloom, eyes fixed on his eyes.

"The Paulls had told you it was going to be tough," she said.

"Yes. We underwent pretty rough mental training from them before leaving the here and now. Many of the men were weeded out. But I got through. They elected me Steersman. I was top of their first class."

Surrey was silent a moment, surprised to hear pride in his own voice. Pride left, after that experience! Yet there was no pride in him; it was just the voice running in an old channel, the naked soul crouching in an ancient husk of character.

The drink arrived. The Chinese girl had one, too, a long one in a misty glass; she put her lute down to drink it. Surrey took a sip of his drink and then resumed the story.

We were travelling ahead! (he said). It was a schoolboy's dream come true. Yet our excitement soon became blunted by monotony. There is nothing simultaneous in time travel, as people have imagined. It took us two ship's months to reach the Paulls' age, and there all but one of them left us to continue on alone into the future.

They had the other ages to supervise, and many organizational problems to attend to: yet I sometimes wonder if they did not use those problems as an excuse, to save their having to visit the age of the Failed Men. Perhaps they thought us less sensitive, and therefore better fitted for the job.

And so we went ahead again. The office of Steersman was almost honorary, entailing merely the switching off of power when the journey was automatically ended. We sat about and talked, we chosen few, reading or viewing in the excellent libraries the Paulls had installed. Time passed quickly enough, yet we were glad when we arrived.

Glad!

The age of the Failed Men is far in the future: many hundred millions of years ahead, or thousands of millions; the Paulls would never tell us the exact number. Does it matter? It was a long time. . . . There's plenty of time—too much, more than anyone will ever need.

We stepped out on to that day's earth. I had childishly expected—oh, to see the sun stuck at the horizon, or turned purple, or the sky full of moons, or something equally dramatic; but there was not even a shadow over the fair land, and the earth had not aged a day. Only man had aged.

The Failed Men differed from us anatomically and spiritually; it was the former quality which struck us first. They just looked like a bunch of dejected oddities sitting among piles of stores, and we wanted to laugh. The humorists among us called them "the Zombies" at first—but in a few days there were no humorists left among us.

The Failed Men had no real hands. From their wrists grew five long and prehensile fingers, and the middle digit touched the ground lightly when they walked, for their spines curved in an arc and their heads were thrust far forward. To counter this, their skulls had elongated into boat shapes, scaphocephalic fashion. They had no eyebrows, nor indeed a brow at all, nor any hair at all, although the pores of their skin stood out flakily, giving them a fluffy appearance from a distance.

When they looked at you their eyes held no meaning: they were blank with a surfeit of experience, as though they had now regained a horrible sort of innocence. When they spoke to you, their voices were hollow and their sentences as short and painful as a child's toothache. We could not understand their language, except through the electronic translator banks given us by the Paulls.

They looked a mournful sight, but at first we were not too disturbed; we didn't, you see, quite grasp the nature of the problem. Also, we were very busy, reclaiming more Failed Men from the ground.

Four great aid centres had been established on the earth. Of the other four races in the I.R.C., two managed sanatoria construction and equipment, another nursing, feeding and staffing, and the fourth communication, rehabilitation and liaison between centres. And we—"the Children!"—our job was to exhume the Failed Men and bring them to the centres: a simple job for the simple group! Between us we all had to get the race of man started again—back into harness.

All told, I suppose there are only about six million Failed Men spread over the earth. We had to go out and dig them up. We had specially made tractors with multiple blades on the front which dug slowly and gently into the soil.

The Failed Men had "cemetery areas"; we called them that, although they had not been designed as cemeteries. It was like a bad, silly dream. Working day and night, we trundled forward, furrowing up the earth as you strip back a soiled bed. In the mould, a face would appear, an arm with the long fingers, a pair of legs, tumbling into the light. We would stop the machine and get down to the body, digging with trowels round it. So we would exhume another man or woman—it was hard to tell which they were: their sexual features were not pronounced.

They would be in coma. Their eyes would open, staring like peek-a-boo dolls, then close again with a click. We'd patch them up with an injection, stack them on stretchers and send them back in a load to base. It was a harrowing job, and no pun intended.

When the corpses had had some attention and care, they revived. Within a month they would be up and walking, trundling about the hospital grounds in that round-shouldered way, with great boat-heads nodding at every step. And then it was I talked to them and tried to understand.

The translator banks, being Paull-made, were the best possible. But their limitations were the limitations of our own language. If the Failed Men said their word for "sun," the machine said "sun" to us, and we understood by that the same thing the Failed Men intended. But away from the few concrete, common facts of our experience, the business was less easy. Less synonyms, more overtones: it was the old linguistic problem, but magnified here by the ages which lay between us.

I remember tackling one old woman on our first spell back at the centre. I say old, but for all I know she was sweet sixteen; they just look ancient.

"I hope you don't mind being dug—er, rescued?" I asked politely.

"Not at all. A pleasure," the banks said for her. Polite stereotypes. No real meaning in any language, but the best machine in the world makes them sound sillier than they are.

"Would you mind if we discussed this whole thing?"

"What object?" the banks asked for her.

"I'd asked the wrong question. I did not mean thing—object, but thing—matter." That sort of trip-up kept getting in the way of our discussion; the translator spoke better English than I.

"Can we talk about your problem?" I asked her, trying again.

"I have no problem. My problem has been resolved."

"I should be interested to hear about it."

"What do you require to know about it? I will tell you anything."

That at least was promising. Willing if not co-operative; they had long ago forgotten the principle of co-operation.

"You know I come from the distant past to help you?" The banks translated me undramatically.

"Yes. It is noble of you all to interrupt your lives for us," she said.

"Oh no; we want to see the race of man starting off again on a right track. We believe it should not die away yet. We are glad to help, and are sorry you took the wrong track."

"When we started, we were on a track others before us— you—had made." It was not defiant, just a fact being stated.

"But the deviation was yours. You made it by an act of will. I'm not condemning, mind; obviously you would not have taken that way had you known it would end in failure."

She answered. I gathered she was just faintly angry, probably burning all the emotion in her. Her hollow voice spanged and doomed away, and the translator banks gave out simultaneously in fluent English. Only it didn't make sense.

It went something like this: "Ah, but what you do not realise, because your realising is completely undeveloped and unstarted, is how to fail. Failing is not failing unless it is defeat, and this defeat of ours—if you realise it *is* a failing—is only a failure. A final failure. But as such, it is only a matter of a result, because in time this realisation tends to breed only the realisation of the result of failure; whereas the resolution of our failure, as opposed to the failure——"

"Stop!" I shouted. "No! Save the incantation or the philosophical treatise for later. It doesn't mean anything to me, I'm sorry. We'll take it for granted there was some sort of a failure. Are you going to be able to make a success of this new start we're giving you?"

"It is not a new start," she said, beginning reasonably

enough. "Once you have had the result, a start is almost a solution. It is merely in the result of failing, and all that is in the case is the start or the failure—depending, for us, on the start, for you on the failure. And you can surely see that even here failure depends abnormally on the beginning of the result, which concerns us more than the failure, simply because it is the result. What you don't see is the failure of the result of the resolution's failure to start an open solution——"

"Stop!" I shouted again.

I went to one of the Paull commanders. He was what my mother would have called "a fine man." I told him the thing was beginning to become an obsession with me.

"It is with all of us," he replied.

"But if only I could grasp a fraction of their problem! Look, Commander, we come out here all this way ahead to help them—and still we don't know what we're helping them *from*."

"We know *why* we're helping them, Edmark. The burden of carrying on the race, of breeding a new and more stable generation, is on them. Keep your eye on that, if possible."

Perhaps his smile was a shade too placating; it made me remember that to him we were "the Children."

"Look," I said pugnaciously. "If those shambling failures can't tell us what's happened to them, you can. Either you tell me, or we pack up and go home. Our fellows have the creeps, I tell you! Now what—*explicitly*—is or was wrong with these Zombies?"

The commander laughed.

"We don't know," he said. "We don't know, and that's all there is to it."

He stood up then, austere, tall, "a fine man." He went and looked out of the window, hands behind his back, and I could tell by his eyes he was looking at Failed Men, down there in the pale afternoon.

He turned and said to me: "This sanatorium was designed for Failed Men. But we're filling up with relief staff instead; they've let the problem get them by the throats."

"I can understand that," I said. "I shall be there myself if I don't get to the root of it, racing the others up the wall."

He held up his hand.

"That's what they *all* say. But there is no root of it to get at, or none we can comprehend, or else we are part of the root ourselves. If you could only *categorize* their failure it would be something: religious, spiritual, economic. . . ."

"So it's got *you* too!" I said.

"Look," I said suddenly. "You've got the time ships. Go back and *see* what their problem was!"

The solution was so simple I couldn't think how they had overlooked it; but of course they hadn't overlooked it.

"We've been," the commander said briefly. "A problem of the mind—presuming it was a mental problem—cannot be seen. All we *saw* was the six million of them singly burying themselves in these damned shallow graves. The process covered over a century; some of them had been under for three hundred years before we rescued them. No, it's no good, the problem from our point of view is linguistic."

"The translator banks are no good," I said sweepingly. "It's all too delicate a job for a machine. Could you lend me a human interpreter?"

He came himself, in the end. He didn't want to, but he wanted to. And how would a machine cope with that statement? Yet to you and me it's perfectly comprehensible.

A woman, one of the Failed Men, was walking slowly across the courtyard as we got outside. It might have been the one I had already spoken to, I don't know. I didn't recognize her and she gave no sign of recognizing me. Anyhow, we stopped her and tried our luck.

"Ask her why they buried themselves, for a start," I said.

The Paull translated and she doomed briefly in reply.

"She says it was considered necessary, as it aided the union before the beginning of the attempt," he told me.

"Ask her what union."

Exchange of dooms.

"The union of the union that they were attempting. Whatever that means."

"Did both 'unions' sound the same to you?"

"One was inflected, as it was in the possessive case," the Paull said. "Otherwise they seemed just alike."

"Ask her—ask her if they were all trying to change themselves into something other than human—you know, into spirits or fairies or ghosts."

"They've only got a word for spirit. Or rather, they've got four words for spirit: spirit of soul; spirit of place; spirit of a non-substantive, such as 'spirit of adventure'; and another sort of spirit I cannot define—we haven't an exact analogy for it."

"Hell's bells! Well, try her with spirit of soul."

Again the melancholy rattle of exchange. Then the commander, with some surprise, said: "She says, Yes, they were striving to attain spirituality."

"Now we're getting somewhere!" I exclaimed, thinking

smugly that it just needed persistence and a twenty-fifth-century brain.

The old woman clanged again.

"What's that?" I asked eagerly.

"She says they're still striving after spirituality."

We both groaned. The lead was merely a dead end.

"It's no good," the Paull said gently. "Give up."

"One last question! Tell the old girl we cannot understand the nature of what has happened to her race. Was it a catastrophe and what was its nature? O.K.?"

"Can but try. Don't imagine this hasn't been done before, though—it's purely for your benefit."

He spoke. She answered briefly.

"She says it was an 'antwerto.' That means it was a catastrophe to end all catastrophes."

"Well, at least we're definite on that."

"Oh yes, they failed all right, whatever it was they were after," the Paull said sombrely.

"The nature of the catastrophe?"

"She just gives me an innocent little word, 'struback.' Unfortunately we don't know what it means."

"I see. Ask her if it is something to do with evolution."

"My dear man, this is all a waste of time! I know the answers, as far as they exist, without speaking to this woman at all."

"Ask her if 'struback' means something to do with a possible way they were evolving or meaning to evolve," I persisted.

He asked her. The ill-matched three of us stood there for a long time while the old woman moaned her reply. At last she was silent.

"She says struback has some vague connection with evolution," the commander told me.

"Is that *all* she says?"

"Oh, God, man! Far from it, but that's what it boils down to! 'Time impresses itself on man as evolution,' she says."

"Ask her if the nature of the catastrophe was at least partly religious."

When she had replied, the commander laughed shortly and said: "She wants to know what 'religious' means. And I'm sorry but I'm not going to stand here while you tell her."

"But just because she doesn't know what it means doesn't mean to say the failure, the catastrophe, wasn't religious in essence."

"Nothing means to say anything here," the commander said angrily. Then he realized he was only talking to one of the Children; he went on more gently: "Supposing that instead of coming ahead, we had gone back in time. Suppose we met a prehistoric tribe of hunters. Right! We learn their language. We want to use the word 'luck.' In their superstitious minds the concept—and consequently the word—does not exist. We have to use a substitute they can accept, 'accident,' or 'good-happening' or 'bad-happening,' as the case may be. They understand that all right, but by it they mean something entirely different from our intention. We have not broken through the barrier at all, merely become further entangled in it. The same trap is operating here.

"And now, please excuse me."

Struback. A long, hollow syllable, followed by a short click. Night after night, I turned that word over in my tired mind. It became the symbol of the Failed Men: but never anything more.

Most of the others caught the worry. Some drifted away in a kind of trance, some went into the wards. The tractors became undermanned. Reinforcements, of course, were arriving from the present. The present! I could not think of it that way. The time of the Failed Men became my present, and my past and future, too.

I worked with the translator banks again, unable to accept defeat. I had this idea in my head that the Failed Men had been trying—and possibly involuntarily—to turn into something superior to man, a sort of super-being, and I was intensely curious about this.

"Tell me," I demanded of an old man, speaking through the banks, "when you all first had this idea, or when it came to you, you were all glad then?"

His answer came: "Where there is failure there is only degradation. You cannot understand the degradation, because you are not of us. There is only degradation and misery and you do not comprehend——"

"Wait! I'm *trying* to comprehend! Help me, can't you? Tell me *why* it was so degrading, why you failed, how you failed."

"The degradation was the failure," he said. "The failure was the struback, the struback was the misery."

"You mean there was *just* misery, even at the beginning of the experiment?"

"There was no beginning, only a finish, and that was the result."

I clutched my head.

"Wasn't burying yourself a beginning?"

"No."

"What was it?"

"It was only a part of the attempt."

"What attempt?"

"You are so stupid. Can you not see? The attempt we were making for the resolution of the problematical problem in the result of our united resolve to solve the overall problem."

"Which overall problem?"

"The problem," he said wearily. "The problem of the resolution of this case into the start of failure. It does not matter how the resolution is accomplished provided all the cases are the same, but in a diversity of cases the start determines the resolution and the finish arbitrarily determines the beginning of the case. But the arbitrary factor is itself inherent in the beginning of the case, and of the case itself. Consequently our case is in the same case, and the failure was because of the start, the start being our resolution."

It was hopeless. "You are really trying to explain?" I asked weakly.

"No, you dull young man," he said. "I am telling you about the failure. You are the struback."

And he walked away.

Surrey looked hopelessly across at the Chinese girl. She tapped her fingers on the table.

"What did he mean, 'You are the struback'?" she asked.

"Anything or nothing," he said wildly. "It would have been no good asking him to elucidate—I shouldn't have understood the elucidation. You see it's all either too complex or too simple for us to grasp."

"But *surely*——" she said, and then hesitated.

"The Failed Men could only think in abstractions," he said. "Perhaps that was a factor involved in their failure—I don't know. You see, language is the most intrinsic product of any culture; you can't comprehend the language till you've understood the culture—and how do you understand a culture till you know its language?"

Surrey looked helplessly at the girl's little lute with its own trapped tongue. Suddenly, the hot silence of the night was shattered by a great orchestral crash half a mile away.

"Another carload of nervous wrecks coming home," he told her grimly. "You'd better go and see to your chickens."

Poor Little Warrior!

CLAUDE FORD KNEW EXACTLY HOW IT WAS TO HUNT A BRON-
TOSAURUS. YOU CRAWLED HEEDLESSLY THROUGH THE GRASS
beneath the willows, through the little primitive flowers with
petals as green and brown as a football field, through the
beauty-lotion mud. You peered out at the creature sprawling
among the reeds, its body as graceful as a sock full of sand.
There it lay, letting the gravity cuddle it nappy-damp to the
marsh, running its big rabbit-hole nostrils a foot above the
grass in a sweeping semi-circle, in a snoring search for more
sausagey reeds. It was beautiful: here horror had reached its
limits, come full circle, and finally disappeared up its own
sphincter movement. Its eyes gleamed with the liveliness of a
week-dead corpse's big toe, and its compost breath and the
fur in its crude aural cavities were particularly to be recom-
mended to anyone who might otherwise have felt inclined to
speak lovingly of the work of Mother Nature.

But as you, little mammal with opposed digit and .65 self-
loading, semi-automatic, duel-barrelled, digitally-computed,
telescopically sighted, ruthless, high-powered rifle gripped in
your otherwise-defenceless paws, as you slide along under the
bygone willows, what primarily attracts you is the thunder liz-
ard's hide. It gives off a smell as deeply resonant as the bass
note of a piano. It makes the elephant's epidermis look like a
sheet of crinkled lavatory paper. It is grey as the Viking seas,
daft-deep as cathedral foundations. What contact possible to
bone could allay the fever of that flesh? Over it scamper—you
can see them from here!—the little brown lice that live in
those grey walls and canyons, gay as ghosts, cruel as crabs. If
one of them jumped on you, it would very likely break your

back. And when one of those parasites stops to cock its leg against one of the bronto's vertebrae, you can see it carries in its turn its own crop of easy-livers, each as big as a lobster, for you're near now, oh, so near that you can hear the monster's primitive heart-organ knocking, as the ventricle keeps miraculous time with the auricle.

Time for listening to the oracle is past: you're beyond the stage for omens, you're now headed in for the kill, yours or his; superstition has had its little day for today; from now on only this windy nerve of yours, this shaky conglomeration of muscle entangled untraceably beneath the sweat-shiny carapace of skin, this bloody little urge to slay the dragon, is going to answer all your orisons.

You could shoot now. Just wait till that tiny steam-shovel head pauses once again to gulp down a quarry load of bullrushes, and with one inexpressibly vulgar bang you can show the whole indifferent Jurassic world that it's standing looking down the business end of evolution's sex-shooter. You know why you pause, even as you pretend not to know why you pause; that old worm conscience, long as a baseball pitch, long-lived tortoise, is at work; through every sense it slides, more monstrous than the serpent. Through the passions: saying here is a sitting duck, O Englishman! Through the intelligence: whispering that boredom, the kite-hawk who never feeds, will settle again when the task is done. Through the nerves: sneering that when the adrenalin currents cease to flow the vomiting begins. Through the maestro behind the retina: plausibly forcing the beauty of the view upon you.

Spare us that poor old slipper-slopper of a word, beauty; holy mom, is this a travelogue, nor are we out of it? "Perched now on this titanic creature's back, we see a round dozen—and folks let me stress that round—of gaudily plumaged birds, exhibiting between them all the colour you might expect to find on lovely, fabled Copacabana Beach. They're so round because they feed from the droppings that fall from the rich man's table. Watch this lovely shot now! See the bronto's tail lift. . . . Oh, lovely, yep, a couple of hayricksful at least emerging from his nether end. That sure was a beauty, folks, delivered straight from consumer to consumer. The birds are fighting over it now. Hey, you, there's enough to go round, and anyhow, you're round enough already. . . . And nothing to do now but hop back up onto the old rump steak and wait for the next round. And now as the sun stinks in the Jurassic West, we say 'Fare well on that diet'. . . ."

No, you're procrastinating, and that's a life work. Shoot

the beast and put it out of your agony. Taking your courage
in your hands, you raise it to shoulder level and squint down
its sights. There is a terrible report; you are half stunned.
Shakily, you look about you. The monster still munches, re-
lieved to have broken enough wind to unbecalm the Ancient
Mariner.

Angered—or is it some subtler emotion?—you now burst
from the bushes and confront it, and this exposed condition
is typical of the straits into which your consideration for
yourself and others continually pitches you. Consideration?
Or again something subtler? Why should you be confused just
because you come from a confused civilization? But that's a
point to deal with later, if there is a later, as these two hog-
wallow eyes pupilling you all over from spitting distance tend
to dispute. Let it not be by jaws alone, O monster, but also
by huge hooves and, if convenient to yourself, by mountain-
ous rollings upon me! Let death be a saga, sagacious, Beo-
wulfate.

Quarter of a mile distant is the sound of a dozen hippos
springing boisterously in gymslips from the ancestral mud,
and next second a walloping great tail as long as Sunday and
as thick as Saturday night comes slicing over your head. You
duck as duck you must, but the beast missed you anyway because it so happens that its co-ordination is no better than
yours would be if you had to wave the Woolworth Building
at a tarsier. This done, it seems to feel it has done its duty by
itself. It forgets you. You just wish you could forget yourself
as easily; that was, after all, the reason you had to come the
long way here. Get Away From It All, said the time travel
brochure, which meant for you getting away from Claude
Ford, a husbandman as futile as his name with a terrible wife
called Maude. Maude and Claude Ford. Who could not adjust to themselves, to each other, or to the world they were
born in. It was the best reason in the as-it-is-at-present-consti-
tuted world for coming back here to shoot giant saurians—if
you were fool enough to think that one hundred and fifty
million years either way made an ounce of difference to the
muddle of thoughts in a man's cerebral vortex.

You try and halt your silly, slobbering thoughts, but they
have never really stopped since the coca-collaborating days
of your growing up; God, if adolescence did not exist it
would be unnecessary to invent it! Slightly, it steadies you to
look again on the enormous bulk of this tyrant vegetarian
into whose presence you charged with such a mixed death-
life wish, charged with all the emotion the human orga-
(ni)sm is capable of. This time the bogey-man is real,

Claude, just as you wanted it to be, and this time you really have to face up to it before it turns and faces you again. And so again you lift Ole Equalizer, waiting till you can spot the vulnerable spot.

The bright birds sway, the lice scamper like dogs, the marsh groans, as bronto rolls over and sends his little cranium snaking down under the bile-bright water in a forage for roughage. You watch this; you have never been so jittery before in all your jittered life, and you are counting on this catharsis to wring the last drop of acid fear out of your system for ever. O.K., you keep saying to yourself insanely over and over, your million-dollar, twenty-second-century education going for nothing, O.K., O.K. And as you say it for the umpteenth time, the crazy head comes back out of the water like a renegade express and gazes in your direction.

Grazes in your direction. For as the champing jaw with its big blunt molars like concrete posts works up and down, you see the swamp water course out over rimless lips, lipless rims, splashing your feet and sousing the ground. Reed and root, stalk and stem, leaf and loam, all are intermittently visible in that masticating maw and, struggling, straggling, or tossed among them, minnows, tiny crustaceans, frogs—all destined in that awful, jaw-full movement to turn into bowel movement. And as the glump-glump-glumping takes place, above it the slime-resistant eyes again survey you.

These beasts live up to three hundred years, says the time travel brochure, and this beast has obviously tried to live up to that, for its gaze is centuries old, full of decades upon decades of wallowing in its heavyweight thoughtlessness until it has grown wise on twitterpated-ness. For you it is like looking into a disturbing misty pool; it gives you a psychic shock, you fire off both barrels at your own reflection. Bang-bang, the dum-dums, big as paw-paws, go.

Those century-old lights, dim and sacred, go out with no indecision. These cloisters are closed till Judgment Day. Your reflection is torn and bloodied from them for ever. Over their ravaged panes nictitating membranes slide slowly upwards, like dirty sheets covering a cadaver. The jaw continues to munch slowly, as slowly the head sinks down. Slowly, a squeeze of cold reptile blood toothpastes down the wrinkled flank of one cheek. Everything is slow, a creepy Secondary Era slowness like the drip of water, and you know that if you had been in charge of creation you would have found some medium less heart-breaking than Time to stage it all in.

Never mind! Quaff down your beakers, lords, Claude Ford has slain a harmless creature. Long live Claude the Clawed!

You watch breathless as the head touches the ground, the long laugh of neck touches the ground, the jaws close for good. You watch and wait for something else to happen, but nothing ever does. Nothing ever would. You could stand here watching for a hundred and fifty million years, Lord Claude, and nothing would ever happen here again. Gradually your bronto's mighty carcass, picked loving clean by predators, would sink into the slime, carried by its own weight deeper; then the waters would rise, and old Conqueror Sea would come in with the leisurely air of a card-sharp dealing the boys a bad hand. Silt and sediment would filter down over the might grave, a slow rain with centuries to rain in. Old bronto's bed might be raised up and then down again perhaps half a dozen times, gently enough not to disturb him, although by now the sedimentary rocks would be forming thick around him. Finally, when he was wrapped in a tomb finer than any Indian rajah ever boasted, the powers of the Earth would raise him high on their shoulders until, sleeping still, bronto would lie in a brow of the Rockies high above the waters of the Pacific. But little any of that would count with you, Claude the Sword; once the midget maggot of life is dead in the creature's skull, the rest is no concern of yours.

You have no emotion now. You are just faintly put out. You expected dramatic thrashing of the ground, or bellowing; on the other hand, you are glad the thing did not appear to suffer. You are like all cruel men, sentimental; you are like all sentimental men, squeamish. You tuck the gun under your arm and walk round the land side of the dinosaur to view your victory.

You prowl past the ungainly hooves, round the septic white of the cliff of belly, beyond the glistening and how-thought-provoking cavern of the cloaca, finally posing beneath the switch-back sweep of tail-to-rump. Now your disappointment is as crisp and obvious as a visiting card: the giant is not half as big as you thought it was. It is not one half as large, for example, as the image of you and Maude is in your mind. Poor little warrior, science will never invent anything to assist the titanic death you want in the contra-terrene caverns of your fee-fo-fi-fumblingly fearful id!

Nothing is left to you now but to slink back to your time-mobile with a belly full of anti-climax. See, the bright dung-consuming birds have already cottoned on to the true state of affairs; one by one, they gather up their hunched wings and fly disconsolately off across the swamp to other hosts. They know when a good thing turns back, and do not wait for the vultures to drive them off; all hope abandon, ye who entrail here. You also turn away.

You turn, but you pause. Nothing is left but to go back, no, but A.D. 2181 is not just the home date; it is Maude. It is Claude. It is the whole awful, hopeless, endless business of trying to adjust to an over-complex environment, of trying to turn yourself into a cog. Your escape from it into the Grand Simplicities of the Jurassic, to quote the brochure again, was only a partial escape, now over.

So you pause and, as you pause, something lands socko on your back, pitching you face forward into tasty mud. You struggle and scream as lobster claws tear at your neck and throat. You try to pick up the rifle but cannot, so in agony you roll over, and next second the crab-thing is greedying it on your chest. You wrench at its shell, but it giggles and pecks your fingers off. You forgot when you killed the bronto that its parasites would leave it, and that to a little shrimp like you they would be a deal more dangerous than their host.

You do your best, kicking for at least three minutes. By the end of that time there is a whole pack of the creatures on you. Already they are picking your carcass loving clean. You're going to like it up there on top of the Rockies; you won't feel a thing.

Man on Bridge

VIEW SLIDING DOWN OUT OF THE WEST-MOVING CLOUDS, AMONG THE MOUNTAINS, TO THE ROADS THAT HALT AT THE barbed wire. Sight of electrified fences, ray-gun posts on stilts, uniformed guards, readily familiar to any inhabitant of this continent for the last two hundred, three hundred years. Sun comes out onto dustbins and big slosh buckets behind low cookhouse; guards cuddle rifles, protecting cookhouse and slosh buckets. Flies unafraid of rifles.

Chief living thing in camp: man. Many of them walking or being marched between buildings, which are long-established without losing air of semi-permanence. The inhabitants of this camp have an identification mark which merely makes them anonymous. On their backs is stuck a big yellow C.

C for Cerebral, yellow as prole-custard.

C for Cerebral, a pleasant splash of brains against the monochrome of existence.

A group of C's pushing a cart of refuse over to the tip, conversing angrily. . . .

"Nonsense, Megrip, methadone hydrochloride may be a powerful analgesic, but its use would be impossible in those circumstances, because it would set up an addiction."

"Never liked the ring of that word analgesic. . . ."

"Even postulating addiction, even postulating addiction, I still say——"

The wind blows, the cart creaks.

More C's, swabbing latrines, four of them in dingy grey, talking as the C's always talk, because they have joy in talking and wrangling. Never forget that this is a report of happiness, following the dictum of the great prole-leader, Keils: however much he may appear to suffer, the C is inwardly happy as long as he is permitted to talk freely; with cerebrals, debate replaces the natural prole urges such as action and drinking and procreation. The C's conversing airily in the jakes. . . .

"No, what we are witnessing today are the usual after-effects of any barbarian invasion: the decline of almost all standards causes the conquered race to turn in despair to extremes of vice. This isn't the first time Europe has had to suffer the phenomenon, God knows."

"That would be feasible enough, Jeffers, if there had indeed been an invasion." This one talks intelligently, but through a streaming cold.

"The intelligent have been overwhelmed by the dull. Is not that an invasion?"

"More, I would say, of a self-betrayal, in that——"

Unison flushing of twenty closets drowns sound of cranky voices. The situation is analysed shrewdly enough; they mistake in thinking that analysis is sufficient, and swab contentedly in the grey water round their ankles.

Sun returning fitfully again. It penetrates a drab damp camp room where stand three men. Two are anxious at their approaching visit to the camp commander. One is indifferent to the universe, for he has had half his brain removed. They call him Adam X. He can: stand, sit, lie down, eat and defecate when reminded to do so; he has no habits. One of the other two men, Morgern Grabowicz, thinks Adam X is free, while the other, Jon Winther, regards him as dead.

Adam stands there while the other two argue over him. Sometimes changes of expression steal over his face, gentle smiles, sadnesses, extreme grimaces, all coming and going gradually, as the part of his brain that is left slyly explores territory that belongs to the part of his brain that is gone. The smiles have no relation to the current situation; nor have the sadnesses; both are entirely manifestations of his nervous system.

The chief intelligence behind the complex system of operations he has undergone is Grabowicz, cold and clever old Grabowicz. Winther was involved at every stage, but in a subordinate role. In long months and mazes of delirium, Adam has been where they could not follow. Now Adam is newly out of bed, and Roban Trabann, the camp commander, is prepared to take an interest in his maimed existence.

Grabowicz and Winther wish to converse with Adam, but

as yet conversation is not possible in their meaning of the word. Jon Winther bears the C on his back with an air. He should have been a prole rather than a cerebral, for he has the warmth. He has kept the warmth because he sometimes sees his family, which is solid-prole. The other man, the older, is Morgern Grabowicz, brought here from Styria: hard, cunning, cold, should have two C's on his back. He made Adam X.

Adam X was once just another young C, born Adran Zatrobik, until Grabowicz began the operations on his brain, whittling it away, a slice here, a whole lobe there . . . carving the man himself, until he made Adam X.

Grabowicz is looking remote and withdrawn now, as some C's will when they are angry, instead of letting the true emotion show. Winther is speaking to him in a low voice, also angry. Their voices are relayed to the camp commander because the electricians have finally got the microphones going again in Block B. Two years they have been out of order, despite the highest priority for attention. There are too many cogs in the clumsy machine. The two C's have observed the electricians at work, but are indifferent to what is overheard.

Winther is talking.

"You know why he wants to see us, Morgern. Trabann is no fool. He is going to ask us to take more men like Adam X, and we can't do that."

Grabowicz replies: "As you say, Jon, Trabann is no fool —therefore he will see that we can make more men like Adam. What has once been done can be done again."

Winther replies: "But he doesn't care what happens to any C, or to anyone, for that matter. In your heart, you know that what we have done to Adam is to commit murder, and we cannot do it again!"

"In your descent into melodrama, you neglect a couple of points in logic. Firstly, I care no more than Trabann what is to be the fate of any individual, since I believe the human race to be superfluous; it fulfils no purpose. Secondly, since Adam lives, he cannot be murdered within the legal definition of the term. Thirdly, I say as I have before, that if Trabann gives us the facilities, we can very easily repeat our work, this time improving greatly on the prototype. And fourthly——"

"Morgern, I beg of you, don't go on! Don't make yourself into something as inhuman as we have made Adam! I've only been your friend here so long because I know that within you there is someone who suffers as much as—and for—the rest of us. . . . Drop this stupid estranged attitude! We don't want to collaborate with proles, even gifted ones like Trabann, and we know—you know, that Adam represents our failure, not our success."

Grabowicz paced about the room. When he replied, his voice came distantly.

"You should have been a prole yourself," he told his friend, in that cold flat voice, still without anger. "You have lost the scientific spirit, or you would know that it is still too early to use emotive words like 'success' or 'failure' of our experiment here. Adam is an unknown factor as yet. Nor have scientists ever been morally responsible for the results of their work, any more than the engineer is responsible for the vehicles that collide on the bridge he has built. As to your claim on what you call friendship between us, that can only be based on respect, and in your case——"

"You feel nothing!" Jon Winther exclaims. "You are as dead as Adam X!"

Listening to this argument, Commander Trabann is interested to hear a C using the very accusation the Prole Party brings against all the C's. Since the world's C's were segregated in camps, the rest of the world has run much more smoothly—or run *down* much more smoothly, you may prefer to say—and the terrible rat-race known to both the old communist and capitalist blocks as "progress" has given way to the truly democratic grandeur of the present staticist utopia, where not only all men but all intelligences are equal.

Now Grabowicz speaks to Adam, saying, "Are you ready to go and meet the camp commandant, Adam?"

"I am fully prepared, and await the order to move." Adam's voice is a light one, almost female, but with a slight throatiness. He rarely looks at the men he addresses.

"Are you feeling well this morning, Adam?"

"You will observe that I am standing up. That is to accustom myself to the fits of dizziness to which I am subject. Otherwise, I have no feelings in my body."

Winther says: "Does your head ache, Adam?"

"By my body I implied my whole anatomy. I have no headache."

To Grabowicz, Winther says: "An absence of headache! He makes it sound like a definition of happiness!"

Ignoring his assistant, Grabowicz asks Adam, "Did you dream last night, Adam?"

"I dreamed one dream, of five minutes' duration."

"Well, go on then, man. I have told you before to be alert for the way several following questions may be inferred from a lead question."

"I recall that, Morgern," Adam says meekly, "but I supposed that we were waiting for the signal to leave this room and go to the commander's office. The answer to what I judge your implied question to be is that I dreamed of a bench."

"Ah, that's interesting! You see, Jon? And what was this bench like?"

Adam says: "It has a steel support at each end. It was perfectly smooth and unmarked. I think it stood on a polished floor."

"And what happened?"

"I dreamed of it for five minutes."

Winther says: "Didn't you sit down on the bench?"

Adam: "I was not present in my dream."

Winther: "What happened?"

Adam: "Nothing happened. There was just the bench."

Grabowicz: "You see, Jon! Even his dreams are chemically clean! We have eradicated all the old muddle of the hypothalamus and the visceral areas of the brain. You have here your first purely cerebral man. Putting sentiment aside, you can see what our next task is; we must persuade Trabann to let us have, say, three male C's and three female. They will all undergo the same treatment that Adam has done, and we then segregate them—it will need much co-operation from Trabann and his bosses, of course—and let them breed and rear their children free from outside interference. The result will be the beginning of a clique dominated by pure intellect."

"They'd be incapable of breeding!" Winther said disgustedly. "By by-passing Adam's visceral brain, we've deprived him of half his autonomic nervous system. He could no more get an erection than fly!"

Then the guards came shouting, cursing the three C's out of their refuge of words into the real world of hard fact.

Patched boots on the patched concrete. On the distant mountains, sunshine, lingering, then sweeping down towards the town of Saint Praz, below the camp. Sky almost all blue. Adam X walking carefully among them, looking at the ground to keep his balance as he is marched to the office.

Trabann makes a good camp commander. Not only is he formidably ugly, he has some pretention of being "brainy," and so is jealous of the two thousand C's under him, and treats them accordingly.

All the while Grabowicz is delivering his report, Trabann sits glaring at Adam X, his bulbous nose shining over the bristles of his moustache. Of course Trabann can come to no decision: everything must be passed on to his superiors: but he does his best to look like a man about to come to a decision, as he stirs and shuffles inside his heavy clothes.

While Winther stands by, Grabowicz does most of the talking, going into lengthy technical details of the surgery, and quoting from his notes. Trabann becomes bored, ceasing to listen since this is all being recorded on a tape machine by a secretary. He becomes more interested when Grabowicz puts forward his idea for creating more men and women like Adam and trying to breed from them. Breeding Trabann understands, or at least the crude mechanics of it.

Finally, Trabann examines Adam X, speaking to him, and questioning him. Then he purses his lips and says slowly to Grabowicz, "What you do, told in plain language, is wipe out this man's subconscious."

Grabowicz replies: "Don't give me that antiquated Freudian nonsense. I mean, sir, that the body of theoretic work incorporating the idea of the sub-conscious mind was discountenanced over a century ago. At least, in the C camps it was."

Trabann makes a note that once Grabowicz has served his purpose he undergoes treatment B35, or even B38. He sharply dismisses Grabowicz, who is marched off protesting, while Jon Winther and Adam X are made to stay. Trabann considers Winther a useful man for making trouble among C's themselves; he has some prole features, despite such typical cerebral habits as habitual use of forbidden past and future tenses in his speech.

Trabann says to Winther: "Suppose we are breeding these purely intellectual children, are they cerebrals or proles?"

Winther: "Neither. They will be new people, if they can be bred. I have my doubts about that."

Trabann: "But *if* they are bred—they are on your side?"

Winther: "Who can say? You are thinking of something twenty years ahead."

Trabann: "You are trying to trap me for you know that such thinking is treasonable. It is not for a prisoner to trap his commandant."

Winther, shrugging his shoulders: "You know why I am a prisoner—because the laws are so stupid that we prefer to break them than live by them, although it means life-long imprisonment."

Trabann: "For that retort, distorting reality of world situation, an hour's D90 afterwards. You can admit to me freely that you and all C's wish to rule the world."

Winther: "Need we have that one again?"

The guards are summoned to administer the D90 on the

spot. Before it is carried out, Winther defiantly claims cerebrals more capable of governing well than what he terms
"anti-intellectuals." He adds that C's undergo much of what
they suffer as a sort of self-imposed discipline, since they believe that one must serve to rule. So again we meet this dangerous C heresy, first formulated in the forty-fifth chapter of
the prime work of our great master Keils. How wise he was
to categorise this belief that dominance lies through servitude
as "extreme cerebral terrorism."

When the D90 is over, Adam X is given a few blows
across the face, and the two C's are dismissed and returned to
the square.

That day, Trabann works long over his report. Dimly, he
senses great potential. He does not understand what Adam X
can do. He gets bored with the effort of trying to think, and
is unhappy because he knows thinking, or at least "thinking-
to-a-purpose" is on the black list of party activities.

But two nights later, Camp Commander Trabann is much
more happy. The local militia brings him a document written
by the C Jon Winther that tells Trabann things he feels his
superiors desire to know. It tells them certain things about
Adam's abilities. He passes it on with a memorandum ex-
pressing his detestation at the cerebral attitudes expressed in
the manuscript. Here follows the Winther manuscript, which
begins as Winther is recovering from the administration of
the D90 already mentioned.

There was a long period when I lay between consciousness
and unconsciousness, aware only of the palsy in my body
(Jon Winther writes). They had injected the mouth of a
quick-vacuum pump into one of my arteries and sucked all
my blood from my body, syphoning it rapidly back again as I
fell senseless. What finally drew my attention away from the
jarring of my bruised heart was the sound of Adam X,
breathing heavily near me.

I rolled myself over onto my stomach and looked at him.
His nose was still bleeding slightly, his face and clothes disfig-
ured with blood.

When he saw me looking at him, he said, "I do not wish to
live, Jon."

I don't want to hate them, but I hated them when I looked
at Adam; and I hated our side too, for Adam could be reck-
oned a collaboration between the two sides. "Wipe your face,
Adam," I said. He was incapable even of thinking of doing
that for himself.

We lay about in a stupor of indifference until a guard came and told us it was time to move. Shakily, I got to my feet and helped Adam up. We moved outside, into warm and welcome afternoon sun.

"Time's so short and so long," I said. I was light-headed; even at the time, the words sounded foolish. But feeling that sun, I knew myself to be a living organism and blessed with a consciousness that lasted but a flash yet often seemed, subjectively, to be the burden of eternity.

Adam stood woodenly by me and said without changing his expression, "You see life as a contrast between misery and pleasure, Jon; that is not a correct interpretation."

"It's a pretty good rule of thumb, I should have thought."

"Thought and non-thought is the only valid line of comparison."

"Bit of a bird's-eye view, isn't it? That puts us on the same level as the proles."

"Exactly."

Suddenly angry, I said, "Look, Adam, let me take you home. I'd like to get you away from the camp atmosphere. My sisters can look after us for a few hours. Knowing Trabann, I think there's a pretty good chance the guard will let us through the gates."

"They will not let me through because I am a specimen."

"When Trabann is not sure what to do, he likes a bit of action."

When he nodded indifferently, I took his arm and led him towards the gates. It was always an ordeal, moving towards those slab-cheeked Croat guards, so contemptuous of eye, so large in their rough uniforms and boots, as they stood there holding their rifles like paddles. We produced our identity sticks, which were taken from us, and were allowed to pass, and go through the side-gate, between the strands of barbed wire, into the free world outside.

"They enjoy their show of might," Adam said. "These people have to express their unhappiness by using ugly things like guns and ill-fitting uniforms, and the whole conception of the camp."

"We are unhappy, but we don't find that sort of thing necessary."

"No, Jon, I am not unhappy. I just feel empty and do not wish to live."

His talk was full of that sort of conversation-stopper.

We strode down the road at increasing pace as the way steepened between cliffs. The ruined spires and roofs of the town were rising out of the dip ahead, and I wanted only to get home; but since I had never caught Adam in so communicative a frame of mind, I felt I had to take advantage of it and find out what I could from him.

"This not wishing to live, Adam—this is just post-operational depression. When it wears off, you will recover your spirits."

"I think not. I have no spirits. Morgern Grabowicz cut them away. I can only reason, and I see that there is no point to life but death."

"That I repudiate with all my heart. On the contrary, while there is life, there is no death. Even now, with all my limbs aching from that filthy prole punishment, I rejoice in every breath I take,, and in the effect of the light on those houses, and the crunch of this track under our feet."

"Well, Jon, you must be allowed your simple vegetable responses." He spoke with such finality, that my mouth was stopped.

The little town of Saint Praz is just above the line of the vine, though the brutal little river Quiviv that cuts the town in two goes hurtling down to water the vineyards only ten kilometres away. The bridge that spans the Quiviv marks the beginning of Saint Praz; next to it stands the green-domed church of Saint Praz And The Romantic Agony, and next to the church is the street in which the remains of my family live. As we climbed its cobbled way, I saw my sister Bynca leaning out of the upper window, talking to someone below. We went into the house, and Bynca ran to welcome me with cries of delight.

"Darling Jon, your face is so drawn!" she cried when she came almost to the end of hugging me. "They've been ill-treating you up in the C camp again! We will hide you here and you shall never go back to them."

"Then they will come and burn this house down and chase you and poor Anr and Pappy into the mountains!"

"Then instead we will leave all together for some far happy country, and keep a real cow, and Pappy and you can grow figs and catch tunny in the sea."

"And you can start slimming, Bynca!"

"Pah, you're jealous because I'm a well-built girl and you're a reed."

When I introduced her to Adam, some of her smile went. She made him welcome, nonetheless, and was getting us glasses of cold tea when my father came in. Father was thin and withered and bent, and smelt as ever pleasantly of his home-grown tobacco; like my sisters, he had the settled expression of a certain kind of peasant—the kind that accepts, with protest but without malice, the vagaries of life. It is the gift life sends to compensate for the lack of a high I.Q.

"It's a long time since we saw you, son," he said to me. "I thought you'd come down before the winter fell. Things don't get any better in Saint Praz, I can tell you. You know the power station broke down in July and they still haven't mended it—can't get the parts, Geri was telling me. We go to bed early, these cold nights, to save fuel. And you can't buy a candle these days, not for love nor money."

"Nonsense, Pappy, Anr brought us two last week from Novok market."

"Maybe, my girl, but Novok's a long way away."

When my sister Anr came in, our family was complete again—as complete as it will be on this Earth, for my mother died of a fever a dozen years ago, my elder sister Myrtyr was killed in riots when I was a child, and my two brothers walked down the valley many years since, and have never been heard of again. There's another sister, Saraj, but since she married, she has quarrelled with Pappy over a question of dowry, and the two sides are not on speaking terms.

Adam sat in our midst, sometimes sipping his tea, looking straight ahead and hardly appearing to bother to listen to our chatter. After a while, my father brought out a little leather bottle of plum brandy and dosed our coffees with some of its contents.

"Disgusting habit," he said, winking at me, "but p'raps it'll put a bit of life into your friend, eh, Jon? You're mighty like my idea of a cerebral, Mr. Adam, too intelligent to trouble yourself with poor people like us."

"Do not become curious about me, Mr. Winther," Adam said. "I am different from other men."

"Is that a boast or a confession?" Anr asked, and she and Bynca went off into peals of laughter. I saw an old woman outside in the sunlight turn her head and smile at the sound as she went past. My cheeks flushed as I sensed the hostility between Adam and the others; it leapt into being as if a tap had been turned on.

"Adam has just come through a series of painful operations," I said, trying to apologise to both sides.

"Are you going to show us your scars, Mr. Adam?" Anr asked, still giggling.

"You don't get any fancy hospital treatment in Saint Praz if you're classified as prole," father said. I knew that he threw it in as a general observation, as a shrewd bit of information he felt was part of his life's experience. But Adam's chip of brain would not register such undertones.

"I have become a new sort of man," he said flatly.

I saw their faces turned to him, flat and unreceptive. He did not amplify. They did not ask. Caught between them, I knew he did not think it worth while explaining anything to them; like most C's, he reciprocated the dislike of the proles. They, in their turn, suspected him of boasting—and although there were many boasters in Saint Praz, the convention was that one did it with a smile on one's face, to take away the sting, or the wrath of the devil, should he be listening.

"The curse of the human race has been animal feeling," Adam said. He was staring up at the dark rafters, his face stiff and cold, but made ludicrous for all that by his red swollen nose. "There was a time, two or three centuries ago, when it looked as if the intellect might win over the body, and our species become something worthwhile. But too much procreation killed that illusion."

"Are you—some sort of a better person than the rest of us?" father asked him.

"No. I am only a freak. I do not belong anywhere."

Silence would have fallen had I not said roughly, "Come off it, Adam—you're welcome here, or I wouldn't have brought you."

"And as usual you must be famished, poor things," Bynca said, jumping up. "We'll have a feast tonight, that's what! Anr, run down to old Herr Sudkinzin and see what he has left of that sow his son slaughtered on Monday. Pappy, if you light up the fire, these two convicts can have a turn in the tub tonight. I think Jon smells a bit high, like an old swine in from a muck-wallow!"

"Very like, Bynca," I said, laughing, "but if so I'm perfectly ready to be home-cured."

With a gesture that seemed half-way between reverence and contempt, my father pushed away the electric fire—useless since the power station ceased to function—from the centre of the hearth and began preparations to light the ancient iron stove. My sisters began bustling about, Anr fetching in kindling from the stack under the eaves. I stood up. They loved me here, but there was no real place for me. My real place was up in the camp, I thought—not without self-pity, but with truth; up there was my own room, shabby, yes, yet full of my books, shabby too, but duplicated right there on the camp press.

Christ's blood, that was the place my kind had chosen, over a century ago. The common people had often revolted against the rich—but the rich were not identifiable once shorn of their money; then the tide of anger turned against the intelligent. You can always tell an intellectual, even when he cowers naked and bruised before you with his spectacles squashed in the muck; you only have to get him to talk. So the intellectuals had elected to live in camps, behind wire, for their own safety. Things were better now—because we were fewer and they infinitely more; but the situation had changed again: the stay was no longer voluntary, for we had lost our place in the world. We had even lost our standing in the camps. Throughout the more-than-mediaeval darkness that had fallen over Europe, our cerebral monasteries were ruled over by the pistol and whip; and the flagellation of the new order of monks was never self-inflicted.

"Some visitors coming to see you, son," father said, peering through the tiny panes of the window. He straightened his back and brushed at his coat, smiling and nodding to himself.

There was no time for thinking from then on. As Anr went down through the town to see the butcher, she called out to her friends that I was home and had brought along a strange man. Gradually those friends straggled round, to look in and drink my health in some of my father's small store of wine, and cast many a curious look at Adam, and ask many a question about what happened in the camp—was it true that we were going to invent a sort of ray that would keep the frost from the tender spring crops, and so on.

When I was tired of talking to them, and that moment came soon, they talked amiably to each other, exchanging the gossip of Saint Praz, drinking the wine. The butcher came back with Anr, his son beside him carrying half a side of pig, and disappeared into the kitchen to help my sisters cook it. The son pushed himself a place beside our stove, and faced up to the wine with gusto. In time, my sisters, very red of cheek, returned to the room, thick by now with smoke and rumour, bearing with them a big steaming goulash, which the company devoured, laughing and splashing as they did so. We ate it with chunks of bread and followed it with black coffee. Afterwards, the visitors wished to stay and see Adam and me in the tub; but, with lewd jokes and roars of mirth, Anr and my father finally saw them off. We could hear them laughing and singing as they made their way down the street.

"You should come home more often, my boy," father said, mopping his brow as he laced the latch on the last of his guests.

"So I would, Father, if your neighbors didn't descend on you and eat you out of house and home every time I put in an appearance."

"Spoken like a damned cerebral," he said. "Always the thought for the morrow! No offence to you, son, but there'd be no joy in the world at all if your sort ruled . . . Life's bad enough as it is. . . . Eh, wish your mother were alive this night, Jon. The good wine makes me feel young and randy again."

He staggered round the room while my sisters brought in the great tub in which the family's infrequent baths had been taken since the day—some years back now—when the reservoir up in the hills was ruptured by earth tremors, and the taps in the bathroom ceased to yield anything but rust.

"Where's your fragile friend Adam?" Anr asked.

For the first time, I noticed Adam was not there. His presence had been so withdrawn that his absence had left no gap. Tired though I was, I ran upstairs calling him, hurried into the yard at the back and called him there. Adam did not appear.

"Eh, leave him—he must have cleared off with the folks," father said. "Let him stay away. We shall hardly miss him."

"He's not fit to wander around alone," I said. "I must go and find him."

"I'll come with you," Bynca said, slipping into an old fur wrap that had belonged to my mother. Anr called derisively that we were wasting our time, but Bynca could see how worried I was, seized my arm, and hustled out of the door with me.

"What's so important about this man? Can't he look after himself like any other young chap?" she asked.

I tried to answer, but the cold had momentarily taken my breath away. The stars froze in the sky overhead; Jupiter steered over the shoulder of the mountain behind us, and beneath our feet the cobbles sparkled and rang. The cold immediately set up a strongpost of frost in my chest, which I tried to dislodge by coughing.

At last I said to her, "He's important—had a brain operation. Could be the beginning of a pure brain kind of man who would overturn the regime—could be a mindless kind that would give the regime a race of slaves. Naturally, both regime and the C's are interested in finding out which he is."

"I wonder they let him come out if he's so important."

"You know them, Bynca—they're keeping watch. They want to see how he behaves when he is free. So do I."

The sound of the river, tumbling in its broken bed, accompanied us down the street. I thought I could also hear voices, although the street was deserted. As we rounded the bulk of the church, the voices came clear, and we saw the knot of people standing on the bridge.

Perhaps a dozen people clustered there, most of them lately the guests of my father's house. Two of them carried lanterns, one a splendid pitch torch, which the owner held aloft. This beacon, smoking and flickering, gave the scene most of what light it had. So unexpected was the sight of them gathered there that instinctively Bynca and I stopped in the middle of the road.

"Sweet Saviour!" Bynca exclaimed. I saw as she spoke what made her exclaim. Of the crowd that now partly turned to face us—was it imagination or a primitive visceral sense that instantly read their hostility?—only one figure was indifferent to our arrival. That figure was apart from the rest. It stood with its back partly turned to Bynca and me and, with its arms extended sideways at shoulder level in an attempt at balance, was trying to walk the narrow parapet that bounded the north side of the bridge.

So alarmed was I that anyone should undertake so foolish a feat, that I did not realise for a moment that it was Adam X, even though I saw the yellow C on his back. The bridge over the Quiviv has stood there for many centuries, and has probably not been repaired properly since the days of the Dual Monarchy, a couple of centuries ago at least. The chest-high walls that guard either side of it are crumbled and notched by the elements and the urchins who for generations have used the bridge as their playground. But it takes a bold urchin, even bare-foot and on a bright morning, to jump up onto the top of the wall and ignore the drop onto the rocks below. And now Adam, subject to giddiness, was walking along the wall by the fitful light of a torch.

As I ran forward, I shouted, "Who put him up to doing that? Get him down at once. That man is ill!"

A hand was planted sharply in the middle of my chest. I came face to face with the butcher's son, Yari Sudkinzin. I'd watched him earlier, when he was sitting against our stove, contriving to get more than his fair share of the wine.

"Keep out of this, you C!" he said. "Your buddy friend here is just showing us what he can do."

"If you made him get up there, get him down at once. He'll slip to his death at any minute."

"He insisted on doing it, get it? Said he would show us he was as good as us. You'd better stand back if you know what's good for you."

And as he was speaking, the women with him clustered

about us, telling me earnestly, "We told him he was mad, but he would do it, he would do it, he would climb up there!"

Breaking through them, I went to Adam, carefully now, so that I would not startle him. His broken shoes rasped against the crumbled stone at the level of my chest. He moved very slowly, one small step at a time. He would be frozen before he got across, if he got across. He was coming now to the first of the little bays that hung out from the bridge and housed benches for the convenience of pedestrians. The angles he would have to turn would make his task more dangerous. Below us, the Quiviv roared and splashed without cease.

"Come down, Adam," I said. "It's Jon Winther here. Let me help you down!"

He said only one thing to me, but it explained much that had led to his climbing up where he was: "I will show them what a superman can do."

"Adam—it's time we were tucked in a warm bed by the side of the fire. Give me your hand."

For an answer, he kicked out sideways at me.

His shoe caught me a light knock on the cheek. He lost his footing entirely, and was falling even as he struck me. I grabbed at his foot, at his trousers, cried aloud, felt myself dragged sharply against the parapet, my elbows rasped over it, as his weight came into my grasp, and his body disappeared over the wall.

He made no sound!

For a ghastly moment, I thought I too was going to be carried below with him. The roar of the Quiviv over its rocks sounded horribly loud. Without thought, I let go of him— perhaps because of fear, perhaps because of the pain in my arms, or the cold in my body, or perhaps because of some deeper, destructive thing that emerged in me for a second. I let go of him, and he would have fallen to his death had not two of the men in the party managed to grasp him almost as I let go.

Panting and cursing, they pulled Adam up over the wall, and dumped him like a sack of potatoes onto the bench. His nose was bleeding, otherwise he seemed unharmed. But he did not speak.

"That's all your doing!" young Yari Sudkinzin said to me. "He was nearly a dead 'un, thanks to you!"

"I could draw a moral far less comforting to you," I told him. "Why don't you clear off home?"

In the end they did go, leaving Bynca and me to return with Adam's two rescuers, who supported Adam up the street. In the way that news travels in our towns, several people were already lighting up their lamps and peering from their windows and doors to see what was going on; along the road, I heard the militia questioning—I hoped—the butcher's son. With this prompting, we made what haste we could home.

Father and Anr made a great bother when we got back. I went to lie down and warm myself by the fire, while all the aspects of what had happened were thrashed out with Bynca. After a while, Adam, who had bathed his face in a bucket outside, came and slumped down beside me, stretching as I did on the reed mats before the stove.

"There is less irrationality up in the camp," he said. "Let us go back. At least we understand that they hit us because they hate us."

"You must tell me, Adam—Grabowicz will want to know —why you did that foolish thing on the bridge. To accept a stupid dare like that is the work of a child, but to show such a lack of fear is unhuman. What are you, how do you analyse yourself?"

He made a noise that imitated a laugh. "Nobody can understand me," he said. "I can't understand myself until there are more like me."

I told him then. "I can't work on these brain operations any more."

"Grabowicz can. Grabowicz will. You're too late to be squeamish, Jon; already there is a new force in the world."

After what I had seen on the bridge, I felt he might be right. But a new force for good or bad? How would the change come? What would it be? I closed my eyes and saw clearly the sort of world that Grabowicz and I, with the unwitting co-operation of the prole leaders, might have already brought into being. Given enough men and women like Adam, with their visceral brains removed, they would bring up children unswayed and unsoftened by human emotion, whose motives were inscrutable to the rest of mankind. The rulers of our world would find such people very useful at first, and so a place would be made for them. And from being instruments of power, they would turn into a power in their own right. It was a process often witnessed by history.

I rolled over and looked at Adam. He appeared to be already asleep. Perhaps he was dreaming one of his sterile dreams, without incident, or body, or turmoil. Despairing, I too tried to close down my mind.

As I lay there with my eyes shut, my old father, thinking me asleep, stooped to kiss my forehead before settling himself to sleep on the fireside bench.

"I must go back to camp tomorrow, father," I murmured.

But in the morning—this morning—father and my sisters prevailed on me to stay till the afternoon, to share their frugal midday meal with them and then go.

I sit now in the upstairs room where Anr and Bynca sleep, catching the first of the sun as it struggles clear of the mountain ridge, and trying to write this account. I feel that something awful is about to happen, that we are at one of those turning points in the story of the world. A secret record may be useful for those who come after.

Adam sits downstairs, silent. It is strange that one feeble man——

The militia are downstairs! They forced their way in, and I hear them shout for me and Adam. Of course the tale of last night got back up there. Dear Bynca will be downstairs, confronting them with her plump arms folded, giving me time to get away. But I must go back with them, to the camp. Perhaps if I killed Grabowicz . . .

This manuscript shall go under the loose floorboard that we used to call "Bynca's board," when we were kids, so long ago. They'll never find it there, or get it except over her dead body.

The Impossible Star

WHEN CONDITIONS VEER AWAY FROM NORMAL, HUMAN REASON TENDS TO SLIP INTO MADNESS.

Eddy Sharn looked at the sentence in his notebook and found it good. He sat with the notebook clutched in tight to his chest, so that Malravin could not see what he wrote. "Tends to slip into madness" he particularly liked; the "tends" had a note of scientific detachment about it, the "madness" suggested something altogether more wild than "insanity." Which was appropriate, since they were a scientific detachment out in the wilds.

He was still savouring his little joke when the noises began in the hatch.

Malravin and Sharn exchanged glances. Malravin jerked his head towards the hatch.

"You hear that fool fellow Dominguey? He makes all that noise on purpose, so that we'll know he's coming. What a big-headed joker to chose for a captain!"

"You can't help making a noise in that hatch," Sharn said. "It was badly designed. They missed out on the soundproofing and the noise carries round in the air circuits. Besides, they're both in there making a noise. Jim Baron's with him."

He spoke pleasantly enough, but of course Malravin's had been a loaded remark. The great Siberian oaf knew that among the four antagonisms that had sprung up between the four men on the ship, some sort of an alliance had grown between Sharn and Dominguey.

The hatch opened, and the other members of the crew of the "Wilson" entered and began to remove their bulky suits.

Neither Malravin nor Sharn moved to help them. Dominguey and Baron helped each other.

Billy Dominguey was a striking young man, dark and sinewy, with a wonderfully gloomy cavern of a face that could break into laughter when anyone responded to his peculiar sense of fun.

Jim Baron was another doleful-looking type, a little compact man with a crew-cut and solid cheeks that had turned red from his exertions outside.

He eyed Sharn and Malravin and said, "Well, you'd better get your sacks on and go out and have a look at it. You won't grasp its full impact until you do."

"It's a real little education, Jim, isn't it?" Dominguey agreed. "A higher education—I just wish they hadn't 'highered' me to get it."

Baron put his arms out with his fingers extended and touched the plastic of the bulkheads. He closed his eyes.

"I didn't think I'd ever make it back into here, Billy. I'm sorry if I went a bit——"

Quickly, Dominguey said, "Yes, it's good to be back in the ship. With the artificial ½ G being maintained in here, and the shutters down, this dump seems less like a cast-off version of hell, doesn't it?" He took Baron's arm and led him to a chair. Sharn watched curiously; he had not seen the stolid and unimaginative Baron so wild-eyed before.

"But the weight business," Baron was saying. "I thought—well, I don't know what I thought. There's no rational way of putting it. I thought my body was disintegrating. I——"

"Jim, you're over-excited," Dominguey said harshly. "Keep quiet or get yourself a sedative." He turned to the other two men. "I want you two to get outside right away. There's nothing there that can possibly harm you; we're down on a minor planet, by the looks of things. But before we can evaluate the situation, I want you to be properly aware of what the situation is—as soon as possible."

"Did you establish the spectroscope? Did you get any readings?" Sharn asked. He was not keen to go outside.

"They're still out there. Get your suit on, Eddy, and you, Ike, and go and look at them. Jim and I will get a bite to eat. We set the instruments up and we left 'em out there on the rock, pointing at Big Bertha, but they don't give any readings. Not any readings that make sense."

"For God's sake, you must have got something. We checked all the gear before you carted it outside."

"If you don't believe us, you get out there and have a god-damned good look for yourself, Sharn," Baron said.

"Don't shout at me, Baron."

"Well, take that sick look off your face. Billy and me have done our stint—now you two get outside as Billy says. Take a walk around as we did. Take your time. We've got plenty till the drive is mended."

Malravin said, "I'd prefer to get on straightening out the coil. No point for me to go out there. My job is in the ship."

"I'm not going out there alone, Ike, so don't try to worm out of it," Sharn said. "We agreed that we should go out there when these two came back."

"If we came back, conquering heroes that we are," Dominguey corrected. "You might have had a meal ready to celebrate our return, Eddy."

"We're on half rations, if you remember."

"I try never to remember a nasty fact like that," Dominguey said good-humouredly.

A preoccupation with food signifies a childish nature, Eddy thought. He must write it down later.

After more quarrelling, Sharn and Malravin climbed into their suits and headed for the hatch. They knew roughly what they would see outside—they had seen enough from the ship's ports before they had agreed to close down all the shutters—but to view it from outside was psychologically a very different matter.

"One thing," Baron called to them. "Watch out for the atmosphere. It has a way of wandering."

"There can't be an atmosphere on a planetoid this size!" Sharn protested.

Baron came up to him and peeped through the helmet at him. His cheeks were still hectically flushed, his eyes wild.

"Look, clever dick, get this into your head. We've arrived up in some ghastly hole in the universe where the ordinary physical laws don't apply. This place can't exist and Big Bertha can't exist. Yet they do. You're very fond of paradoxes —well, now one has gobbled you up. Just get out there quickly, and you won't come back in as cocky as you are now."

"You love to blow your mouth off, Baron. It didn't do you much good out there. I thought you were going to die of fright just now."

Dominguey said urgently, "Hey, you two sweet little fellows, stop bitching. I warn you, Eddy, Jim is right. You'll see when you get outside that in this bit of heaven the universe is horribly out of joint."

"So will someone's nose be," Sharn promised.

He tramped into the hatch with Malravin. The burly Siberian thumbed the sunken toggle switches on the panel, and the air lock sank to ground level, its atmosphere exhausting as it went.

They unsealed the door and stepped out onto the rough surface of the planetoid Captain Dominguey had christened Erewhon. They stood with the doughnut shape of the "Wilson" on stilts behind them and tried to adjust to the prospect. If anything, they seemed to weigh slightly more than they had in the ship's artificially maintained ½ G field, although the bulk of their suits made this hard to tell.

At first it was difficult to see anything; it was always to remain difficult to see anything well.

They stood on a tiny plain. The distance of the horizon was impossible to judge in the weird light. It seemed never more than a hundred yards away in any direction. It was distorted; this seemed to be because the plain was irregular. High banks, broken hollows, jagged lips of rock, formed the landscape, the features running higgledy-piggledy in a way that baffled sense. There was no sign of the atmosphere Baron had mentioned; the stars came down to the skyline and were sharply occulted by it.

With the hand claws of their suits touching, the two men began to walk forward. They could see Baron's instruments standing deserted a short way off, and instinctively moved towards them. There was no need for lights; the entire bowl of the sky was awash with stars.

The "Wilson" was a deep penetration cartographic ship. With two sister ships, it was the first such vessel to venture into the heart of the Crab Nebula. There, weaving its way among the endless abysses of interstellar dust, it lost contact with the "Brinkdale" and the "Grandon." The curtains of uncreated matter closed in on them, baffling even the subradio.

They went on. As they went, the concepts of space they had once held were erased. This was a domain of light and matter, not of emptiness and dark. All about them were coils of smoke—smoke set with sequins!—and cliffs of shimmering dust the surface of which they could not have explored in two lifetimes. To begin with the four men were elated at the sheer magnificence of the new environment. Later, the magnificence seemed not of beauty but of annihilation. It was too big, they were too insignificant. The four men retreated into silence.

But the ship continued on its course, for they had their orders and their honour, and their pay. According to plan, the

"Wilson" sank into the heart of the nebula. The instrumentation had developed an increasing fault until it became folly to go farther, but fortunately they had then come to a region less tightly packed with stars and star matter. Beyond that was space, light years across, entirely free of physical bodies —except one.

They found soon enough that it was no stroke of fortune to be here. Swilling in the middle of the gigantic hole in space was the phenomenon they christened Big Bertha.

It was too big. It was impossible. But the instruments ceased to be reliable; without instruments, human senses were useless in such a region. Already bemused by travel, they were ill-equipped to deal with Big Bertha. To add to their troubles, the directional cyboscope that governed the jets in the ship's equator broke down and became unreliable.

They took the only course open to them: they landed on the nearest possible body, to rest there while they did a repair job and re-established contact with their sister ships. The nearest possible body happened to be Erewhon.

Touchdown on Erewhon had been a little miracle, accomplished with few other instruments than human eyes, human hands, and a string of human blasphemies. The hammer of static radiated by Big Bertha rendered radio, radar, and radix all ineffective.

Now the sky was a wonder painful to view. Everywhere were the glittering points of stars, everywhere the immense plumes and shawls of inchoate matter illuminated by starshine. Yet it was all far away, glittering beyond the gravitational pull of Bertha. In her domain, only the wretched planetoid the "Wilson" rested on seemed to exist. It was like being a bone alone in an empty room with a starving dog.

"Gravitation can be felt not only in the muscles but in the thalamus. It is a power of darkness, perhaps the ultimate power."

"What's that?" Malravin asked, startled.

"I was thinking aloud." Embarrassed, Sharn added, "Bertha will rise in a minute, Ike. Are you ready for it?"

They stopped by the pathetic cluster of instruments. They just stood there, rooted to the spot with a tension that could not be denied. Bertha had already begun to rise.

Their eyes were bad judges of what happened next, even with the infra-red screens pulled down over their faceplates. But they partly saw—and partly they felt, for a tidal sensation crawled across their bodies.

Above the eastern horizon, a section of the star field began to melt and sag. Star after star, cluster after cluster, uncoun-

tably stratified and then wavered and ran towards the horizon
like ill-applied paint trickling down a wall. As if in sympathy,
distortion also seized the bodies of Sharn and Malravin.

"An illusion, an optical illusion," Malravin said, raising a
hand to the melting lines of stars. "Gravity bending light. But
I've—Eddy, I've got something in my suit with me. Let's get
back to the ship."

Sharn could not reply. He fought silently with something
inside his own suit, something closer to him than his muscles.

Where the stars flowed, something was lumbering up over
the horizon, a great body sure of its strength, rising powerfully from its grave, thrusting up now a shoulder now a torso
into the visible. It was Bertha. The two men sank clumsily to
their knees.

Whatever it was, it was gigantic. It occupied about twenty
degrees of arc. It climbed above the horizon—but more and
more of it kept coming, and it seemed to expand as it came
—it rose tall, swallowing the sky as it rose. Its outline indicated that it was spherical, though the outline was not distinct,
the wavering bands of starlight rendering it impossible to see
properly.

The sensation in Sharn's body had changed. He felt lighter
now, and more comfortable. The feeling that he was wearing
someone else's body had disappeared. In its place had come
an odd lopsidedness. Drained, he could only peer up at the
disturbance.

Whatever it was, it ate the sky. It did not radiate light. Yet
what could be seen of it was clearly not seen by reflected
light. It darkled in the sky.

"It—emits black light," Sharn said. "Is it alive, Ike?"

"It's going to crush us," Ike said. He turned to crawl back
to the ship, but at that instant the atmosphere hit them.

Sharn had drawn his gaze away from that awesome monster in space to see what Malravin was doing, so that he saw
the atmosphere arrive. He put a claw up to shield his face as
it hit.

The atmosphere came up over the horizon after Bertha. It
came in long strands, travelling fast. With it came sound, a
whisper that grew to a shriek that shrilled inside their faceplates. At first the vapour was no more than a confusion in
the gloom, but as it thickened it became visible as drab grey
cloud. There were electrical side effects too; corposants
glowed along the ridges of rock about them. The cloud rose
rapidly, engulfing them like an intangible sea.

Sharn found he was on his knees beside Malravin. They
both had their headlights on now, and headed for the ship in

a rapid shuffle. It was hard going. That lopsided effect spoilt their instinctive placing of their limbs.

Once they were touching the metal of the "Wilson's" air-lock, some of the panic left them. Both men stood up, breathing heavily. The level of the greyish gas had risen above their heads. Sharn moved out from under the bulk of the "Wilson" and looked into the sky. Bertha was still visible through haze.

It was evident that Erewhon had a rapid rotation speed. The monstrous black disc was already almost at zenith; surrounded by a halo of distorted starglow, it loured over the little ship like a milestone about to fall. Hesitantly, Sharn put up his hand to see if he could touch it.

Malravin tugged at his arm.

"There's nothing there," he said. "It's impossible. It's a dream, a figment. It's the sort of thing you see in a dream. And how do you feel now? Very light now, as in a dream! It's just a nightmare, and you'll——"

"You're talking bloody nonsense, Malravin. You're trying to escape into madness if you pretend it isn't there. You wait till it falls down and crushes us all flat into the rock—then you'll see whether it's a dream or not!"

Malravin broke from him and ran to the air lock. He opened the door and climbed in, beckoning to Sharn. Sharn stood where he was, laughing. The other's absurd notion, so obviously a product of fear, had set Sharn into a high good humour. He did—Malravin was right there—feel much lighter than he had done; it made him light-headed.

"Challenge," he said. "Challenge and response. The whole history of life can be related in those terms. That must go into the book. Those that do not respond go to the wall."

"It's some sort of a nightmare, Eddy! What is that thing up there? It's no sun! Come in here, for God's sake!" Malravin called from the safety of the air lock.

"You fool, this is no dream or I'd be a figment of it, and you know that's nonsense. You're losing your head, that's all."

In his contempt for Malravin, he turned his back on the man, and began to stride over the plain. Each stride took him a long floating way. He switched off his intercom, and at once the fellow's voice was cut out of existence. In the helmet fell a perfect peace.

He found he was not afraid to look up at the lumbering beast in the sky.

"Put anything into words and it loses that touch of tabu to which fear attaches. That thing is a thing overhead. It may be some sort of a physical body. It may be some sort of a whirl-pool operating in space in a way we do not yet understand. It may be an effect in space itself, caused by the stresses in the heart of a nebula. There must be all sorts of unexpected pressures there. So I put the thing into words and it ceases to worry me."

He had got only to chapter four in the autobiography he was writing, but he saw that it would be necessary at some point—perhaps at the focal point of the book—to explain what prompted a man to go into deep space, and what sustained him when he got there. This experience on Erewhon was valuable, an intellectual experience as much as anything. It would be something to recall in the years to come—if that beast did not fall and squash him! It was leaping at him, directly overhead.

Again he was down full length, yelling into the dead microphone. He was too light to nuzzle properly, heavily, deeply, into the ground, and he cried his dismay till the helmet rang with sound.

He stopped the noise abruptly.

"Got dizzy," he told himself. He shut his eyes, squeezing up his face to do so. "Don't relax your control over yourself, Ed. Think of those fools in the ship, how they'd laugh. Remember nothing can hurt a man who has enough resilience."

He opened his eyes. The next thing would be to get up. He switched on his helmet light.

The ground was moving beneath him. For a while he stared fascinated at it. A light dust of grit and sand crawled over the solid rock at an unhurried but steady pace. He put his metal claw into it, and it piled against the barrier like water against a dam. Must be quite a wind blowing, Sharn told himself. Looking along the ground, he saw the particles trundled slowly towards the west. The west was veiled in the cloud-like atmosphere; into it, the great grinding shape of Big Bertha was sinking at a noticeable rate.

Now other fears overcame him. He saw Erewhon for what it was, a fragment of rock twirling over and over. He—the ship—the others—they clung to this bit of rock like flies, and —and—no, that was something he couldn't face, not alone out here. Something else occurred to him. Planetoids as small as Erewhon did not possess atmospheres. So this atmosphere had been something else fairly recently; he saw it as an ice casing, embalming the rock. Suddenly, more than irrational fear made him want to run—there was a logical reason as well. He switched on his mike and began to shout as he stumbled back towards the ship: "I'm coming back, fellers, open up! Open up, I'm coming back!"

Some of the drive casing was off. Malravin's feet protruded from the cluttered cavity. He was in there with an arc lamp, still patiently working on the directional cyboscope.

The other three sat round in bucket seats, talking. Sharn had changed his clothes, towelled himself down, and had a hot cup of Stimulous. Baron and the captain smoked mescahales.

"We've established that Erewhon's period of rotation is two hours, five minutes odd," Dominguey told Sharn. "That gives us about an hour of night when the ship is shielded from Big Bertha by the bulk of the planetoid. Sunset of the night after next will fall just before twenty hours, Galactic Mean. At twenty hours, all governmental ships keep open-listed for distress signals. Shielded from Bertha's noise, we stand our best chance of contacting the 'Grandon' and the 'Brinkdale' then. There's hope for us yet!"

Sharn nodded, Baron said, "You're too much the optimist, Billy. Nobody can ever get to rescue us." He spoke in an amused, confident tone.

"How's that again?"

"I said nobody can ever reach us, man. Consider it like this, man. We left ordinary space behind when we started burying into the nebula to get here. This little spot involves a number of paradoxes, doesn't it? I mean, we agree that there's nowhere else like this place in the universe, don't we?"

"No we don't," Dominguey said. "We agree that in less than eleven hundred years of galactic exploration we have covered only a small section of one arm of one galaxy. We don't know enough as yet to be capable of labelling an unusual situation paradoxical. Though I'll agree it's a poor spot for a picnic. Now, you were saying?"

"Don't try and be funny, Billy. This is not the place for humour—not even graveyard humour." Baron smiled as if the remark had a significance only he knew. He gestured with one hand, gracefully. "We are in a place that cannot possibly exist. That monstrous thing up in space cannot be a sun or any known body, or we would have got a spectroscopic reading from it. It cannot be a dead sun, or we would not see it as we do. This planetoid cannot be a planetoid, for in reality it would be so near Bertha it would be swept into it by irresistible gravitational forces. You were right to call it Erewhon. That's what it is—Nowhere."

Sharn spoke. "You're playing with Malravin's silly theory,

Baron. You're pretending we are in a nightmare. Let me assure you such assumptions are based entirely on withdrawal——"

"I don't want to hear!" Baron said. The smile on his lips became gentler. "You wouldn't understand, Sharn. You are so clever you prefer to tell me what I think rather than *hear* what I think. But I'm going to tell you what I think. I don't think we are undergoing a nightmare. I think we are dead."

Sharn rose, and began pacing behind his seat.

"Dominguey, you don't think this?"

"I don't feel dead."

"Good. Keep feeling that way or we're going to be in trouble. You know what the matter is with Baron. He's a weak character. He has always supported himself with science and the methods of science—we've had nothing but a diet of facts from him for the last thousand light years. Now he thinks science has failed him. There's nothing else left. He can no longer face the physical world. So, he comes to this emotional conclusion that he is dead. Classic withdrawal symptoms."

Dominguey said, "Someone ought to kick your ass, Eddy Sharn. Of all the glib and conceited idiots I ever met. . . . At least Jim has come out with an idea. It's not so far-fetched at that, when you consider we know nothing about what happens after death. Think about it a bit, think about the first few moments of death. Try to visualise the period after heart action had ceased, when the body, and particularly the brain inside its skull case, still retains its warmth. What goes on then? Suppose in that period of time everything in the brain drains away into nothing like a bucket of water leaking into sand. Don't you think some pretty vivid and hallucinatory things would happen inside that head? And, after all, the sort of events happening to us now are typical of the sort that might occur to spacers like us in that dying period. Maybe we ran smack into a big chunk of dead matter on our way into the Crab. Okay, we're all dead—the strong feeling of helplessness we all have is a token of the fact that we are really strewn over the control cabin with the walls caved in."

Lazily clapping his hands, Baron said, "You put it even better than I could have put it myself, Billy."

"Don't think I believe what I am saying, though," Dominguey said grimly. "You know me, laddie: ever the funny man, even to death."

He stood up and confronted Sharn.

"What I am trying to say, Eddy, is that you are too fond of your own opinions. I know the way your mind works—you're much happier in any situation if you can make yourself

believe that the other people involved are inferior to you.
Now then, if you have a theory that helps us tackle this particular section of hell, Jim and I would be pleased to hear it."

"Give me a mescahale," Sharn said. He had heard such
outbursts from the captain before, and attributed them to
Dominguey's being less stable than he liked to pretend he
was. Dominguey would be dangerous in a crisis. Not that this
was less than a crisis. Sharn accepted the yellow cylinder, activated it, stuck it into his mouth, and sat down. Dominguey
sat down beside him, regarding him with interest. They both
smoked in silence.

"Begin then, Eddy. It's time we took a quick sleep, the lot
of us. We're all exhausted, and it's beginning to show."

"On you maybe, Dominguey." He turned to Baron, languid-
ly sunk in his chair.

"Are you listening, Baron?"

Baron nodded his head.

"Go ahead. Don't mind me."

Things would be so much simpler if one were a robot,
Sharn thought. Personalities would not be involved. Any situation has to be situation plus character. It's bad enough to be
burdened with one's own character; one has to put up with
other people's as well. He pulled out his little notebook to
write the thought down, saw Dominguey was eyeing him, and
began to speak abruptly.

"What's your silly fuss about? We're here to do a job of
observation—why not do it? Before Ike and I went outside,
you told us to watch for the atmosphere. I did just that, but
from the nonsense you talk about being dead I'd say you
were the ones who should have watched it. And this peculiar
bodily sensation—you let it rattle you. So did Ike—so did I
—but it doesn't take much knowledge to realise that the horrible sensation as if something were climbing about inside the
suit with you has a rational and obvious explanation."

Baron got up and walked away.

"Come back when I'm talking, Baron," Sharn said, angrily.

"I'm going to see how Malravin is getting on, then I'm
going to bunk down. If you have anything interesting to say,
Billy can give it to me in a nutshell later. Your double talk
holds nothing for me. I'm tired of your speeches."

"Tired?—When you're dead? Needing to bunk down?—
When you're dead?"

"Leave him, for God's sake, and get on with what you
were saying," Dominguey said with a yawn. "Look, Eddy,
we're in a nasty spot here—I don't just mean stuck on Erewhon, though that's bad enough. But much more getting on

each other's nerves and there will be murder done. I'd say you were turning into a very good candidate for the axe."

"You toying with the idea of murder, Dominguey? I suppose that could be another refuge from the realities of the position."

"Knock off that line of talk, Sharn, and that's an order. You were talking about this strange bodily sensation we felt out on the rock. Don't be so coy about it. It's caused by the fact that most of our weight out there comes by courtesy of Big Bertha, not Erewhon. Your mass orients itself partly according to where Bertha is, and not according to the body you are standing on. Of course it causes some odd sensations, particularly with respect to your proprioceptors and the balance in your inner ear. When the sun first rises, your intellect has to fight your body out of its tendency to regard the east as *down*. When the sun's overhead, the situation's not so bad, but your mass will always act as a compass, as it were, tending towards the sun—if Bertha is a sun. Have I taken the words out of your mouth?"

Sharn nodded.

"Since you're so smart, Billy, you've probably worked out that Bertha is a star—a big star . . . a star, that is, with an abnormally large mass. And I do mean abnormally—it's got an unique chance to grow here. It has accumulated bulk from the nebula. Its mass must be something above twenty-five million times the mass of Sol."

Dominguey whistled. "A pretty tall order! Though I see it is well placed for stellar growth processes. So you think it is just a gigantic accumulation of dead matter?"

"Not at all. There's no such thing as dead matter in that sense. Baron's the scientist—he'd tell you if he wasn't heading for catatonia. You get such a mass of material together and terrific pressures are set up. No, I'm saying Bertha is a tremendous live sun built from dead nebular matter."

"That's all nonsense, though, Eddy. We don't even see it properly except as a shimmering blackness. If your theory were correct, Bertha would be a white giant. We'd all be scorched out of existence, sitting here so close to it."

"No, you're forgetting your elementary relativity. I've worked this out. This is no fool hypothesis. I said Bertha had twenty-five million times Sol's mass for a good reason. Because if you have a sun that big, the force of gravity at its surface is so colossal that even light cannot escape off into space."

Dominguey put his mescahale down and stared at the nearest bulkhead with his mouth open.

"By the saints . . . Eddy, could that be so? What follows from that? I mean, is there any proof?"

"There's the visible distortion of distant starlight by Bertha's bulk that gives you some idea of the gravitational forces involved. And the interferometer offers some guide. It's still working. I used it out on the surface before I came back aboard. Why didn't you try it? I suppose you and Baron panicked out there, as Malravin did? Bertha has an angular diameter of twenty-two degrees of arc. If the mass is as I say, then you can reckon its diameter in miles. Should be 346 times the sun's, or about some 300 million miles. That's presuming a lot, I know, but it gives us a rough guide. And from there a spot of trig will tell you how far we are from Bertha. I make it something less than one billion six hundred million miles. You know what that means—we're as far from Bertha as Uranus is from Sol, which with a body of Bertha's size means we're very nearly on top of it!"

"Now you're beginning to frighten me," Dominguey said. He looked frightened, dark skin stretched over his cheekbones as he pressed his temples with his fingertips. Behind them, Baron and Malravin were quarrelling. Baron had tripped over the other's foot as he lay with his head in the drive box, and they were having a swearing match. Neither Dominguey nor Sharn paid them any attention.

"No, there's one hole in your theory," Dominguey finally said.

"Such as?"

"Such as if Erewhon was as close as that to its primary, it could never hold its orbit. It would be drawn into Bertha."

Sharn stared at the captain, mulling over his answer. Life was a misery, but there was always some pleasure to be wrung from the misery.

"I got the answer to that when I was outside rolling on the sterile stinking rockface," he said. "The vapour came pouring over the ground at me. I knew Erewhon was too small to retain any atmosphere for any length of time. In fact it was diffusing into space fast. Therefore, not so long ago, that atmosphere was lying in hollows on the surface, liquid. Follow me?"

Dominguey swallowed and said, "Go on."

"*You* made the assumption that Erewhon bore a planetary relationship to Bertha, Dominguey. You were wrong. Erewhon is spinning in from a colder region. The rocks are heating up. We haven't settled on a planetoid—we're squatting on a hunk of rock spiralling rapidly into the sun."

There came the sound of a blow, and Malravin grunted. He jumped at Baron and the two men clinched, pummelling each other's backs rather foolishly. Dominguey and Sharn ran up and pulled them apart. Dead or not, Baron was giving a fair account of himself.

"All right," Dominguey said angrily. "So we've run ourselves ragged. We need sleep. You three bunk down, give yourselves sedatives. I'll get on fixing the cybo, Malravin. Set the alarm signal for nineteen hours fifty, G.M., so that we don't miss calling 'Grandon' and 'Brinkdale,' and bunk down. We want to get out of here—and we all want to get out of here. Go on, move—you too, Eddy. Your theory has me convinced. We're leaving as soon as possible, so I'm having peace while I work."

In turn they all protested, but Dominguey was not to be over-ruled. He stood with his hands on his hips, his dark face unmoving as they climbed into their bunks. Then he shrugged, set the alarm on the communication panel, and crawled into the drive compartment.

It was not a matter of simple replacement. Fortunately they had spares for the little sinecells which studded the main spiral of the cyboscope that steered the ship. But the spiral itself had become warped by the extra strains placed on it during their penetration of the nebula. Malravin had drained its oil bath and removed its casing, but the business of setting it back into true was a slow precision job, not made easier by the awkward angle at which it had to be tackled.

Time passed. Dominguey was listening to the sound of his own heavy breathing when the alarm bell shrilled.

He crawled out into the cabin. Sharn and Malravin were already rousing and stretching.

"That's four hours' hard grind I just put in," he said, pushing his words through a yawn. "Eddy, see if you can raise the other ships, will you? I must have a drink and get some shut eye. We're nearly set to blast off."

Then he pointed to Baron, his ashen face, the crimson stain over his chest. In two steps he was over to his bunk. Baron lay contorted on his left side, gripping a handful of blanket. He was dead with a knife in his ribs. Dominguey let out a cry that brought the other two down onto their feet.

"He's been murdered! Jim's been murdered! One of you two. . . ." He turned to Sharn. "Sharn, you did this. You've killed him with his own explorer's knife. Why? Why?"

Sharn had gone as pale as Dominguey.

"You're lying, I never did it. I was in my bunk asleep! I had no quarrel with Baron. What about Malravin? He'd just had a fight with Jim. He did it, didn't you, Malravin?"

The alarm was still shrilling away. They were all shouting. Malravin said, "Don't you call me a murderer. I was fast asleep in my bunk, under sedation as ordered. One of you two did it. It was nothing to do with me."

"You've got a black eye coming on, Malravin," Dominguey said. "Jim Baron gave you that before you hit the sack. Did you stab him to even up the score?"

"For God's sake, man, let's try and raise the other ships while we've the chance. You know I'd not do anything like that. You did it yourself, most likely. You were awake, we weren't."

"I was stuck with my head in the drive all the time."

"Were you? How do we know?"

"Yes, he has a point, Dominguey," Sharn said. "How do we know what you were up to? Didn't you arrange for us all to get a bit of sleep on purpose, so that you could bring this off?"

"So he did, the filthy murderer," Malravin shouted. "I wonder you didn't finish us all while you were about it." Putting his hands up, he charged at Dominguey.

Dominguey ducked. He jumped to one side and hit Malravin as he lumbered past. The blow was a light one. It served merely to make Malravin bellow and come on again. On the table lay a wrench they had used earlier on the cybo casing. Dominguey hit Malravin with it at the base of the neck. The big fellow collided with a chair and sprawled with it to the floor, catching his head sharply against the bulkhead as he went.

"You want any?" Dominguey asked, facing Sharn with the wrench ready.

Shaking, Sharn formulated the word "No".

"See to Ike then, while I try to raise a signal." Nodding curtly, he went over to the communications panel and cut off the alarm. The sudden silence was as chilling as the racket had been a moment before. He opened up the subradio and began to call.

Sharn slipped to his knees and pulled Malravin's head up as gently as he could. The man did not stir. Groaning, Sharn tried to adjust to what had happened. He tried to concentrate his thoughts. He muttered, "Humans instigate events; events affect humans. Once a man has started a chain of events, he may find himself the victim of the events. When I entered star service, this was a decisive action, but readers may think that since then I have been at the mercy—the mercy——"

He began to weep. Malravin was also dead. His neck was broken. Inside his head, still warm, thoughts pouring out into oblivion. . . .

After some indefinite period of time, Sharn realised that Dominguey had stopped speaking. Only a meaningless gibber and squeak of static came from the subradio. He looked up. The captain was pointing an iongun at him.

"I know you killed Jim Baron, Sharn," he said. His face was distorted by tension.

"I know you killed Malravin. I saw you do it, and there is the murder weapon on the floor."

The iongun wavered.

"Ike's dead?"

"Dead, just as you killed Baron. You're clever, Dominguey, the real silent superman type, always in command of his environment. Now I suppose you will kill me. With three bodies out of the hatch, the 'Wilson' will lift a lot more easily, won't it? You'll need all that lift, Dominguey, because we are getting nearer to Bertha every minute."

"I'm not going to kill you, Sharn, just as I didn't kill Baron. Just as killing Malravin was an accident. You know—— Wait! Don't move! There's a signal."

He slightly swivelled his chair and turned up the volume of the set. Below the crackle of static, a faint voice called them. It said, "Can you hear me, 'Wilson'? Can you hear me, 'Wilson'? Grant of the 'Brinkdale' here. Come in, please."

"Hello, Grant! Hello, Grant!" As he spoke, the captain moved the mike so that he could continue to cover Sharn with his iongun. "Dominguey of 'Wilson' here. We're down on an asteroid for repairs. If I send a carrier, will you get a fix on us? Situation very urgent—dawn is less than an hour away, and static will cancel reception then."

Far away, down a great well of time and space, a tiny voice asked for the carrier wave. Dominguey switched to send and turned to face Sharn.

Sharn still crouched over Malravin. He had brought himself under control now.

"Going to finish me at once, Dominguey?" he asked. "Don't want any witnesses, do you?"

"Get up, Sharn. Back over to the wall. I want to see if Malravin is really dead, or if you are up to some stupid deception."

"Oh, he's dead all right. I'd say you did a very good job. And with Baron too, although there it was easier because the poor fellow was not only asleep but believed himself already dead."

"You're sick, Sharn. Get over against that wall when you're ordered to."

They moved into their new positions, Sharn by the wall near the shuttered ports, Dominguey by the ugly body on the floor. Both of them moved slowly, watching each other, their faces blank.

"He's dead all right," Sharn said.

"He's dead. Sharn, get into your space suit."

"What are you planning, a burial service? You're crazy Dominguey! It's only a few hours before our mass cremation."

"Don't you call me crazy, you little snake. Get into your space suit. I can't have you in here while I'm working. I don't trust you. I know you killed Baron; you're mad and he had less patience with your talk and theories than any of us. You can't tolerate anyone who won't enlist as your audience, can you? But you're not going to kill me. So you wait outside until we are ready to go, or until the 'Brinkdale' comes to pick us up, whichever is soonest. Move fast now, man, into your suit."

"You're going to leave me out there, you swine! What are you doing, compiling an anthology of ways to murder in galactic space? Beyond the solar system, the word of man becomes the word of God."

Moving fast, Dominguey slapped him across the cheek.

"—And the hand of God," Sharn muttered. He moved towards his suit. Reluctantly, he climbed into it, menaced continually by the iongun. Dominguey propelled him towards the lock.

"Don't send me out there again, Dominguey, please. I can't stand it. You know what Big Bertha's like—— Please! Tie me to my bunk——"

"Move, man. I have to get back to the set. I won't leave without you."

"Please, Dominguey, Captain, I swear I'm innocent. You know I never touched Baron. I'd die out there on the rock! Forgive me!"

"You can stay if you'll sign a confession that you murdered Baron."

"You know I never did it! You did it while we were all asleep. You saw how his idea about our all being dead was a menace to the general sanity, and so you killed him. Or Malravin killed him. Yes, Malravin killed Jim, Dominguey, it's obvious! You know we were talking together while they were quarrelling! We're not to blame. Let's not be at each other's throats now we're the only two left. We've got to get out of here quickly—you need help. We always get on well together, we've covered the galaxy——"

"Confess or get out, Sharn. I know you did it. I can't have you in here or you'll kill me."

Sharn stopped protesting. He ran a hand through his damp hair and leant back against the bulkhead.

"All right. I'll sign. Anything rather than go out there again. I can always say I signed under duress."

Dominguey dragged him to the table, seized a scratch pad from the radio bench, and forced Sharn to write out a brief confession to the murder of Jim Baron. He pocketed it and levelled the iongun again.

"Now get outside," he said.

"Dominguey, no, no, you lied to me—please——"

"You've got to get out, Sharn. With this paper in my pocket, you'd not hesitate to kill me now, given half a chance."

"You're mad, Dominguey, cunning mad. You're going to get rid of me and then blame it all onto me——"

"I'll count five, Sharn. If you're not on your way to that lock by then, I swear I'll fry your boots off."

The look on his face was unmistakable. Sharn backed into the lock, weeping. The door closed on him. He heard Dominguey begin to exhaust the air from the room panel. Hurriedly, he screwed down his faceplate. The air whispered away and the lock descended to ground level.

When it stopped, he opened the door, unscrewed one of the levers from the control panel, and wedged it in the doorway so that the door could not close. It could not retract until it was closed, so his way to the ship was not withdrawn. Then he stepped out onto the surface of Erewhon for a second time.

Conditions were changing. Bertha came ripping up into the sky, surrounded by a shock wave of star-blur. The farther stars lent it a halo of confused light. It was rising ahead of the time-table the humans had worked out. So communication with "Brinkdale" would now be effectively cut off. Also, the perceptible disc of the body was larger. They were indeed falling towards it.

Sharn wondered why he was not already fried to smears of carbohydrate on the rock, despite the refrigeration unit in his suit. But if Bertha was so gigantic, then she would not even be able to release her own heat. What a terrible unstable thing it was! He looked up at it, in a sort of ecstasy transcending fear, feeling in his lack of weight that he was drifting out towards it. The black globe seemed to thunder overhead, a symbol—a symbol of what? Of life, of fertility, of death, of destruction? It seemed to combine aspects of all things as it rode omnipotently overhead.

"The core of experience—to be at the core of experience transcends the need for lesser pleasures," Sharn told himself. He could feel his black notebook in his hip pocket. It was inaccessible inside the space-suit. For all his inability to get at it, it might as well have been left back on Earth. That was a terrible loss—not just to him, but to others who might have read and been stimulated by his work. Words were coming to him now, thick and rich as blood, coming first singly like birds alighting on his shoulder, then in swarms.

Finally he fell silent, impaled under that black gaze. The isolation was so acute, it was as if he alone of all creation had been singled out to stand there . . . there under something that was physically impossible.

He switched on his suit mike and began to speak to Dominguey.

"I want to come back aboard. I want to make some calculations. I'm beginning to understand Bertha. Her properties represent physical impossibilities. You understand that, don't you, Dominguey? So how can she exist? The answer must be that beneath her surface, under unimaginable conditions, she is creating anti-matter. We've made a tremendous discovery, Dominguey. Perhaps they'll name the process after me: the Sharn Effect. Let me come back, Dominguey. . . ."

But he spoke to himself, and the words were lost in his helmet.

He stood mute, bowing to the black thing.

Already Bertha was setting. The foggy blanket of atmosphere was whipped off the bed of rock, following, following the sun round like a tide. The vapour was thinner now, and little more than shoulder high as its component molecules drained off into space.

The weight-shift took place. Sharn's body told him that *down* was the monstrous thing on the horizon and that he walked like a fly on the wall across Erewhon. Though he fought the sensation, when he turned back towards the "Wilson," he moved uphill, and the vapours poured across him in a dying waterfall.

Taking no notice of the vapours, Sharn lumbered back to the air lock. He had remembered the thick pad of miostrene that hung clipped to one wall of the lock, a stylo beside it. It was placed there for emergencies, and surely this was one. As he reached for it, Dominguey's voice came harshly through his headphones.

"Stay away from that lock, Sharn. I've got the casing back on the cyboscope and am preparing to blast off. I shall have to take a chance on manoeuvring. Get away from the ship!"

"Don't leave without me, Dominguey, please! You know I'm an innocent man."

"We're none of us innocent, Sharn, isn't that true?"

"This is no time for metaphysics, Dominguey. We'll discuss it when you let me back inside."

"You killed Jim Baron, Sharn, and I'm not letting you back on board in case you kill me."

"I didn't kill Baron, and you know it. I'm not the killer type. Either you killed him, or else Malravin did. It wasn't me."

"I've got your confession! Stand clear for blast-off!"

"But I've made an important discovery!"

"Stand clear!"

The connection went dead. Sharn cried into his suit. Only the universe answered.

Clutching the miostrene pad, he ran from the lock. He ran after the last disappearing strand of vapour, sucked along the ground like a worm withdrawing. He lumbered down a cliff that began to see-saw back towards horizontal. The big sun had disappeared below a group of rocks that did rough duty for a horizon.

A tower of distorted strata rose before him. He stooped behind it as quickly as the suit would allow him, and looked back.

A golden glow turned white, a plump pillow of smoke turned into flat sheets of vapour that flapped across the rock towards him, the ship rose. Almost at once, it was hidden behind the northern horizon. The movement was so sudden and unpredictable that Sharn thought it had crashed, until he realised how fast ship and planetoid were moving in relation to each other. He never caught another glimpse of it.

Calmer now, he stood up and looked round. In the rock lay a great crater. The last of the smoke was sucked into it. He hobbled over to it and looked down. A great eye looked back at him.

Sharn staggered away in alarm, running through the passages of his mind to see if delusion had entered there. Then he realised what he had seen. Erewhon was a thin slab of rock holed right through the middle. He had seen Bertha louring on the other side. In a minute, it would rise again in its tireless chase of this splinter of flotsam.

Now the illusion of day and night, with its complementary implication that one was on a planet or planetoid, was shattered. That great eye held truth in its gaze: he clung to an infinitesimal chunk of rock falling ever faster towards its doom.

As he squatted down with his pad, the sun came up again. It rushed across the arch of space and disappeared almost at once. Erewhon bore no trace of any vapour to follow it now. And another illusion was gone: now, plainly, it was the chunk of rock that turned, not the mighty ball that moved—that was stationary, and all space was full of it. It hung there like a dull shield, inviting all comers.

He began to write on his pad in big letters. "As this rock is stripped of all that made it seem like a world, so I become a human stripped of all my characteristics. I am as bare as a symbol myself. There are no questions relevant to me; you cannot ask me if I murdered a man on a ship; I do not know; I do not remember. I have no need for memory. I only know what it is to have the universe's grandest grandstand view of death. I——"

But the rock was spinning so fast now that he had to abandon the writing. A spiral of black light filled space, widening as he drew nearer to Bertha. He lay back on the rock to watch, to stretch his nerves to the business of watching, holding on as his weight pulsed about him in rhythm with the black spiral.

As he flung the pad aside, the last word on it caught his eye, and he flicked an eyebrow in recognition of its appositeness:

"I——"

Basis for Negotiation

THE UNIVERSITY OF EAST LINCOLN IS A MUDDLE OF BUILD-
INGS. IN THE CENTRE STANDS THE THEATRICALLY BAROQUE
pile still called Gransby Manor, while round it lie the pencil-
boxes of glass and cedar and cement that are our century's
contribution to the treasury of world architecture. John
Haines-Roberts and I walked round the grounds in agonized
discussion, viewing our conglomeration of a college from all
its meaningless angles.

When I tell you the date was July 1st, 1971, you will know
what was the subject under discussion.

"I tell you I cannot just stay here, John, idle, isolated, ignorant," I said. "I must go to London and find out what the
devil the government is doing."

Most of the conversations that follow, I feel confident, are
word for word what was said at the time. My memory is generally eidetic; in times of stress such as this, it records everything, so that I see John Haines-Roberts now, his head thrust
forward from those heavy shoulders, as he replied, "I will
offer you no platitudes about considering your reputation at
such a grave time. Nevertheless, Simon, you are a public
figure, and were before your knighthood. You have a foot in
both worlds, the academic and the world of affairs. Your
work on the Humanities Council and the Pilgrim Trust has
not been forgotten. You were M.P. for Bedford under Mac-
leon. That has not been forgotten. At such a trying time,
any untoward move by somebody of your stature may fatally
prejudice the course of events, marring——"

"No, no, John, that's not it at all!" I stopped him with a
curt movement of my hand. He talked that awful dead lan-

guage of English newspaper leaders; with his evasions and eu-
phemisms, his "untoward moves" and "trying times." I could
not bear to listen to him. He believed as I did on that one
fundamental point, that the British Government had made
the most fatal error any government could have done; but
this apart we could have nothing in common. His woolly language only reflected the numbness of his intellect. At that terrible moment, one more prop fell away. I began to hate John.
The man who had been my friend since I took the specially
created chair of Moral History two years before suddenly became just another enemy of my country, and of me.

"We cannot discuss the problem in these terms," I told
him. He stopped, peering forward in that intense way of his.
In the distance, I saw some undergraduates bunched together
in the tepid sunshine and watching us with interest. "The
British have turned basely against their dearest friends and allies. Either this wounds you to the heart or it doesn't——"

"But the Americans can manage alone perfectly well——"
he began, with all the patience and reason in the world in his
voice. John Haines-Roberts was a saint; nothing in the world
could ruffle him in debate. I knew he would be standing reasoning in some quiet corner of University College when the
H-bombs fell.

"I'm sorry, John, I'm not prepared to go into it all again.
The sands have run out—right out of the bottom of the glass.
This is no time for talk. You don't think the Communists are
standing talking, do you? I'm going to London."

He saw I was making to go and laid a placatory hand on
my sleeve.

"My dear fellow, you know I wish you well, but you have
a reputation for being over-hasty. Never, never let action become a substitute for thought. You'll recall what that great
and good man Wilberforce said when——"

"Damn Wilberforce!" I said. Turning away, I strode off.
The undergraduates saw me coming and fanned out to inter-
cept me on my way to Manor, pouring out questions.

"Is it true the Americans have cordoned off Holy Loch?
Sir Simon, what do you think of the news about the International Brigade? Did you see C. P. Snow on TV, blasting poor
old Minnie?" "Minnie" was their nickname for Sir Alfred
Menhennick, the Prime Minister.

Behind my back, John was still calling, "Simon, my dear
fellow. . . ." To my audience, I said, "Gentlemen, from this
week onwards, only shame attaches to the name of England.
You know how I feel on this subject. Please let me pass."

Their faces were before me, troubled, angry, or snivelling.

They began bombarding me with preposterous questions—
"Who do you think will win, America or China?" as if it
were a boat-race staged for their delight.

"Let me through!" I repeated.

"Why don't you join up, if you feel so strongly?" "We
don't owe the Americans anything." "We'll still be here when
they're one big hole in the ground." And so on.

I said: "You had the police in here last night. Rowdyism
will get you nowhere. Why don't you go somewhere quietly
and consult your history books if you have no consciences to
consult?" I hated them, though I knew they half-sided with
me.

"Consult our history books!" one of them exclaimed.
"He'll tell us to cultivate our gardens next!"

Angrily I pushed through them, making my way towards
my rooms. That last remark echoed through my head; obviously many of them could not differentiate between my
convictions and those of, say, Haines-Roberts. In the final
judgement, he and I would be lumped together as men who sat
by and let it happen—or, even worse, would be cheered as
men who had not interfered.

With distaste I surveyed the comfortable room with Adam
fireplace and white panelling that I had chosen in preference
to an office in Whitehall, asking myself as I took in—through
what a scornfully fresh vision!—the untidy bookcases and
neat cocktail cabinet, if there was still time left to do something effective. How terribly often in the past must English-
men have asked themselves that!

Momentarily I surveyed myself in the looking-glass. Grey-
haired, long in the nose, clear of eye, neat in appearance. Not
a don. More a retired soldier. Certainly—oh yes, my God,
that certainly—a gentleman! A product of Harrow and Balliol and a Wiltshire estate. With the international situation
what it was, it sounded more like a heresy than a heritage.
Nothing is more vile (or more eloquent of guilt) than to hate
everything one has been: to see that you have contaminated
the things that have contaminated you.

Taking a deep breath, I began to phone my wife at home.
When her voice came over the line, I closed my eyes.

"Jean, I can't bear inaction any longer. I'm going up to
London to try to get through to Tertis."

"Darling, we went over all this last night. You can't help
by going to see Tertis—no, don't tell me you can't help by
not going either. But it becomes more and more obvious each
hour that public opinion here is with Minnie, and that your
viewpoint . . ."

By ceasing to listen to her meaning, I could concentrate on her voice. Her "all" was pronounced "arl," her "either" was an "eether"; her tone had a soft firmness totally unlike the harshness of so many Englishwomen!—no, comparisons were worthless. It was stupid to think in categories. She was Jean Challington, my beloved wife. When I had first met her in New York, one fine September day in 1942, she had been Jean Gershein, daughter of a magazine publisher. At twenty-six, I was then playing my first useful role in affairs on the British Merchant Shipping Mission. Jean was the most Anglophile, as well as the most lovely, of creatures; I was the most Americanophile and adoring of men. That hasty wartime wedding at least was a success; no better Anglo-American agreement ever existed than our marriage.

This was the woman on whose breast I had wept the night before last, wept long and hard after the bleak TV announcement that in the interests of future world unity the British Government had declared its neutrality in the American-Chinese war. Last night I had wept again, when the U.S.S.R. had come in on the side of the People's Republic and Sir Alfred Menhennick himself had smiled to viewers under his straggling moustache and reaffirmed our neutrality.

Now, with the phone in my hand and Jean's voice in my ear, I could not but recall Menhennick's hatefully assured delivery as he said, "Let us in this darkest period of civilized history be the nation that stands firm and keeps its lamps alight. It is a difficult—perhaps you will agree that it is the most difficult—role that I and my government have elected to play. But we must never forget that throughout the quarter century of the Cold War, Great Britain's path has been the exacting and unrewarding one of intermediary.

"We must remember, too, that the United States, in facing Communist China, faces an enemy of its own creating. One of the most fatal failures of this century was the failure of the U.S. to participate in world affairs during the twenties and thirties, when Britain and France strove almost single-handedly to preserve the peace. Despite constant warnings, the U.S. at that time allowed their enemy Japan to grow strong on the spoils of an invaded China. As a consequence, the broken Chinese peoples had to restore their position as a world power by what means they could. It is not for us to condemn if in desperation they turned to Communism. That their experiment, their desperate experiment, worked must be its justification. At this fateful hour, it behoves us to think with every sympathy of the Chinese, embroiled yet again in another terrible conflict. . . ."

The hypocrisy! The sheer bloody wicked hypocrisy, the lies, the distortions, the twists of logic, the contortions of history! My God, I could shoot Menhennick!

"Darling, I hadn't mentioned Menhennick," Jean protested.

"Did I say that aloud?" I asked the phone.

"You weren't listening to a word I said."

"I'll bet you were telling me to pack a clean shirt!"

"Nothing of the sort. I was saying that here in Lincoln there are some demonstrations in progress."

"Tell me about them."

"If you'll listen, honey. The best-organized procession carries a large banner saying, 'Boot the Traitors out of Whitehall.' "

"Good for them."

"My, yes, good for them! The odd thing is, those boys look like exactly the same crowd we used to see marching from Aldermaston to Trafalgar Square shouting, 'Ban the Bomb.' "

"Probably they are. If you think with your emotions, slight glandular changes are sufficient to revise your entire outlook. In the Aldermaston days, they were afraid of being involved in war; now that Russia has come in on China's side, they're afraid that the U.S. will be defeated, leaving us to be picked off by Big Brother afterwards. Which is precisely what will happen unless we do something positive now. What else goes on in Lincoln?"

Jean's voice became more cautious. "Some anti-Americanism. The usual rabble with ill-printed posters saying, 'Yanks, Go Home' and 'Britain for the British.' One of them spells Britain 'B-R-I-T-I-A-N.' So much for the ten thousand million pounds spent on education last year. . . . It feels funny, Simon—to be an alien in what I thought was my own country."

"It's not my country either till this is all put right. You know that, Jean. There's never been such a time of moral humiliation. I wish I'd been born anything but British."

"Don't be silly, Simon."

Foreseeing an argument, I changed the line of discussion.

"You've got Michael and Sheila and Adrian there with you?"

"Oh yes, and Mrs. B. And a platoon or so of sheepish English soldiers drilling opposite the Post Office."

"Fine. You won't be lonely. I'll be back as soon as I can."

"Meaning just when?"

"Soonest possible, love. 'Bye. Be good."

I put the phone down. I looked distractedly round the room. I put pipe and tobacco into one jacket pocket, opened a drawer, selected three clean handkerchiefs, and put them into the other pocket. I wondered if I would ever see the room—or Jean—again, and strove at the same time not to dismiss such speculations as simply dramatic.

London, I knew, could turn into a real trouble centre at any hour. Early news bulletins had spoken of rioting and arrests here and there, but these were mere five-finger exercises for what was to come.

Until now, the sheer momentousness of world events had deadened reactions. After a month of mounting tension, war between the U.S. and China broke out. Then came Menhennick's unexpected tearing up of treaties and declaration of neutrality. Initially, his action came as a relief as well as a surprise; the great bulk of the electorate saw no further than the fact that an Armageddon of nuclear war had been avoided. The U.S.S.R.'s entry into hostilities was more a shock than a surprise, again postponing real thinking.

Now—as I foresaw the situation—a growing mass of people would come to see that if they were to have any hope for a tolerable future, it would be fulfilled only by throwing in our lot heart and soul with our allies, the Americans. We had behaved like vermin, deserting in an hour of need. Even Neville Chamberlain returning from Munich in 1938 to proclaim "Peace in our time" had not brought the country into such disgrace as Minnie with his "nation that keeps the lamps alight."

Soon the English would realize that; and I wanted to be there when trouble broke.

As I was heading for the door, David Woolf entered, quickly and without knocking. David was University Lecturer in Nuclear Physics, with a good but troubled record from Harwell. Three years back, he had run for Parliament, but an ill-timed tariff campaign had spoilt his chances. Though his politics were opposed to mine, his astute and often pungent thinking was undeniably attractive. Tall and very thin, with a crop of unbrushed hair, he was still in his thirties and looked what he undoubtedly was: the sort of man who managed always to be unhappy and spread unhappiness. Despite this—despite our radically different upbringings—his father had been a sagger-magger's bottomer in a Staffordshire pottery—David and I saw much of each other.

"What is it?" I asked. "I can't stop, David."

"You're in trouble," he said, clicking his fingers.

I had not seen him since the Chinese declaration of war forty-eight hours before. His face was drawn, his shirt dirty. If he had slept, clearly it had been in his clothes.

"What sort of trouble?" I asked. "Aren't we all in trouble?"

"The Dean has you marked down as a dangerous man, and at times like this the Dean's kind can cause a hell of a lot of grief."

"I know that."

Dean Burroughs was a cousin of Peter Dawkinson, the reactionary old editor of the *Arbiter,* the newspaper as firmly entrenched behind out-dated attitudes as *The Times* had ever been at its worst period—and as powerful. Burroughs and I had been in opposition even before my first day at East Lincoln, back when I edited Garbitt's short-living independent *Zonal.*

"What you don't know is that the Dean has started vetting your phone calls," David said. "I was by the exchange just now. You made an outgoing call; Mrs. Ferguson had it plugged through to old Putters, the Dean's fair-haired boy."

"It was a private call to my wife," I said furiously.

"Are you leaving or something? Don't mind my asking."

"Yes, I'm leaving, though by God what you tell me makes me want to go and sort things out with Burroughs first. No, that luxury must wait; time's short. I must leave at once."

"Then I warn you, Simon, that they may try to stop you."

"Thanks for telling me."

He hesitated, knowing I wanted him to move away from the door. For a moment we stood confronting each other. Then he spoke.

"Simon—I want to come with you."

That did surprise me. The news about the phone did not; in the present tense atmosphere, it merely seemed in character, a small sample of a vast untrustworthiness. I accepted David's words as truth; David, though isolated from the rest of the teaching body by his political and sexual beliefs, had a way of knowing whatever was happening in the college before anyone else.

"Look, David, you don't know what I am doing."

"Let me guess then. You are going to drive to London. You have influential friends there. You are going to get in contact with someone like Lord Boulton or Tertis, and you are going to throw in your lot with the group trying to overthrow the government."

This was so good a guess that he read his answer in my face. I said, with some bitterness, "Your politics are no secret to me. For years you have preached that we should disarm, that we should cease to behave like a first-rate power, with all the assumptions of a first-rate power, when we are really a second-rate power——"

He seized my arm, only to release it at once. Behind his spectacles, his eyes brimmed with anger.

"Don't be a bloody fool, Simon! We *are* a second-rate power, but now the moment of truth is upon us, isn't it? The bastards who misgovern us would not climb off their silly perches when they had a chance, when we were warning them. Now, *now,* they just *must* honour agreements. You know I've no time for America, but by God we owe it to them to stick by them: we owe it to ourselves! We mustn't behave like a fifth-rate power: that at least we're not."

"So we've both arrived on the same side?"

From his pocket he produced a revolver.

"You could have worse allies than me, Simon. I don't go to Bisley every year for nothing. I'm prepared to use this when needed."

"Put it away!"

Savagely he laughed.

"You're a gentleman, Simon! That's your trouble. It's the only really vital difference between us. You don't enjoy force! You're as like Minnie as makes no difference! In the ultimate analysis, his faults are yours—and it's a class fault."

I grabbed his jacket, clenching a fist in his face and choking with rage.

"You dare say that! Even you've not opposed Minnie as bitterly as I. I hate all he stands for, hate it."

"No you don't. You both belong to the same league of gentlemen—Balliol and all that. If it wasn't that your wife happened to be American, you'd feel as Minnie does. It's you blasted gentlemen putting the social order before the country that have got us into this bloody disgraceful muddle. . . ." With an effort, he broke off and pushed my hand roughly away, saying, "And I'm in danger of doing the same thing myself. Sir Simon, my apologies. Our country has disgraced us before the world. Please let me come to London with you. I'm prepared to do anything to boot out the Nationalist party. That's what I came here to say."

He put out his hand; I shook it.

We were round at the car port getting my Wolseley out when Spinks, the head porter, came thudding up at the double.

"Excuse me, Sir Simon, but the Dean wants you very urgently, sir. Matter of importance, sir."

"All right, Spinks. I'll just drive the car round to the front of Manor and go in that way. He's in his rooms, I take it?"

His round heavy face was troubled.

"You will go straight in to him *now*, sir, won't you? He did stress as it was urgent."

"Quite so, Spinks. Thank you for delivering the message."

I drove round to the front of Manor, accelerated, and in next to no time we were speeding down the drive. David Woolf sat beside me, peering anxiously back at the huddle of buildings.

"Relax," I said, knowing it would anger him. "Nobody's going to shoot us."

"The war's forty-eight hours old—I wonder how many people have been shot already?"

Not answering, I switched on the car radio as we struck the main road. I tried the three channels, General, Popular, and Motorway. On the first, a theatre organ played *Roses of Picardy*. On the second, a plummy woman's voice said, ". . . when to my bitter disappointment I found that all the jars of strawberry jam had gone mouldy; however, this tragedy——" On the third, a disc jockey announced, "That was *My Blue Heaven*, and while we're on the subject of colour, here are Reggy Palmer and his Regiment in a colourful arrangement of another old favourite, *Chinatown*."

"I wonder they didn't censor that one out for reasons of political expediency," David said sourly.

We stayed with the jocular jockey, hoping to catch a news bulletin, as I drove south. Avoiding Lincoln, we entered the newly opened M13 at Hykeham and increased speed. Noticing the number of Army vehicles heading south with us, David started to comment when the news came through.

"This morning has been punctuated by disturbances and demonstrations in most of the larger towns throughout Britain. Some arrests have been made. In Norwich, a man was fined twenty pounds for defacing the Town Hall. The Sovereign's visit to Glasgow has been postponed until a later date."

"Royalty!" David grunted.

"Tautology!" I grunted.

"The Soviet Ambassador to Britain said today that the Soviet peoples greatly sympathised with the wisdom shown by the British in remaining neutral. They themselves had been drawn into the conflict with the deepest reluctance, and then only because vital interests were at stake. M. Kasinferov went on to say that he was sure that guided by our example the rest of Europe would remain neutral, thus saving itself from what could only be complete annihilation."

"Bloody flatterers," David growled.

"Concealed threats," I growled.

"In the United States of America, our neutrality has been

generally condemned, although as one Washington correspondent points out, 'Had Britain not torn up her treaties
with us, she might well have been obliterated by now.' Dis-
cussions over the immediate evacuation of U.S. air, naval,
and military bases in this country are taking place in Whitehall. A government spokesman said they were proceeding in
what he described as 'a fairly cordial atmosphere.' "

"How English can you get?" David asked.

"They're probably tearing each other's throats out," I said,
instinctively pressing my foot down on the accelerator. I
looked at my watch; an idea had occurred to me. From the
dashboard, the gentlemanly voice continued in the same tones
it had used in happier years to describe the Chelsea flower
show.

"Last night saw little aerial activity, though reliable U.S.
sources report aerial reconnaissance from points as far apart
as the Arctic Circle and Hawaii. Formosa is still under heavy
bombardment from shore batteries. Units of the British Fleet
stand ready to assume defensive action in Singapore harbour.
The fighting between Chinese Airborne forces and units of
the Indonesian army in Northern Central Sumatra and near
Jakarta in Java still continues. Peking yesterday reported the
evacuation of Medan in Sumatra, but Indonesian sources
later denied this, whilst admitting that the city was 'almost
uninhabitable' by now. The landing of U.S. troops near Pa-
lembang continues. So far only conventional weapons are
being used on all fronts."

"So far . . . so far," David said. "They're only limbering
up yet."

That was where all the trouble had begun, in Sumatra, little more than a month ago. Peking had protested that the
large population of overseas Chinese there were being victim-
ized. Jakarta had denied it. A bunch of bandits shot a promi-
nent Indonesian citizen in the Kesawan, Medan. President
Molkasto protested. Tempers flared. Fighting broke out. The
U.N. were called in. The U.S.S.R. protested against this un-
warranted interference in national affairs. A plane full of
U.S. experts was shot down near Bali, possibly by accident.
The slanging started. Three weeks later, the People's Republic declared "a crusade of succour": war.

"David, we're going to London via Oxford," I said.

He looked curiously at me.

"What the hell for? It's a long way round. I thought you
were in a hurry?"

"The motorway will take us as far as Bicester. The delay
won't be too great. As you know, I'm a Fellow of Saints; I

want to call in there and have a word with Norman, if possible."

His reaction was predictable. Among the less informed on his side of the political arena, Saints had an undeserved reputation for being a sort of shadow Establishment from which the country was governed. This legend had been fostered by the fact that Saints, as a compromise between Princeton's Institute for Advanced Studies and Oxford's own All Souls, naturally contained the influential among its members.

"Who is Norman?" David inquired. "Do you mean Norman Parmettio, the Contemporary Welfare chap?"

"If you like to put it like that, yes, 'the Contemporary Welfare chap.' He's in his eighties now, but still active, a sage and lovable man. He drafted the Cultural Agreement of '69 with Russia, you know. He's seen academic and public service, including working as an aide to old Sir Winston at Yalta in the forties."

"Too old! What do you want to see *him* for?"

"He's an absolutely trustworthy man, David. You forget how cut of touch I am. We can't just drive into London knowing absolutely nothing of what is going on behind the scenes. Norman will put us in the picture as to what's happening in the Foreign Office and to who's changed sides in the last forty-eight hours."

"Touché. Carry on. You know I only came for the ride—but for God's sake let something happen. My stomach's turning over all the time; I have a presentiment of evil. I'm sick!"

"So's the whole confounded country."

We felt sicker before we reached Bicester. Another news bulletin gave us more details of local events. International news, as I had suspected, was being heavily censored; there was no mention of what was happening in Europe, or of what the Commonwealth was saying or doing.

Several members of the government had resigned—the predictable ones like Hand, Chapman, and Desmond Cooney, with a few unexpecteds such as poor old Vinton and Sep Greene. Martial law had been proclaimed in Liverpool and Glasgow. In the interests of public safety, a curfew would operate tonight and until further notice in the following cities: London, etc. . . . Airline services between Britain and the U.S. and Britain and the U.S.S.R.. were temporarily suspended. The L.C.C. were all out at Lords for 114.

At Fogmere Park we ran into trouble. There was a big U.S.A.F. base at Fogmere. You could see the planes and runways from the road at one point. A knot of people perhaps a hundred strong—a fair number for such a country spot—

filled the road. Several cars were parked on the verges, some with men standing on top of them. Banners waved, many of them bearing the usual disarmament symbol. One florid individual was haranguing the crowd through a megaphone.

"This'll take your mind off your stomach," I told David, rolling forward at 20 m.p.h. and sounding my horn. I glanced sideways at him. He sat rigid with his fists clenched in his lap —presumably nursing his presentiment of evil.

The crowd that had been facing the other way turned to look at us, parting instinctively to clear the road. The fellow with the megaphone, a big man with a red face and black moustache, dressed in a loud tweedy suit—how often one saw his type about the country!—bore down on us and tried to open my door.

"It's locked, old fellow," I said, rolling down my window. "Looking for a lift to somewhere?"

He got his big fingers over the top of the window and poked the moustache in for me to inspect. His eyes went hotly from me to David and back to me.

"Where do you two think you are going?" he asked.

"Straight down this road. Kindly get your face out of the way. You are being obstructive."

He was running to keep up with us. I could hear the crowd shouting without being able to grasp what they were saying.

"Don't annoy him," David said anxiously.

"I want to talk to you," the heavy man said. "Slow down, will you. Where are you going? What's the ruddy hurry?"

His head was outside the car door. The window closed electrically, catching his fingers. He roared in anger, dropping the megaphone to clasp his bruised knuckles. As we surged forward, it became apparent why the crowd had gathered. Beyond them had been established a check-point with a black-and-white bar across the road and the legend: "UNITED STATES AIR COMMAND. HALT." Behind sandbags were armed men and a couple of hefty tanks, besides several light vehicles, including a British Army Signals truck. It all appeared very efficient in the colourless sunshine.

As I halted at the barrier, two Americans in uniform stepped forward, a corporal and a sergeant, one on either side of the Wolseley. Again my window came down. The sergeant looked round and amiable. I thrust my face out before he could get his in.

"What's happening here, Sergeant?"

"U.S. Air Command check point. Just a formality to check for weapons. We have to stop all vehicles." This in an East Coast accent: Maine, I guessed.

"Have to? Whose orders?"

"Look, my orders, sir. It's only a formality. We don't want trouble."

"It's we English, unfortunately, who don't want trouble, Sergeant, but I'm curious to know by whose authority you have closed a main British road."

The crowd behind, divided in loyalty as in understanding, called, "Lock 'em up!" and "Let 'em go!" indiscriminately.

The corporal on David's side of the car, a yellow-complexioned fellow I had already marked as a trouble-maker, since his type was prevalent in the British Army, said, "You Limey copsuckers, you'd always argue rather than act."

"Simon, don't be difficult; tell him what he wants to know and let's get on," David implored. Turning to the corporal, he added, "Don't make any mistake, we're really on your side."

"Oh, no you ain't, Mac. You're just a neutral. You ain't on anyone's side."

"A very apposite answer, if I may say so," I replied. "I still wish to know by whose orders you have erected this barrier across the highway."

"Let's not argue, mister. Let's just say it's necessary, or I wouldn't be here wasting my time," said the sergeant patiently. A British Army officer, a dapper captain, was coming from behind the barrier towards us. I beckoned to him and repeated my question.

Instinctively he summed me up, just as I summed him up the moment he spoke. Under his Sandhurst veneer I recognized the Birmingham middle-class accent, just as I saw he had identified my Balliol honk, accentuated for the occasion. The moment would be lost on our American sergeant, a breed without many subtleties.

"There's been a spot of trouble, sir," the captain said, very politely. "A small private van passed along the road a couple of hours ago and machine-gunned the American planes over on the runway. So we are just taking precautions to see that such a breach of neutrality doesn't happen again."

"Captain, I am a friend of Lord Waters, the Lord Lieutenant of the county. Who has sanctioned this road block?"

"We naturally have official permission, sir, which I could show you."

"Get 'em moving, Captain, before we all die of boredom," urged the sergeant. Two other cars had arrived behind us and were hooting.

"Do you mind me asking, sir, have you any weapons in the car?"

"No, Captain. No bombs, no machine-guns."

"Splendid. Carry on to the next check-point, sir, and try to keep moving all the time."

"I will try," I assured him earnestly, and we rolled under the barrier arm as it lifted. A mile down the road was the other point, stopping vehicles coming from Oxford; it let us through without comment.

"Rather a comic incident that, eh?" I said.

David's face was wooden.

"Your sort loves to make trouble and humiliate people, doesn't it?" he said.

"Not at all. You can't have every Tom, Dick and Harry blocking the roads, or where would we be? I just asked a question I was perfectly entitled to ask."

"It comes to the same thing in the end."

"It's people like you who fail to ask pertinent questions that get misled. Your party, for instance."

"You dare mention parties after the tragic mistakes *yours* has made this last week?" He was furious. Debate always made his temper rise.

Quietly I said, "You know I know my party has behaved indefensibly, David—quite indefensibly. But your party's unreal dreams of collective security without armament, of nuclear disarmament in a nuclear age, have hampered the country's striking power so effectively that our shame must also be yours. Remember the TSR 2? When you were the ones who pulled our teeth, how could you expect us to bite? What curb could we offer the Red powers? At least these traitors like Minnie and Northleech can plead they had no alternative but to act badly."

"Christ, you wriggle on the hook as deftly as they do! What about the torn-up treaties? What about the promises? What about the Anglo-American alliance? All hot air, I suppose?"

"Here's Oxford," I said, as we came on to the top of the Banbury Road.

We were stopped again, this time by an exotic crowd of R.A.F. Regiment, Army, Civil Defence, and police, with a couple of A.A. men for luck. Plus a cheerful bunch of civilians doing good business with an ice-cream van.

"Sorry, sir, can't go through Oxford unless you've got a good reason for it." This was a well-scrubbed corporal with a tommy-gun over his shoulder, ambling up to the car.

"Such as? I am a fellow of Saints and am on my way there now."

"Better make it next week instead, sir. There's been a bit of trouble in the town. A fire or two and some hooliganism.

We're trying to keep the city centre clear. Try the by-pass, sir, if you were thinking of going through. Keep moving and you won't get into no trouble."

He wasn't to be budged.

"There's a phone box over there," David pointed. "Try phoning Norman."

"Good idea. Thanks, Corporal."

"Thank you, sir. Nice day, anyhow, isn't it?"

"Yes, lovely. Except for the L.C.C., eh?"

"What, sir? Oh yes, quite, sir. They didn't put up much of a show, did they?"

We left him beaming as I drove over to the side of the road. David laughed with an angry face.

"You love playing the decent chap and you love playing the cad, Simon. Which are you really?"

"The common man, David, *l'homme moyen sensuel*. In other words, a bit of both. Buy yourself an ice-cream while I'm phoning."

I got through to Saints straight away and recognized the head porter's voice at once, strained as it was through thickets of phlegm. Legend has it they built the college round him.

"That you, Dibbs? Challington here. Would you put me through to Professor Norman Parmettio."

"Hello, sir, nice to hear your voice. We haven't seen you here for months. You used to be so frequent."

"Pressure of work, I fear. Is the professor there?"

"Well, we had a bit of trouble last night, sir."

"Trouble? What sort of trouble?"

"Well, sir, we had to have the fire brigade round, sir. Some young hooligans threw petrol bombs over the east wall, sir. Terrible it was, sir. Fortunately I was all right in here. I phoned the police and the fire brigade and anyone I could think of. Proper scaring it was. I've never seen nothing like it."

"Indeed, anyone killed?"

"Not to speak of, sir. But the east wing's ruined. Your old room gone, sir, and part of the chapel. By a miracle of good fortune my lodge was preserved, but——"

"It seems impossible such things could happen in Oxford, Dibbs. The time is out of joint. Where's Professor Parmettio?"

"Those are my feelings exactly, sir. There you have it. Terrible it was. As for the professor, bless his soul, he committed suicide the day before yesterday, an hour or so after the Prime Minister spoke about us British being neutral and keeping the lamps alight. At least he missed the fire and all the fuss——"

"Parmettio dead? Do you say he's dead?"

"No, he committed suicide, sir, up in his bedroom. Left a note to say his country had dishonoured him and that he was taking the only possible course open to him. A fine old fellow he was, sir. . . ."

As I climbed back into the car, David dropped a newspaper he was scanning.

"You're as pale as a ghost, Simon. What's the matter?"

"How's your presentiment of evil, David? Norman's dead. Committed suicide—couldn't bear the dishonour. Poor dear old Norman! The porter told me and put me on to the Warden."

"On to Starling? He's a true blue government man. What did he have to say?"

"He's not so true blue as we thought; frankly I feel sorry for him. He sounded like a sick man over the phone. He told me that several of the clearer-thinking younger Fellows, Thorn-Davis, Shell, Geoffrey Alderton, and one or two more, tried to charter a private plane to fly to America. Foolish, I suppose, but quite understandable. They were apparently arrested at the aerodrome and haven't been heard of since. Starling went round and saw the local superintendent of police in person but couldn't get a word out of the man. He was almost weeping as he told me. And then——"

"Then?"

"Starling was cut off."

We sat in silence.

At last David said, "I'm sorry if I sounded stupid before. It's all a bit nastier than we thought."

"No nastier than we had a right to expect. We'd better get to London while we still have the chance."

"You think all potential trouble-makers are being arrested?"

"What else? And I'd hazard that by now you and I are on the list. Got that gun of yours ready?"

He had bought a local paper from a vendor while I was phoning. As we drove off I caught sight of its headlines: RUSSIAN NUCLEAR SATELLITE IN ORBIT: Ultimate Weapon, Moscow Claims; For Emergency Only.

At one point, David leant over and switched the radio on, but they were playing *Roses of Picardy* again.

We drove into and through the outskirts of London without being stopped. By noon we were crawling through Hammersmith, moving in fits and starts through dense traffic.

"How about stopping for a drink and some sandwiches?" David asked. "We don't really know when we'll eat again, do we?"

"Good idea. There's a pub over there that looks likely."

London was far from normal. In the centre of town we would see processions and meetings. Here were only people in small groups, hanging about or strolling. Some of the smaller shops were closed. Never had I seen such a large percentage of the population with their eyes buried in newspapers, not even at the time of the Suez crisis, back in '56—when the Americans had failed to support us, came the treacherous thought to my brain. Momentarily irritated with myself, I ushered David into the pub.

As I ordered drinks, I saw him cast his eye over the men present. One of them next to him, a man in voluble conversation with his mate, mistaking the intent of David's look, leant towards him and said, "You agree, don't you, mate?"

I could not be sure what David replied in the general hubbub, but I heard the other fellow say, "Why should we go to war for a lot of black men in Sumatra? I'd never even heard of Sumatra till last week! I reckon the government did right. Old Minnie has my vote every time. Let the blighters fight their own battles."

At last I got served. Carrying a tray with a Guinness and a pale ale and expensive chicken sandwiches over to David's table, I was in time to hear David say, "I can't see that neutrality *is* a way of saving our skins."

The two men, who worked, or so I surmised, at the big cake factory nearby, were on him with glee.

"You mean you think it would be *safer* to have declared war on the Chinks and Ruskies?"

"I mean that once global war breaks out, safety axiomatically disappears."

"Never mind axiomatically, mate! As long as we aren't in it, it's not global, is it? 'Ere, Bill, there's a bloke here thinks we ought to be fighting for the bloody Yanks!" They motioned to a couple of their mates, and soon there was a ring of them round our table. David's nervousness increased.

"If they wants a war, let them have it, I say," Bill opined. His cheeks were heavy with woe and drink-fat. "It's none of our business."

"But that's precisely what it is, Bill," I said. "You've heard of N.A.T.O., the North Atlantic Treaty Organization, I expect?"

Howls of derision greeted this. The first speaker—Harry, I believe he was—leant over our table and said, "Are you honestly going to sit there and tell me that you want to see this country blown to bits just because the Americans have come a cropper in Sumatra?"

"That's not a proper question. But if you are trying to ask me whether I support the democratic way of life, then I must answer yes——"

"Democracy! Wrap up!"

"—because I believe, like many another Englishman, that it is better to die fighting than die under Communist bombs or whips."

"That's all bloody propaganda!"

"Who's he think he is?"

"Go and join the Army!"

"You're a right one," Bill said to me. "What have the Yanks done for you to make you so fond of them?"

"You ought to ask yourself that," David said angrily. "You're old enough to remember the last war—yes, and the war before that! How do you think we'd have managed without American aid then?"

"Okay then," Bill said in gloomy triumph. "Then we'll hang on for three years and *then* we'll come in to help them, the way they did with us before!"

This sally drew a howl of laughter, and they turned away from us, losing interest and going back to a game of shove-ha'penny.

"Bill certainly averted a nasty moment," David said with rancour. He drank deeply into his Guinness. "Thank God for this poisonous British ability to laugh at themselves."

"And at others."

We drank up, ate our sandwiches, and rose to go.

"See you on the Russian Steppes—scrubbing them!" Harry called. Their laughter followed us into the sunshine.

We drove down the Mall and so to the Foreign Office, where I hoped to see Tertis. We had passed the marchers and the speakers, the ragged and the angry; but the prevalent mood was distastefully light-hearted. Although many of the shops had closed, cafés and pubs were open, and people were treating the whole thing as a grand unplanned holiday, lying in the parks caressing each other or buying each other ice-cream.

All this angered David much more than it did me; he had always been the one with faith in the masses.

I thought of the cities I knew thousands of miles away,

their grandeurs and their shortcomings: Washington, New York, San Francisco (my favourite American city), Chicago, Kansas City, and others I had never had the opportunity to visit. Yes, and I thought of Moscow and Leningrad, Baku and Tiflis, each of which I had visited on trade missions in the fifties; and of the teeming cities of the Orient, Canton, Shanghai, Peking with its factories and Ming tombs, Amoy, all cities I had not visited and now never would visit.

What was happening in them now? Were they being crushed to the ground even while London lazed in the sun? I looked up to the sky, half expecting to see—I knew not what.

"Not yet," David said grimly, interpreting my look. "But it will come."

We parked the car with difficulty and made our way to the F.O.

On the drive down from Oxford, after hearing of Norman Parmettio's death, my mind had become clear. If it were possible to help overthrow Minnie's government, I would help. If I were needed to take part in a new government, in whatsoever capacity, again I would help. Throughout the fifties and the early sixties, when the Cold War had shown signs of thawing (largely because of the then Russian leader Khrushchev's love-hate affair with the West) I had remained convinced that Communism was a declared enemy. Nothing I had written or spoken publicly had wavered from that belief. My record was clean. There were not so very many like me left in Britain. If I were needed, I would serve.

Although I did not know if Tertis was accessible, he was my best line of approach. I had worked with him often; we knew and trusted each other. If he were not available, I would try elsewhere, probably with the Athenaeum as first call.

At the doors of the F.O., David and I were stopped. We had to give our names, after which I was allowed to write a note for a messenger to take up to Tertis. The messenger was gone for a long while; only when fifteen minutes had elapsed did he return and request us to follow him.

Leo Tertis was assistant head of the Military Relations Department formed in the sixties and lately of growing importance. We walked down a corridor I remembered well, with messengers lounging by doorways and chandeliers hanging overhead. Nobody knocks on doors in the F.O., the assumption, I suppose, being that anyone admitted to the building in the first place will be birds of a feather. When our messenger indicated the second room of the Department, I walked straight in.

Tertis was there, five years my junior and at fifty a curiously youthful figure with plump pale cheeks, almost white hair and dark eyebrows. He looked, not unexpectedly, exceedingly grave and very tired. A vacuum flask of coffee stood on his desk; though the window was open, a smell of stale cigarette smoke pervaded the room.

He had been sitting talking to a short plump man. As David and I entered, he broke off, rose, and came round the desk to shake my hand. I introduced David; Tertis eyed him appraisingly.

"David Woolf; I remember the name. You stood for Fleetwood in the by-election, didn't you?" he asked.

"I did."

"Then you're a unilateralist. What are you doing here with Sir Simon?"

Give David his due, he hardly hesitated before replying, "I've seen the error of my ways."

"You're too late, my boy," Tertis said grimly, turning away to add, "I won't pretend I'm particularly glad to meet either of you just now, but while you're here you'd better be introduced to the Minister of Economic Affairs, Mr. Edgar Northleech."

I had already recognized the plump man as Northleech. For me he represented one of the country's worst enemies, a crony of Menhennick's, and one of the prime movers for increased appeasement towards the U.S.S.R. since the retirement of Macmillan had allowed his sort to get into power. Northleech moved heavily towards us now, his white hair flowing round his head, paunch well out, beaming through his spectacles as he extended his hand. David took it; I did not.

Moving round to Tertis, I said, "We don't have to tell each other where we stand. What can I do to help, Leo?"

"I'll give you the true picture in a moment; it's bad. Friend Northleech, like your friend Woolf here, is busy changing sides. These are men of straw, Simon, blowing with the wind. I would rather ditch them than use them."

Northleech came into the conversation saying, in the rambling manner he maintained even when angry, "The ability to change should not be despised. I can help you, Tertis. I can get you to Menhennick; he's ready to discuss anything; pressure of events makes him feel he may have been misled."

"Misled!" David exclaimed. "We don't want to *talk* to you and Minnie. We want to shoot you. Don't you realize that revolution or civil war is brewing up and down the country? Misled, be damned!"

"Enough of that talk, Mr. Woolf," said Northleech. "We have the situation in hand, you know. Anybody can be misled."

"It's the duty of men in office not to be misled. You've failed in your duty—abysmally. The Communist bloc's intentions have been clear since the forties."

Red in the face, Northleech pointed a fat and shaking finger at David and said, "That comes well from a unilateralist and a homosexual!"

"Leave personalities out of this! At least I and my party acted from our convictions. We advocated national disarmament as a first step towards general international disarmament. We advocated neutrality because as a neutral power Britain could weld other neutrals into a powerful enough group to break the deadly *status quo* of Big Two power ideologies that have frozen the world since the close of World War II. But your people, Northleech—yes, and I include you in this, Simon, and you, Mr. Tertis—what were you up to all the time?"

Tertis banged furiously on his desk.

"That's enough," he said. "If you wish to remain in here, hold your tongue."

But David went straight on, levelling one finger like a firearm at the three of us.

"Your sort had no real thought for world peace, or even for the country. You were after preserving the social structure to which you belonged, just as Halifax, Baldwin, Chamberlain, and the other hangers-on did in the thirties. You're the damned middle-class powermongers, with no knowledge of Russian or Chinese language and culture, or of what goes on in their dangerous skulls. It's your unspoken assumptions that have ruined Britain, not Communism or Socialism or all the other isms put together—your assumption that the best thing that can happen to anyone is that he can become a conformist and a gentleman, your assumption that your own narrow way of life is the only fit way of life. What happened to the workers? Once they got an education—*your* type of education, with a smattering of Shakespeare and a veneer of B.B.C. accent—then they too were hell-bent on becoming gentlemen, poor carbon-copy gentlemen."

"Paranoia!" I exclaimed.

"Why?" he demanded explosively, turning on me. "Because I don't subscribe to your conventions? Don't worry, you had nearly everyone else subscribing. You fools, you've ended by deluding yourselves. That's why we're all on the brink of disaster: you said to yourselves, 'Oh, the Chinese leaders are gentlemen. Treat them like gentlemen and they'll behave like gentlemen!' Look where it's got you."

"You're a very foolish young man," Northleech said. "There is no historical basis for your remarks. If we have in this country a rule by gentlemen, as you claim, then it is simply because the hoi-polloi have proved themselves unfit to rule. Besides, there is no conspiracy. Sir Simon and I went to the same public school, but we never had one opinion in common, then or since."

"Except the unspoken assumption that you were both of leader material!"

"Bringing you to the F.O. has gone to your head, David," I said. "Your speech would have been more effective delivered to rabble in Trafalgar Square."

"It may be yet. I'd still like to know why Northleech should be here, rather than with Minnie, palling up to the Chinese."

With a brow of thunder, Tertis said, "If you'd had the courtesy to keep quiet when you came in here, you would have heard why the Minister is here. It's too late for your type of speechifying, Mr. Woolf, just as it's too late for a lot else. Edgar, you'd better tell them why you came."

Northleech cleared his throat, glanced anxiously at Tertis, removed his spectacles to polish them furiously as he said, "It is no longer possible to keep peace with the People's Republic. Three hours ago—probably at about the time you were leaving your university—the first nuclear weapon of World War III was detonated. A 'clean' one-megaton bomb was dropped on Hong Kong. It fell at about six in the evening, local time, when the maximum number of people was about in the streets. We are as yet unable to obtain coherent accounts of the extent of the destruction."

In the silence that followed, Tertis's internal phone rang. He picked it up, listened, said, "Bring him in."

Looking up at us, he said wearily, "Our country is fatally split, gentlemen. That's the curse of it: when we come to discuss any detail, the opinions on it are infinite, and one man's vote is as good as another's. Perhaps it's the democratic system itself that has brought us to this humiliating position; I don't know. But I must ask you now to put personal considerations aside if you wish to remain here. We are about to be visited by General Schuller, Deputy Supreme Commander of N.A.T.O."

This I scarcely heard. I was still overwhelmed by the news of the Hong Kong catastrophe and trying to assess its meaning. As a result, I had one of the briefest and most significant exchanges that ever passed between two men.

I asked Northleech, "Then I suppose we are now actually at war with Communist China?"

Northleech said, "No. Their Ambassador has apologized. He claims the bomb was dropped by accident."

There seemed to me no possible reply ever to this, but David asked, "And you believed him?"

"It seemed politic to do so," Northleech said stonily.

"Politic! My gods alive, there's a term being used appositely for once!" David broke into ragged laughter.

Hopelessness came up and overwhelmed me. The terrible betrayal all round was at last revealing itself, and not a man in the country was innocent. Faintly, I said to Tertis, "You were going to put us in the picture. What of the countries of the Commonwealth?"

A deep voice from the door said, "Canada declared war on the common enemy two hours after the U.S. did so. It was expedient for the defence of the North American continent. Australia entered the war as soon as Sydney got news of the Hong Kong disaster. Your government promptly tore up the S.E.A.T.O. agreement. Seems the one thing it *is* efficient at is the gagging of news."

General Schuller did not introduce himself. He marched into the room and planted himself by Tertis. He was brusque and angry and had cut himself shaving with an old-fashioned razor that morning. His German-American accent was thick and nasal. Dark, handsome, very neat and be-medalled, he dominated the room with compressed fury.

"Well, Tertis, here I am. Who are these men? We were to be alone, as I understood it."

Tertis stood up, listing us without introducing us. I felt like an undergraduate again under that black stare. The General made no comment, save for a snort when Northleech's identity was made known to him. Plainly he dismissed David and me from his calculations. David, with his sensitive nature, would not stand for this. Stepping forward, he produced his revolver and said, "I am an enemy of your enemies. I'm prepared to shoot any traitors, sir."

Schuller never paused.

"Shoot Northleech," he ordered.

As my body seemed to freeze, so the tableau did. Even Northleech only cringed without moving from where he stood. David Woolf remained absolutely immobile. Then he returned the gun to his pocket and spoke contemptuously, in perfect command of himself.

"I kill from conviction, not to pass a personality quiz."

Schuller grunted again, outwardly unmoved, but from that moment the first impact of his personality was weakened.

"I won't mince matters," he said, swinging his head so that he spoke directly to Tertis. "Britain has never added anything to the power of America. Rather, it's been a liability, a weak partner to be helped along, mind without muscle. Get it?"

"There to aid your muscle without mind," I interposed tartly, but he continued without condescending to notice the interruption.

"We could have done without Britain as a partner once. But because she needed us, we've got bases and personnel and war material over here to defend our friends. Now at the eleventh hour—no, by Jesus, nearer half-past midnight!—your Prime Minister announces that Britain is to be neutral. Egged on by Red threats and encouragement, he says America must withdraw from these Isles. Right?

"It so happens it is no longer strategy for us to withdraw. We cannot withdraw. We are not going to withdraw. What's going to happen now, Tertis?"

Without hesitation, Tertis said, "As things are now, with the present government, we shall fight you to turn you out."

"Get in the picture, man! You *are* fighting us. Norfolk's a battleground right now. Outside Glasgow, the R.A.F. is bombing our installations."

"I don't believe it!" I said.

"You'd bloody better believe it, *Sir* Simon, because it's happening right enough."

"I believe it, General," Northleech said. "You presumably want to know what can be done to change the situation?"

"No. I'm going to tell *you* what can be done."

"You need our help, General. Don't interfere with our offering it to you. What are the alternatives as you see them?"

"The alternatives are brutal. Either you get Minnie Menhennick and his boys out of the way and replace him by a reliable anti-Red government, or—or London is going to be destroyed and this island will become an American forward base. You've got till sundown to act. We can't let you have any further time."

Put the way he put it, it sounded all wrong. Without American interference, we would have set our house in order anyway. Made to do it under threats, we would become inglorious traitors. After all, what future was there for Britain in a nuclear war? Suddenly before my eyes rose a picture of our cities all in ruins, women and children dying, even as they were dying now in Hong Kong . . . and it could happen within five minutes of our declaration of war. All the same, Schuller's view was understandable, inevitable even. I just wished it could have been put by someone less obviously a gunman.

Dismissing that hopeless argument *ad hominem,* I asked Northleech, "Where is Minnie? Can you get us to him? Is he at Chequers, or No. 10, or where?"

"He's in London, in an underground H.Q. I could get us there in twenty minutes in my car, if you're sure it's the right thing. . . ."

"It's too late to *talk.* We have to act," General Schuller said. "Yes, let's for God's sake go in your car. My Thunderbird might be a little kind of conspicuous."

"I'm staying here," Tertis said. He was the least ruffled of any of us. "Though I'm under suspicion, I can be more use by keeping in touch at this end. My boss feels as I do, and there are plenty more in responsible positions who will back a change of government. You're comparatively unknown, Simon, but they'd accept you for P.M. in the emergency. You go with the Minister."

As the others moved towards the door, I shook Tertis by the hand and said, "I'll do whatever I can."

"One word of warning," he said. "The country is now under martial law. Conscription for Civil Defence starts tomorrow, and you, Simon, have been officially declared an agitator—by the Dean of your college, so I hear. There's a warrant out for your arrest, so mind how you go."

"It should improve my reputation if I stand for office," I said. "And David?"

Tertis nodded.

"They want him too."

I turned round just too late to see what happened then. David had evidently gone first into the corridor. Northleech was frozen in the threshold with General Schuller close behind. Shouts came from along the corridor, shouts and the sound of running feet.

David pulled out that wretched revolver and fired twice, backing into the room as he did so. Someone screamed and the running stopped. Belatedly, one shot was fired in reply. It splintered through the door, which David had shut by then.

Gasping, he looked round at me and said, "They're after us, Simon. Now what the hell do we do?"

"Rubbish," Schuller growled. "They're after me: who else? What is this, a trap or something? Northleech, Tertis, get that desk across the door before they rush us."

He strode across the room as Tertis and Northleech went into action. He wrenched open the side door leading into the third room of Tertis's department. This was the secretaries' room. There were three of them, nice fresh young fellows all looking rather identical with identical suits and their hands raised above their heads. The General had brought two majors and a signalman with him, to wait for him in this outer office. The majors had already attended to the secretaries, while the signalman worked at his walkie-talkie, speaking into it in unhurried code.

"Nice fast work, Farnes and Able," General Schuller said, striding into the third room and adding to the secretaries, "Sorry about this, boys, but if I'm in a trap you'll have to play hostage."

"They're after Woolf and Sir Simon, General, not you," Tertis said, following Schuller. "Let me go out into the corridor and explain to them."

"You'll stay where you are. I'm sorry not to trust you, Tertis, but right now the British aren't my favourite nation. I'm taking no chances with anyone. Farnes and Able, bring those three hostages into the other room. Get the desk in too and barricade the side door with it. Look slippy. Operator, get Green Devil One on the air."

"Right to hand, sir," the operator said, looking up and handing a scramblerphone to Schuller.

Both majors carried light machine-guns. The one addressed as Farnes covered Tertis, David, Northleech and me, while Able directed the three secretaries. The latter worked efficiently, dragging in the desk, even smiling as they did so; for them this seemed just a break in F.O. routine. I wondered whether they were displaying British nonchalance or if they genuinely did not grasp the seriousness of the situation.

For myself, I expected a grenade to come through the door at any moment, until it occurred to me that the guards outside were holding their fire in case they injured the General. Everything happened in such rapid succession that it was difficult to think clearly. Although I did not know in what tone Dean Burroughs had reported my hurried exit from East Lincoln, it seemed likely that he would have exaggerated enough for the group in the corridor to regard me as a potential killer.

The General handed the scramblerphone back to his operator, informing the majors as he did so, "They're going to have a whirlybird at this window in two minutes minus."

Instinctively we all glanced over at Tertis's long windows with the balcony looking out across Horse Guards' Parade.

Later it occurred to me that here was a moment for clear thought—the first since the General had entered the room. He filled it by striding from one desk to the other with his jaw forward, saying with heavy sarcasm, "And now, my friend Tertis, we'll test out your theory that the guards outside aren't gunning for me at all. Farnes, throw this guy David Woolf out into the corridor."

You understand there were ten of us in the room. The place was comparatively crowded. I saw David's face shift as he ducked and moved. He looked rat-like: both frightened and frightening.

"You can't do this, Schuller. I'm on your side. Take me in the helicopter with you!"

He dodged behind Northleech, who whinnied with fright, and behind Schuller, pulling out his gun as he went. The crazy scheme no doubt was to hold Schuller at pistol-point until we were all safe in the copter. Doubtless David fell between self-preservation and patriotism and saw this idea as offering more hope than being pushed out into the corridor.

"Hold still, General, I won't harm——" he began, his voice shrill. But Farnes moved too. He sprang two paces across the room, dropped to one knee, and fired an automatic, one short and deafening burst.

The long window splintered and fell in. Northleech dropped next—through sheer panic reaction. For a second, dazed, I thought David had not been hit. Then dark blood gouted out of three holes in his shirt, spreading fast.

General Schuller swung round on him. David closed his eyes and fired one shot. Schuller blundered forward on to him. The two men fell together, breaking a chair as they went. Appalled, the two majors ran forward.

In moments of extreme crisis, a governing mechanism seems to take over from the rational centres of the brain. Without reflecting at all on what I was doing, I went to the outer door, pushed aside the desk that barricaded it, and threw it open.

Behind an open doorway opposite, armed men watched from cover. I saw their weapons come up. Down the corridor one way, another group had gathered, dark suits mingling with khaki.

"General Schuller has been assassinated! Help!" I called.

Framed in the doorway with smoke drifting past me, I must have looked a wild enough figure. But it was that pregnant cry "Assassination," echoing down the corridors of the Foreign Office, that brought them all running. As they came, I turned and beckoned Northleech.

In the excitement, the two of us left unnoticed. My last glimpse into the room caught a sudden shadow falling over it. Schuller's helicopter was arriving—on time, but too late. We ran down the corridor, Northleech puffing hard. As we descended the grand staircase, more shots rang out. Another fool had gone trigger-happy. Long bursts of automatic fire indicated that the helicopter was returning as good as it got.

We met several people. To all of them I uttered my formula and they scattered. Even at the door, where a no-nonsense captain in the South Wales Borderers moved to block our escape, I said, "Captain, General Schuller has been assassinated and you people will have to answer for it. See you get reinforcements and surround the building. Nobody whatsoever must leave until further orders. Clear?"

"I'm not in charge here, sir——"

"Then consider yourself so immediately. Get half a dozen men up on the second floor at once."

He jumped to it and we were through.

"My car!" Northleech puffed. "It's got a radio link. I must speak to Whitehall as we go. Over this way."

He headed towards the Chiefs' Park and I followed, blinking in the sunshine.

"We're going to Menhennick?" I asked.

"Yes."

His car was one of the new J.C. wagons, with a chauffeur lounging near who threw open the rear door smartly as we approached.

"The Tower, James—fast," Northleech ordered.

We climbed in and I asked, "You mean to say Menhennick's in the Tower of London? How singularly appropriate."

"Underneath it."

Northleech was just recovering his breath. As we rolled forward he opaqued the bullet-proof glass so that we could see out and not be seen. At the press of a button, a small bar slid out at knee level. At the press of another, his radiophone opened before him. We were of course completely soundproofed off from the driver.

The screen before the Minister lit. A severe matron appeared, with behind her a crowded Whitehall room where people came and went.

"Give me Bawtrey, General Intelligence," Northleech said, still puffing slightly.

"There may be a moment's delay, Minister. Routine is a little disturbed at present."

"Fast as you can, miss. Emergency."

She turned away. Northleech stabbed a finger at the screen.

"I'll give her 'routine disturbed.' Look, there's some bugger walking round that room with a cup of tea in his hand. Do you wonder the country's going to the dogs!"

I bit off the obvious answer that it was people like him who helped it go. He poured us some drinks, looked more cheerful, and began to grumble, all the while tapping one knee impatiently and staring at the screen before him.

"Sorry we had to leave Leo Tertis with his hands full like that. . . . Expedient, however. Look, Simon, I don't want you to feel disappointed, but Tertis was flannelling you in there."

"In what way?"

"This incredible stuff about the possibility of your becoming P.M. No offence, but it just shows how far poor old Tertis's judgement is awry. I urged the Foreign Secretary to get him into something safe like Housing years ago. . . . I mean, for P.M. we need a man of experience, a young man, a man in the public eye, a man who knows the ropes, knows where to turn for guidance."

"To you for instance?"

"I'll serve as long as the public need me, Simon. I'm an old warhorse."

"You're a bloody pacifist, Edgar. Appeasement's the be-all and end-all of your philosophy."

He looked broodingly at me, entirely without taking offence.

"You don't really want to see this grand little country blown to bits just to gratify your ambition, do you?"

"My record——"

"Bugger your record! You can't help being what you are, I know. You've never held office and you can't see the reason for being guided by necessity occasionally. There's none of the sticker about you, Simon, that's what's lacking. In my young days, I had the fortune to be guided by the great Lord Halifax——"

"You know what I think of Halifax!"

"I don't care what you think. You don't think enough. That's the world's trouble. Look at Schuller: the action school, as much brain power as a bull. Need never have been killed if he'd spent thirty seconds cogitating instead of emoting. *Non cogitavit ergo fuit.* Same with Woolf—an anarchist and subversive like all his kind. He had no idea he was shooting Schuller; it was simple father-hatred squeezed the trigger."

"Package reasoning! There was a lifetime's conviction behind that bullet of David's. He had a reasoned hatred of big and noisy men who use their position to make more noise——"

"Putting you through," said the panel. Simultaneously, a bearded man in shirt sleeves with a cup at his elbow and a pile of flimsies in his fist blinked into being on the screen.

"Hello, Bawtrey," Northleech said, with a parade of affability. "What's happening since I called you last?"

"Everything," Bawtrey said, taking a swig from his cup. "What do you want to know, Minister?"

"Relevant events of the last two hours. Hong Kong?"

"Nothing fresh. No new H-bombs dropped. First casualty estimate, one hundred fifty thousand dead, wounded, and missing. Singapore on general alert, Aussie fleet engaging Chinese warships off New Guinea. Three Russian nuclear subs detected and destroyed off Alaska coast——"

"What else? Washington?"

"Contact with America is just about defunct," Bawtrey said, looking at us under his eyebrows. "They're tearing their hair here, Minister. Not a peep from Washington, New York, Ottawa, Toronto—the whole blessed continent might just as well have disappeared. All cables are reported temporarily out of order, and all wavelengths blanketed with unusually strong interference."

Northleech and I looked at each other.

"How long has this been the case?" Northleech asked.

Bawtrey glanced at his watch.

"I've been on shift two hours. Two and a half hours, at a guess. There may be something through in a few minutes. Meanwhile, hang on, here's something else of interest."

As he was speaking, Bawtrey leafed through his flimsies. "The first space battle is now in progress. U.S. Orbitters attacking the Red nuclear satellite, meeting opposition from Tsiolkos and China bugs."

"Europe?"

"Mobilization in France, Italy, and the Scandinavian countries. Every man in Western Germany at the frontier, Reuter reports. Same in Turkey, Greece. Main impression seems to be that they're waiting to see what Great Britain decides."

As the man talked, I stared out of the window. We moved with unconscionable slowness, though Northleech's driver took short cuts when he could. Trafalgar Square was crowded, and not only with soap-box orators. A figure in a white cassock was holding a service on the steps of St. Martin's-in-the-Fields. Down the Strand, traffic was entirely at a standstill. We detoured round Covent Garden, to squeeze into a Fleet Street almost as crowded.

In contrast to the sightseers round the Park, people here looked grave. Outside a Civil Defence recruitment booth, both men and women queued. The military was out in strength; a column of light tanks added to the traffic congestion. I thought of the other grey old capitals of Europe, members of the same dying yet grand order, all teetering on the brink of annihilation.

Bawtrey shuffled up another piece of paper as we approached Ludgate Circus.

"Dame reaffirms Sark's neutrality," he read disgustedly, screwing it up. "And here's one more in your line, Minister. Deputy Supreme Commander of N.A.T.O., General Gavin T. Schuller, was assassinated within the last twenty-five minutes by Derick Woolf, described as a member of the British Communist Party. Members of the Special Police shot Woolf before he could escape. Fighting is still——"

He paused. Someone visible to us only as a torso tapped Bawtrey's shoulder and handed him a fresh communiqué. He read it out slowly, squinting now and again at Northleech as he did so.

"Here's one for the general circuits. Sounds like big stuff. Seems they finally got through to Washington and Ottawa. This one's datelined Washington and reads: 'Mr. Martin Mumford, President of the United States, will make a special address to the world at 1500 hours, British Summer Time, today.' That's in about twenty-eight minutes' time. 'This address will transcend in importance any previous statement ever made by a U.S. President.' Hm, some billing. 'It is of the utmost importance that the largest possible audience in all countries sees and hears the President speak.' Sounds as if the Martians have stepped in, doesn't it?"

"That will be all, thank you, Bawtrey," Northleech said, obviously disapproving such facetiousness. As he switched off, the bearded man picked up his cup, swigged it and faded into nothing. The set folded neatly back into its compartment.

The traffic thinned; we accelerated along the last stretch of the way, and the Tower swung into sight ahead. The bright dress uniforms had gone. Light tanks had replaced the sentry-boxes. Everything was handled efficiently. Northleech produced a pass for the guard officer, which was okayed. Nevertheless, we and the driver had to climb out and be searched for fire-arms, while two plain-clothes men simultaneously examined our vehicle.

They gave us clearance in about forty-five seconds, saluting us as we drove on under Byward Tower with a guard riding beside the driver.

We drove over to the Queen's House and climbed out. I followed Northleech inside. Another guard stationed by a wooden staircase was replacing the receiver on a handphone as we entered; the main gate had warned him we were about to arrive. He flicked over a switch normally concealed behind oak panelling.

The wooden staircase hinged at the sixth step up, yawning open to reveal a flight of carpeted stone stairs descending underground. Motioning to me, Northleech started down them, his untidy white hair fluttering round his head in the warm updraught of air.

I recognized that smell of canned air, sweet with disinfectant. It reminded me of the underground H.Q. of my department in Hyde Park during World War II. This was a much more elaborate and larger subterranean system. At the bottom of the stairs was a chain of three airlocks giving one on to each other, their indicators all at a neutral green. They opened on to a large circular space, well-lit but almost deserted. Here stood a magazine and paper stall, a tobacconist's, and a café, all open. Piped music played softly. I noticed other stairs leading down into this foyer.

Without hesitation, Northleech led over to a central block of lifts, a row of perhaps a dozen of varying sizes, each with an ancient male attendant waiting by the doors. We entered the nearest.

"Level X," Northleech said crisply.

Glancing at me with a sly humour, he remarked, "You see the government hasn't been entirely unprepared for emergencies."

"Every man for himself," I replied.

It was an express lift. I climbed out at the bottom feeling slightly sick. For a second we had been in free fall.

Here was a maze of corridors, with many people moving fast with set faces. After some slight confusion and a word or two of barked argument, Northleech got us into an anteroom, where a smartly formidable secretary left us, returning in two minutes.

While he was out of the room, Northleech said, "I know this man, this secretary. Obviously Menhennick is still in full control. We'll have to watch our step until we see how the land lies. Agreed?"

"It seems inevitable."

"Keep it that way. We don't want trouble if it can be avoided."

"Spoken in character, Minister."

"Don't be a bloody fool, Simon. You're out of your depth and you know it."

The secretary, returning, said, "The P.M.'s with the Indian Premier and other Commonwealth gentlemen. You may go in, but don't intrude."

We went in.

We did not intrude.

The room was impressive. Some fifty men were gathered there, many of them leading diplomats. Waiters with trays unobtrusively served drinks. On the surface it appeared incongruously peaceful. I recognized Mr. Turdilal, the Indian Premier, at once. He stood on a raised platform with Minnie slightly behind him. Minnie looked worn and shrunken; his face reminded me of the ill look I had seen on the face of Sir Anthony Eden at the time of Suez.

Turdilal seemed incongruously cheerful. He was in full spate as we entered, waving a relaxed right hand in time with his phrases.

". . . and furthermore, gentlemen, you need no reminding from me that India has always stood for the peace of the world. We are an old nation and we have always stood for peace. That is why we are standing now at this terribly black hour of international conflict solidly behind the British government and most of the other members of the Commonwealth for neutrality. We——"

"What about the invasion of Indonesia?" a voice called.

Turdilal smiled a charming smile.

"What about the invasion, indeed, my South American friend? Carnage added to carnage does not equal peace, my friend. We are not Gadarene swine, may I remind you. Your country is also on friendly terms with Indonesia, but you are not hurrying to bear arms on their behalf. No. You are wise. Instead you are stepping up armament production to sell to China, I guess."

Ugly murmurs greeted this, but Turdilal flowed on.

"South America must remain neutral. And that is what I am saying also about Britain and the Commonwealth. Someone must rebuild out of the ashes. That is a harder task than creating the ashes. So I for one applaud Mr. Menhennick's stand against the pressure of power politics."

A hubbub arose as he finished, angry cries mingling with cheers and the odd handclap.

Minnie came forward, clapped Turdilal weakly on the

back, and held up his hand for silence. When it came, he rubbed the hand over his moustache and said, "Thank you for your support, gentlemen. I realize our country is in an invidious position, I realize it only too well. But we have been in an invidious position for a quarter of a century now, ever since the perfection of this deadly nuclear power and the emergence of the two great powers. Rest assured, I have done all in my power to keep our beloved country safe. Rest assured, I shall not stand down——"

"Shame!" I cried.

"—until I feel the nation has no more need for me. . . ."

"Go, in God's name, go!" I shouted.

Two Ghana ministers looked angrily round and said, "Keep silence while he speaks," and a waiter pressed a large whisky into my hand.

"I will say no more now," Minnie continued, looking at his watch. "In two minutes, the American President, Mr. Mumford, is speaking to the world via Telstar II. We can see it on the wall screen here. I do not know what he is to say, but doubtless it will be of grave import. Just at present our contacts with Washington are disturbed; however, I have been reliably informed that a very few hours ago the American continent was subjected to intense nuclear bombardment on both her seaboards."

A ripple of amusement that grew with the beginning of his last sentence was killed stone dead by the end of it. A terrible silence, a chill, settled over everyone present—myself, of course, included. Everyone present had their differences with the United States, yet in that moment friction died and love came uppermost. Many faces were full of shame. We all stood motionless.

Not a word was spoken until the big wall screen lit. The time was three o'clock.

The Global Viewing sign came on, a spinning world with the illuminated orbits of the TV relay stations surrounding it. How long, I wondered, before they were shot down and TV shrank again into a petty national plaything instead of the transnational communication it had become?

A voice said, "Here is the President of the United States of America, Mr. Martin Wainwright Mumford."

He sat composedly at a desk bare of everything bar one sheet of paper. He wore a neat suit. Behind him hung the American flag. He looked young, determined, and under enormous strain. He launched into what he had to say without preliminaries; he spoke without rhetoric.

"I invited everyone in the world to see and hear me because what I have to say is of personal importance to you all.

"Only a few hours ago, the enemies of the United States launched their mightiest weapons upon us. Intercontinental ballistic missiles carrying nuclear warheads descended on all our major cities almost simultaneously. Their destructive forces when unleashed on their targets were so great that no nation could have survived the blow.

"Happily, all those missiles were checked some miles up in the atmosphere.

"The United States of America now possesses a sure defence against the hideous and hitherto all-conquering weapon of nuclear bombing.

"This defence is of such a nature that it could only be given thorough trial under actual test conditions. We have had to undergo that test, and we have survived. Had the defence failed, I should not be here talking to you now.

"The defence takes the form of a shield, which we call the geogravitic flux. In theory, this form of defence has been known for some time, but its consumption of energy seemed so vast as to render it impracticable. However, our scientists and technologists have perfected a way whereby the shield—which now covers all of North America, our Canadian allies as well as ourselves—the shield draws its power from the nuclear powers it destroys. The greater the force exerted against it, the more greatly the shield is able to resist.

"You will see that we are in consequence impregnable. What is more, we shall remain impregnable for a long time. We have this new defence. Our enemies have new weapons. We were subjected not only to nuclear attack; we were bombarded by a type of anti-matter bomb infinitely more terrible than the nuclear bomb, which must now be regarded as old-fashioned. Our shield effectively repelled all comers."

Almost furtively, I glanced about me. Every face was fixed in fascination on that grave face looming on the screen. An immense pressure of triumph was building up as the President continued his address.

"I confess that this nation—as yet—has no anti-matter bomb. We have been concentrating on methods of defence rather than offence. But we have literally at our finger-tips the mighty power of the atom. So far we have unleashed no retaliatory bombs in reply to the brutal attack of our enemies.

"It is my hope that retaliation will not be necessary. America and Canada cannot be conquered; but we could bring our enemies to their knees two hours from now. We could destroy them utterly, as they well know. We do not desire to take this ultimate step. The collapse of the two vast Communist countries would involve the rest of the free world in decades of rehabilitation too costly to be visualized. So we are stepping forward, laying our cards on the table, and inviting our enemies to make peace with the Free World at once.

"This is an unprecedented step to take. We live in unprecedented times; God grant us unprecedented courage to meet it.

"Such a step would not have been possible had not our friends the British, and the other North Atlantic countries who look to them for leadership, decided to remain neutral. Had they not so decided, then beyond doubt they would have suffered the same terrible bombardment inflicted on us. Without the geogravitic shield, they would never have survived, and we should have been forced to carry out total war to avenge their destruction.

"So I say again, we whole-heartedly and unreservedly offer a fresh chance to make peace. On behalf of my government and people, I invite the leaders of the Communist bloc to meet me personally on neutral ground in London. I give them forty-eight hours to make a just peace. After that time, if they have not shown themselves more than willing to build a lasting agreement—they know what the consequences will have to be.

"They will be shown no mercy then, as they have shown us no mercy. But the United America offers them more than mercy now."

Mumford's image disappeared. At once a subdued uproar broke out in the hall. Like many of the others, I was weeping with an un-British lack of restraint.

Next to the hall was a canteen. As I was eating there a few minutes later, Northleech approached, talking to a secretary. By his manner, I saw he bubbled with excitement. No doubt he was, in his own phrase, being guided by necessity. He broke off his conversation to speak to me.

"Look here, Sir Simon, this wonderful gesture of Mumford's has put a different complexion on matters. I will see to it personally that the warrant for your arrest is cancelled straightaway."

"Thank you. Then I can get back to East Lincoln to see how my wife is. Though I shall have to tender my resignation to the Dean."

"Understandable, quite. Well, that must remain your worry; I can't interfere there, naturally."

"Naturally."

"Though the Dean may not accept it. His anti-American views were always too clear. Since you'll no doubt return there as something of a hero, he may feel that by keeping you on he will gain popularity for himself. I'm sure I should feel like that, in his boots."

I looked down at my plate to conceal my distaste.

"I'm sure you would," I said. "But I'm sick of appeasement in all its forms. A new breeze is blowing from now on, and I'm coming back into politics."

A spark of anger fired in the old boy. He rapped on my table, making my spoon rattle against the plate.

"Before you do that, you'd better learn to distinguish between negotiation and appeasement."

"I can already. You're a great appeaser, Minister; Mumford is a great negotiator. The difference is in the position from which you talk: a position of weakness or a position of strength. Mumford's is one of strength, yours and Minnie's one of weakness—and chiefly moral weakness."

He cleared his throat. His wattle had turned a dusky red. In a low voice he said, "Stop kicking a man when he's down. You saw for yourself how shaken poor old Alfred Menhennick was. He can't resign quickly enough."

There had never been better news. I only wished Jean—and David Woolf—could have shared it with me. Then, sobering my excitement, came the thought that we would have to turn out all of Minnie's sympathizers before the peace contingent arrived from America. When I spoke, the secretary flinched at the poison in my voice.

"Your own position is none too happy, Edgar. Mumford may have granted Britain a face-saver for general consumption, but you well know how Washington must really be feeling about us. Aren't we revealed, every one of us, as a set of cowardly turncoats—not only to the U.S. but to the world? You might alleviate the situation slightly by resigning with Minnie, as quickly and publicly as possible—or perferably by falling on your sword."

He gripped the back of his chair.

"I remember this sort of holier-than-thou cant from you in the Sixth Form," he said. "I'm a politician, not a Roman. I've no time for your sort of dramatics. It's true the world, and the Americans in particular, are going to need a lot of explanations, but I'm not going to quit now—I'm going to give them those explanations. Now more than ever the country needs experienced leaders."

Only for a moment did his face grow ugly; then he smiled with his mouth alone. The secretary aped the gesture of ill-omen.

Old Hundredth

THE ROAD CLIMBED DOWN BETWEEN TREES AS SYMMETRICAL AS UMBRELLAS. ITS LENGTH WAS PUNCTUATED AT ONE POINT by a musicolumn standing on the sandy verge. From a distance, the column was only a faint stain in the air. As sentient creatures neared it, their psyches activated it, it drew on their vitalities, and then it could be heard as well as seen. Their presence made it flower into pleasant noise, instrumental or chant.

All this region was called Ghinomon, for nobody lived here any more, not even the odd hermit Impure. It was given over to grass and the weight of time. Only a few wild goats activated the musicolumn nowadays, or a scampering vole wrung a brief chord from it in passing.

When old Dandi Lashadusa came riding down that dusty road on her baluchitherium, the column began to intone. It was just an indigo trace on the air, hardly visible, for it represented only a bonded pattern of music locked into the fabric of that particular area of space. It was also a transubstantiospatial shrine, the eternal part of a being that had dematerialized itself into music.

The baluchitherium whinnied, lowered its head, and sneezed onto the gritty road.

"Gently, Lass," Dandi told her mare, savouring the growth of the chords that increased in volume as she approached. Her long nose twitched with pleasure as if she could feel the melody along her olfactory nerves.

Obediently, the baluchitherium slowed, turning aside to crop fern, although it kept an eye on the indigo stain. It liked things to have being or not to have being; these half-and-half objects disturbed it, though they could not impair its immense appetite.

Dandi climbed down her ladder onto the ground, glad to feel the ancient dust under her feet. She smoothed her hair and stretched as she listened to the music.

She spoke aloud to her mentor, half the world away, but he was not listening. His mind closed to her thoughts, he muttered an obscure exposition that darkened what it sought to clarify.

". . . useless to deny that it is well-nigh impossible to improve anything, however faulty, that has so much tradition behind it. And the origins of your bit of metricism are indeed embedded in such a fearful antiquity that we must needs——"

"Tush, Mentor, come out of your black box and forget your hatred of my 'metricism' a moment," Dandi Lashadusa said, cutting her thought into his. "Listen to the bit of 'metricism' I've found here, look at where I have come to, let your argument rest."

She turned her eyes about, scanning the tawny rocks near at hand, the brown line of the road, the distant black and white magnificence of ancient Oldorajo's town, doing this all for him, tiresome old fellow. Her mentor was blind, never left his cell in Peterbroe to go farther than the sandy courtyard, hadn't physically left that green cathedral pile for over a century. Womanlike, she thought he needed change. Soul, how he rambled on! Even now, he was managing to ignore her and refute her.

". . . for consider, Lashadusa woman, nobody can be found to father it. Nobody wrought or thought it, phrases of it merely *came* together. Even the old nations of men could not own it. None of them knew who composed it. An element here from a Spanish pavan, an influence there of a French psalm tune, a flavour here of early English carol, a savour there of later German chorals. Nor are the faults of your bit of metricism confined to bastardy. . . ."

"Stay in your black box then, if you won't see or listen," Dandi said. She could not get into his mind; it was the Mentor's privilege to lodge in her mind, and in the minds of those few other wards he had, scattered round Earth. Only the mentors had the power of being in another's mind—which made them rather tiring on occasions like this, they would not get out of it. For over seventy years, Dandi's mentor had been persuading her to die into a dirge of his choosing (and composing). Let her die, yes, let her transubstantiospatialize herself a thousand times! His quarrel was not with her decision but her taste, which he considered execrable.

Leaving the baluchitherium to crop, Dandi walked away from the musicolumn towards a hillock. Still fed by her steed's psyche, the column continued to play. Its music was of a simplicity, with a dominant-tonic recurrent bass part suggesting pessimism. To Dandi, a savant is musicolumnology, it yielded other data. She could tell to within a few years when its founder had died and also what kind of a creature, generally speaking, he had been.

Climbing the hillock, Dandi looked about. To the south where the road led were low hills, lilac in the poor light. There lay her home. At last she was returning, after wanderings covering half a century and most of the globe.

Apart from the blind beauty of Oldorajo's town lying to the west, there was only one landmark she recognized. That was the Involute. It seemed to hang iridial above the ground a few leagues on; just to look on it made her feel she must at once get nearer.

Before summoning the baluchitherium, Dandi listened once more to the sounds of the musicolumn, making sure she had them fixed in her head. The pity was her old fool wise man would not share it. She could still feel his sulks floating like sediment through his mind.

"Are you listening now, Mentor?"

"Eh? An interesting point is that back in 1556 by the old pre-Involutary calendar your same little tune may be discovered lurking in Knox's Anglo-Genevan Psalter, where it espoused the cause of the third psalm——"

"You dreary old fish! Wake yourself! How can you criticize my intended way of dying when you have such a fustian way of living?"

This time he heard her words. So close did he seem that his peevish pinching at the bridge of his snuffy old nose tickled hers too.

"What are you doing *now*, Dandi?" he inquired.

"If you had been listening, you'd know. Here's where I am, on the last Ghinomon plain before Crotheria and home." She swept the landscape again and he took it in, drank it almost greedily. Many mentors went blind early in life shut in their monastic underwater dens; their most effective visions were conducted through the eyes of their wards.

His view of what she saw enriched hers. He knew the history, the myth behind this forsaken land. He could stock the tired old landscape with pageantry, delighting her and surprising her. Back and forward he went, flicking her pictures;

the Youdicans, the Lombards, the Ex-Europa Emissary, the Grites, the Risorgimento, the Involuters—and catch-words, costumes, customs, courtesans, pelted briefly through Dandi Lashadusa's mind. Ah, she thought admiringly, who could truly live without these priestly, beastly, erudite, erratic mentors?

"Erratic?" he inquired, snatching at her lick of thought. "A thousand years I live, for all that time to absent myself from the world, to eat mashed fish here with my brothers, learning history, studying *rapport*, sleeping with my bones on stones —a humble being, a being in a million, a mentor in a myriad, and your standards of judgement are so mundane you find no stronger label for me than erratic? Fie, Lashadusa, bother me no more for fifty years!"

The words nattered and squeaked in her head as if she spoke herself. She felt his old chops work phantom-like in hers, and half in anger half in laughter called aloud, "I'll be dead by then!"

He snicked back hot and holy to reply, "And another thing about your footloose swan song—in Marot and Beza's Genevan Psalter of 1551, Old Time, it was musical midwife to the one hundred and thirty-fourth psalm. Like you, it never seemed to settle!" Then he was gone.

"Pooh!" Dandi said. She whistled Lass.

Obediently the great rhino-like creature, eighteen feet high at the shoulder, ambled over. The musicolumn died as the mare left it, faded, sank to a whisper, silenced: only the purple stain remained, noiseless, in the lonely air. Lass reached Dandi. Lowering its great Oligocene head, it nuzzled its mistress's hand. She climbed the ladder on to that ridged plateau of back.

They made contentedly towards the Involute, lulled by the simple and intricate feeling of being alive.

Night was settling in now, steady as snow. Hidden behind banks of mist, the sun prepared to set. But Venus was high, a gallant half-crescent four times as big as the Moon had been before the Moon, spiralling farther and farther from Earth, had shaken off its parent's clutch to go dance round the sun, a second Mercury. Even by that time Venus had been moved by gravito-traction into Earth's orbit, so that the two sister worlds circled each other as they circled the sun.

The stamp of that great event still lay everywhere, its tokens not only in the crescent in the sky. For Venus put a strange spell on the hearts of man, and a more penetrating displacement in his genes. Even when its atmosphere was transformed into a muffled breathability, it remained an alien world; against logic, its opportunities, its possibilities, were its own. It shaped men, just as Earth had shaped them. On Venus, men bred themselves anew.

And they bred the so-called Impures. They bred new plants, new fruits, new creatures—original ones, and duplications of creatures not seen on Earth for aeons past. From one line of these familiar strangers Dandi's baluchitherium was descended. So, for that matter, was Dandi.

The huge creature came now to the Involute, or as near as it cared to get. Again it began to crop at thistles, thrusting its nose through dewy spiders' webs and ground mist.

"Like you, I'm a vegetarian," Dandi said, climbing down to the ground. A grove of low fruit trees grew nearby; she reached up into the branches, gathered and ate, before turning to inspect the Involute. Already her spine tingled at the nearness of it; awe, loathing and love made a part-pleasant sensation near her heart.

The Involute was not beautiful. True, its colours changed with the changing light, yet the colours were fish-cold, for they belonged to another universe. Though they reacted to dusk and dawn, Earth had no stronger power over them. They pricked the eyes. Perhaps too they were painful because they were the last signs of materialist man. Even Lass moved uneasily before that ill-defined lattice, the upper limits of which were lost in thickening gloom.

"Don't fear," Dandi said. "There's an explanation for this, old girl." She added sadly, "There's an explanation for everything, if we can find it."

She could feel all the personalities in the Involute. It was a frozen screen of personality. All over the old planet the structures stood, to shed their awe on those who were left behind. They were the essence of man. They were man—all that remained of him.

When the first flint, the first shell, was shaped into a weapon, that action shaped man. As he moulded and complicated his tools, so they moulded and complicated him. He became the first scientific animal. And at last, via information theory and great computers, he gained knowledge of all his parts. He formed the Laws of Integration, which reveal all beings as part of a pattern and show them their part in the pattern. There is only the pattern, the pattern is all the universe, creator and created. For the first time, it became possible to duplicate that pattern artificially; the transubstantio-spatializers were built.

All mankind left their strange hobbies on Earth and Venus and projected themselves into the pattern. Their entire personalities were merged with the texture of space itself. Through science, they reached immortality.

It was a one-way passage.

They did not return. Each Involute carried thousands or even millions of people. There they were, not dead, not living. How they exulted or wept in their transubstantiation, nobody left could say. Only this could be said: man had gone, and a great emptiness was fallen over the Earth.

"Your thoughts are heavy, Dandi Lashadusa. Get you home." Her mentor was back in her mind. She caught the feeling of his moving round and round in his coral-formed cell.

"I must think of man," she said.

"Your thoughts mean nothing, do nothing."

"Man created us; I want to consider him in peace."

"He only shaped a stream of life that was always entirely out of his control. Forget him. Get on to your mare and ride home."

"Mentor——"

"Get home, woman. Moping does not become you. I want to hear no more of your swan song, for I've given you my final word on that. Use a theme of your own, not of man's. I've said it a million times and I say it again."

"I wasn't going to mention my music. I was only going to tell you that . . ."

"What then?" His thought was querulous. She felt his powerful tail tremble, disturbing the quiet water of his cell.

"I don't know. . . ."

"Get home then."

"I'm lonely."

He shot her a picture from another of his wards before leaving her. Dandi had seen this ward before in similar dream-like glimpses. It was a huge mole creature, still boring underground as it had been for the last twenty years. Occasionally it crawled through vast caves; once it swam in a subterranean lake; most of the while it just bored through rock. Its motivations were obscure to Dandi, although her mentor referred to it as "a geologer". Doubtless if the mole was vouchsafed occasional glimpses of Dandi and her musicolumnology, it would find her as baffling. At least the mentor's point was made: loneliness was psychological, not statistical.

Why, a million personalities glittered almost before her eyes!

She mounted the great baluchitherium mare and headed for home. Time and old monuments made glum company.

Twilight now, with just one streak of antique gold left in the sky, Venus sweetly bright, and stars peppering the purple. A fine night for being alive on, particularly with one's last bedtime close at hand.

And yes, for all her mentor said, she was going to turn into that old little piece derived from one of the tunes in the 1540 *Souter Liedekens,* that splendid source of Netherlands folk music. For a moment, Dandi Lashadusa chuckled almost as eruditely as her mentor. The sixteenth-century Old Time, with the virtual death of plainsong and virtual birth of the violin, was most interesting to her. Ah, the richness of facts, the texture of man's brief history! Pure joy! Then she remembered herself.

After all, she was only a megatherium, a sloth as big as an elephant, whose kind had been extinct for millions of years until man reconstituted a few of them in the Venusian experiments. Her modifications in the way of fingers and enlarged brain gave her no real qualifications to think up to man's level.

Early next morning, they arrived at the ramparts of the town Crotheria where Dandi lived. The ubiquitous goats thronged about them, some no bigger than hedgehogs, some almost as big as hippos—what madness in his last days provoked man to so many variations on one undistinguished caprine theme?—as Lass and her mistress moved up the last slope and under the archway.

It was good to be back, to push among the trails fringed with bracken, among the palms, oaks, and treeferns. Almost all the town was deeply green and private from the sun, curtained by swathes of Spanish moss. Here and there were houses—caves, pits, crude piles of boulders or even genuine man-type buildings, grand in ruin. Dandi climbed down, walking ahead of her mount, her long hair curling in pleasure. The air was cool with the coo of doves or the occasional bleat of a merino.

As she explored familiar ways, though, disappointment overcame her. Her friends were all away, even the dreamy bison whose wallow lay at the corner of the street in which Dandi lived. Only pure animals were here, rooting happily and mindlessly in the lanes, beggars who owned the Earth. The Impures—descendants of the Venusian experimental stock—were all absent from Crotheria.

That was understandable. For obvious reasons, man had increased the abilities of herbivores rather than carnivores. After the Involution, with man gone, these Impures had taken to his towns as they took to his ways, as far as this was possible to their natures. Both Dandi and Lass, and many of the others, consumed massive amounts of vegetable matter every day. Gradually a wider and wider circle of desolation grew about each town (the greenery in the town itself was sacrosanct), forcing a semi-nomadic life on to its vegetarian inhabitants.

This thinning in its turn led to a decline in the birth rate. The travellers grew fewer, the towns greener and emptier; in time they had become little oases of forest studding the grassless plains.

"Rest here, Lass," Dandi said at last, pausing by a bank of brightly flowering cycads. "I'm going into my house."

A giant beech grew before the stone façade of her home, so close that it was hard to determine whether it did not help support the ancient building. A crumbling balcony jutted from the first floor. Reaching up, Dandi seized the balustrade and hauled herself on to the balcony.

This was her normal way of entering her home, for the ground floor was taken over by goats and hogs, just as the second floor had been appropriated by doves and parakeets. Trampling over the greenery self-sown on the balcony, she moved into the front room. Dandi smiled. Here were her old things, the broken furniture on which she liked to sleep, the vision screens on which nothing could be seen, the heavy manuscript books in which, guided by her know-all mentor, she wrote down the outpourings of the musicolumns she had visited all over the world.

She ambled through to the next room.

She paused, her peace of mind suddenly shattered by danger.

A brown bear stood there. One of its heavy hands was clenched over the hilt of a knife.

"I am no vulgar thief," it said, curling its thick black lips over the syllables. "I am an archaeologer. If this is your place, you must grant me permission to remove the man things. Obviously you have no idea of the worth of some of the equipment here. We bears require it. We must have it."

It came towards her, panting doggy fashion with its jaws open. From under bristling eyebrows gleamed the lust to kill.

Dandi was frightened. Peaceful by nature, she feared the bears above all creatures for their fierceness and their ability to organize. The bears were few: they were the only creatures to show signs of wishing to emulate man's old aggressiveness.

She knew what the bears did. They hurled themselves

through the Involutes to increase their power; by penetrating those patterns, they nourished their psychic drive, so the Mentor said. It was forbidden. They were transgressors. They were killers.

"Mentor!" she screamed.

The bear hesitated. As far as he was concerned, the hulking creature before him was merely an obstacle in the way of progress, something to be thrust aside without hate. Killing would be pleasant but irrelevant; more important items remained to be done. Much of the equipment housed here could be used in the rebuilding of the world, the world of which bears had such high haphazard dreams. Holding the knife threateningly, he moved forward.

The Mentor was in Dandi's head, answering her cry, seeing through her eyes, though he had no sight of his own. He scanned the bear and took over her mind instantly, knifing himself into place like a guillotine.

No longer was he a blind old dolphin lurking in one cell of a cathedral pile of coral under tropical seas, a theologer, an inculcator of wisdom into feebler-minded beings. He was a killer more savage than the bear, keen to kill anything that might covet the vacant throne once held by men. The mere thought of men could send this mentor into shark-like fury at times.

Caught up in his fury, Dandi found herself advancing. For all the bear's strength, she could vanquish it. In the open, where she could have brought her heavy tail into action, it would have been an easy matter. Here, her weighty forearms must come into play. She felt them lift to her mentor's command as he planned for her to clout the bear to death.

The bear stepped back, awed by an opponent twice its size, suddenly unsure.

She advanced.

"No! Stop!" Dandi cried.

Instead of fighting the bear, she fought her mentor, hating his hate. Her mind twisted, her dim mind full of that steely fishy one, as she blocked his resolution.

"I'm for peace!" she cried.

"Then kill the bear!"

"I'm for peace, not killing!"

She rocked back and forth. When she staggered into a wall, it shook; dust spread in the old room. The Mentor's fury was terrible to feel.

"Get out quickly!" Dandi called to the bear.

Hesitating, it stared at her. Then it turned and made for the window. For a moment it hung with its shaggy shabby hindquarters in the room. Momentarily she saw it for what it was, an old animal in an old world, without direction. It jumped. It was gone. Goats blared confusion on its retreat.

"Bitch!" screamed the Mentor. Insane with frustration, he hurled Dandi against the doorway with all the force of his mind.

Wood cracked and splintered. The lintel came crashing down. Brick and stone shifted, grumbled, fell. Powdered filth billowed up. With a great roar, one wall collapsed. Dandi struggled to get free. Her house was tumbling about her. It had never been intended to carry so much weight, so many centuries.

She reached the balcony and jumped clumsily to safety, just as the building avalanched in on itself, sending a great cloud of plaster and powdered mortar into the overhanging trees.

For a horribly long while the world was full of dust, goat bleats, and panic-stricken parakeets.

Heavily astride her baluchitherium once more, Dandi Lashadusa headed back to the empty region called Ghinomon. She fought her bitterness, trying to urge herself towards resignation.

All she had was destroyed—not that she set store by possessions: that was a man trait. Much more terrible was the knowledge that her mentor had left her for ever; she had transgressed too badly to be forgiven this time.

Suddenly she was lonely for his pernickety voice in her head, for the wisdom he fed her, for the scraps of dead knowledge he tossed her—yes, even for the love he gave her. She had never seen him, never could: yet no two beings could have been more intimate.

She missed too those other wards of his she would glimpse no more: the mole creature tunnelling in Earth's depths, the seal family that barked with laughter on a desolate coast, a senile gorilla that endlessly collected and classified spiders, an aurochs—seen only once, but then unforgettably—that lived with smaller creatures in an Arctic city it had helped build in the ice.

She was excommunicated.

Well, it was time for her to change, to disintegrate, to transubstantiate into a pattern not of flesh but music. That discipline at least the Mentor had taught and could not take away.

"This will do, Lass," she said.

Her gigantic mount stopped obediently. Lovingly she patted its neck. It was young; it would be free.

Following the dusty trail, she went ahead, alone. Somewhere far off one bird called. Coming to a mound of boulders, Dandi squatted among gorse, the points of which could not prick through her thick old coat.

Already her selected music poured through her head, already it seemed to loosen the chemical bonds of her being.

Why should she not choose an old human tune? She was an antiquarian. Things that were gone solaced her for things that were to come.

In her dim way, she had always stood out against her mentor's absolute hatred of men. The thing to hate was hatred. Men in their finer moments had risen above hate. Her death psalm was an instance of that—a multiple instance, for it had been fingered and changed over the ages, as the Mentor himself insisted, by men of a variety of races, all with their minds directed to worship rather than hate.

Locking herself into thought disciplines, Dandi began to dissolve. Man had needed machines to help him to do it, to fit into the Involutes. She was a lesser animal: she could unbutton herself into the humbler shape of a musicolumn. It was just a matter of *rearranging*—and without pain she formed into a pattern that was not a shaggy megatherium body . . . but an indigo column, hardly visible. . . .

Lass for a long while cropped thistle and cacti. Then she ambled forward to seek the hairy creature she fondly—and a little condescendingly—regarded as her equal. But of the sloth there was no sign.

Almost the only landmark was a faint violet-blue dye in the air. As the baluchitherium mare approached, a sweet old music grew in volume from the die. It was a music almost as old as the landscape itself and certainly as much travelled, a tune once known to men as The Old Hundredth. And there were voices singing: "All creatures that on Earth do dwell. . . ."

A Kind of Artistry

*It is better to repose in the earth betimes than to
sit up late.*

W. S. LANDOR

A GIANT RISING FROM THE FJORD, FROM THE GREY ARM OF SEA
IN THE FJORD, COULD HAVE PEERED OVER THE CROWN OF
its sheer cliffs and discovered Endehaaven there on the edge,
sprawling at the very start of the island.

Derek Flamifew Ende saw much of this sprawl from his
high window; indeed, a growing unease, apprehensions of a
quarrel, forced him to see everything with particular clarity,
just as a landscape takes on an intense actinic visibility before
a thunderstorm. Although he was warmseeing with his face,
yet his eye vision wandered over the estate. All was bleakly
neat at Endehaaven—as I should know, for its neatness is my
care. The gardens are made to support evergreens and shrubs
that never flower; this is My Lady's whim, that likes a sobriety
to match the furrowed brow of the coastline. The building,
gaunt Endehaaven itself, is tall and lank and severe; earlier
ages would have found its structure impossible: for its thousand built-in paragravity units ensure that column, buttress,
arch, and wall support masonry the mass of which is largely
an illusion.

Between the building and the fjord, where the garden con-
trived itself into a parade, stood My Lady's laboratory, and
My Lady's pets—and, indeed, My Lady herself at this time,
her long hands busy with the minicoypus and the agoutinis. I
stood with her, attending the animals' cages or passing her instruments or stirring the tanks, doing always what she asked.
And the eyes of Derek Ende looked down on us; no, they
looked down on *her* only.

Derek Flamifew Ende stood with his face over the receptor bowl, reading the message from Star One. It played lightly over his countenance and over the boscises of his forehead. Though he stared down across that achingly familiar stage of his life outside, he still warmsaw the communication clearly. When it was finished, he negated the receptor, pressed his face to it, and flexed his message back.

"I will do as you message, Star One. I will go at once to Festi XV in the Veil Nebula and enter liaison with the being you call the Cliff. If possible I will also obey your order to take some of its substance to Pyrylyn. Thank you for your greetings; I return them in good faith. Good-bye."

He straightened and massaged his face: warmlooking over great light distances was always tiring, as if the sensitive muscles of the countenance knew that they delivered up their tiny electrostatic charges to parsecs of vacuum and were appalled. Slowly his boscises also relaxed, as slowly he gathered together his gear. It would be a long flight to the Veil, and the task that had been set him would daunt the stoutest heart on Earth; yet it was for another reason he lingered: before he could be away, he had to say a farewell to his Mistress.

Dilating the door, he stepped out into the corridor, walked along it with a steady tread—feet covering mosaics of a pattern learnt long ago in his childhood—and walked into the paragravity shaft. Moments later, he was leaving the main hall, approaching My Lady as she stood gaunt, with her rodents scuttling at breast level before her and Vatna Jokull's heights rising behind her, grey with the impurities of distance.

"Go indoors and fetch me the box of name rings, Hols," she said to me; so I passed him, My Lord, as he went to her. He noticed me no more than he noticed any of the other parthenos, fixing his sights on her.

When I returned, she had not turned towards him, though he was speaking urgently to her.

"You know I have my duty to perform, Mistress," I heard him saying. "Nobody else but a normal-born Earthborn can be entrusted with this sort of task."

"This sort of task! The galaxy is loaded inexhaustibly with such tasks! You can excuse yourself for ever with such excursions."

He said to her remote back, pleadingly: "You can't talk of them like that. You know the nature of the Cliff—I told you all about it. You know this isn't an excursion: it requires all the courage I have. And you know that only Earthborns, for some reason, have such courage. . . . Don't you, Mistress?"

Although I had come up to them, threading my subservient

way between cage and tank, they noticed me not enough even to lower their voices. My Lady stood gazing at the grey heights inland, her countenance as formidable as they; one boscis twitched as she said, "You think you are so big and brave, don't you?"

Knowing the power of sympathetic magic, she never spoke his name when she was angry; it was as if she wished him to disappear.

"It isn't that," he said humbly. "Please be reasonable, Mistress; you know I must go; a man cannot be for ever at home. Don't be angry."

She turned to him at last.

Her face was high and stern; it did not receive. Yet she had a beauty of some dreadful kind I cannot describe, if weariness and knowledge can together knead beauty. Her eyes were as grey and distant as the frieze of snow-covered volcano behind her. O My Lady! She was a century older than Derek: though the difference showed not in her skin—which would stay fresh yet a thousand years—but in her authority.

"I'm not angry. I'm only hurt. You know how you have the power to hurt me."

"Mistress——" he said, taking a step towards her.

"Don't touch me," she said. "Go if you must, but don't make a mockery of it by touching me."

He took her elbow. She held one of the minicoypus quiet in the crook of her arm—animals were always docile at her touch—and strained it closer.

"I don't mean to hurt you, Mistress. You know we owe allegiance to Star One; I must work for them, or how else do we hold this estate? Let me go for once with an affectionate parting."

"Affection! You go off and leave me alone with a handful of parthenos and you talk of affection! Don't pretend you don't rejoice to get away from me. You're tired of me, aren't you?"

Wearily he said, as if nothing else would come, "It's not that. . . ."

"You see! You don't even attempt to sound sincere. Why don't you go? It doesn't matter what happens to me."

"Oh, if you could hear your own self-pity!"

Now she had a tear on the icy slope of one cheek. Turning, she flashed it for his inspection.

"Who else should pity me? You don't, or you wouldn't go away from me as you do. Suppose you get killed by this Cliff, what will happen to me?"

"I shall be back, Mistress," he said. "Never fear."

"It's easy to say. Why don't you have the courage to admit that you're only too glad to leave me?"

"Because I'm not going to be provoked into a quarrel."

"Pah, you sound like a child again. You won't answer, will you? Instead, you're going to run away, evading your responsibilities."

"I'm not running away!"

"Of course you are, whatever you pretend. You're just immature."

"I'm not, I'm not! And I'm not running away! It takes real courage to do what I'm going to do."

"You think so well of yourself!"

He turned away then, petulantly, without dignity. He began to head towards the landing platform. He began to run.

"Derek!" she called.

He did not answer.

She took the squatting minicoypu by the scruff of its neck. Angrily she flung it into a nearby tank of water. It turned into a fish and swam down into the depths.

II

Derek journeyed towards the Veil Nebula in his fast light-pusher. Lonely it sailed, a great fin shaped like an archer's bow, barnacled all over with the photon cells that sucked its motive power from the dense and dusty emptiness of space. Midway along the trailing edge was the blister in which Derek lay, senseless over most of his voyage.

He woke in the therapeutic bed, called to another resurrection day that was no day, with gentle machine hands easing the stiffness from his muscles. Soup gurgled in a retort, bubbling up towards a nipple only two inches from his mouth. He drank. He slept again, tired from his long inactivity.

When he woke again, he climbed slowly from the bed and exercised for fifteen minutes. Then he moved forward to the controls. My friend Jon was there.

"How is everything?" Derek asked.

"Everything is in order, My Lord," Jon replied. "We are swinging into the orbit of Festi XV now." He gave the co-ordinates and retired to eat. Jon's job was the loneliest any partheno could have. We are hatched according to strictly controlled formulae, without the inbred organizations of D.N.A. that assure true Earthborns of their amazing longevity; five more long hauls and Jon will be old and worn out, fit only for the transmuter.

Derek sat at the controls. Did he see, superimposed on the face of Festi, the face he loved and feared? I think he did. I think there were no swirling clouds for him that could erase the clouding of her brow.

Whatever he saw, he settled the lightpusher into a fast low orbit about the desolate planet. The sun Festi was little more than a blazing point some eight hundred million miles away. Like a riding light of a ship it bobbed above a turbulent sea of cloud as they went in.

For a long while, Derek sat with his face in a receptor bowl, checking ground heats far below. Since he was dealing with temperatures approaching absolute zero, this was not simple; yet when the Cliff moved into a position directly below, there was no mistaking its bulk; it stood out as clearly on his senses as if outlined on a radar screen.

"There she goes!" Derek exclaimed.

Jon had come forward again. He fed the time co-ordinates into the lightpusher's brain, waited, and read off the time when the Cliff would be below them again.

Nodding, Derek began to prepare to jump. Without haste, he assumed his special suit, checking each item as he took it up, opening the paragravs until he floated and then closing them again, clicking down every snap-fastener until he was entirely encased.

"395 seconds to next zenith, My Lord," Jon said.

"You know all about collecting me?"

"Yes, sir."

"I shall not activate the radio beacon till I'm back in orbit."

"I fully understand, sir."

"Right. I'll be moving."

A little animated prison, he walked ponderously into the air lock.

Three minutes before they were next above the Cliff, Derek opened the outer door and dived into the sea of cloud. A brief blast of his suit jets set him free from the lightpusher's orbit. Cloud engulfed him like death as he fell.

The twenty surly planets that swung round Festi held only an infinitesimal fraction of the mysteries of the galaxy. Every globe in the universe huddled its own secret purpose to itself. On some of those globes, as on Earth, the purpose manifested itself in a type of being that could shape itself, burst into the space lanes, and rough-hew its aims in a civilized extra-planetary environment. On others, the purpose remained aloof and dark; only Earthborns, weaving their obscure patterns of will and compulsion, challenged those alien beings, to wrest from them new knowledge that might be added to the pool of the old.

All knowledge has its influence. Over the millennia since interstellar flight had become practicable, mankind was insensibly moulded by its own findings; together with its lost innocence, its genetic stability went out of the galactic window. As Man fell like rain over other planets, so his strain lost its original hereditary design: each centre of civilization bred new ways of thought, of feeling, of shape—of life. Only on old Earth itself did man still somewhat resemble the men of pre-stellar days.

That was why it was an Earthborn who dived head-first to meet an entity called the Cliff.

The Cliff had destroyed each of the few spaceships or lightpushers that had landed on its desolate globe. After long study of the being from safe orbits, the wise men of Star One evolved the theory that it destroyed any considerable source of power, as a man will swat a buzzing fly. Derek Ende, going alone with no powering but his suit motors, would be safe—or so the theory went.

Riding down on the paragravs, he sank more and more slowly into planetary night. The last of the cloud was whipped from about his shoulders and a high wind thrummed and whistled round the supporters of his suit. Beneath him, the ground loomed. So as not to be blown across it, he speeded his rate of fall; next moment he sprawled full length on Festi XV. For a while he lay there, resting and letting his suit cool.

The darkness was not complete. Though almost no solar light touched this continent, green flares grew from the earth, illumining its barren contours. Wishing to accustom his eyes to the gloom, he did not switch on his head, shoulder, stomach, or hand lights.

Something like a stream of fire flowed to his left. Because its radiance was poor and guttering, it confused itself with its own shadows, so that the smoke it gave off, distorted into bars by the bulk of the 4G planet, appeared to roll along its course like burning tumbleweed. Farther off were large sources of fire, impure ethane and methane most probably burning with a sound that came like frying steak to Derek's ears, and spouting upwards with an energy that licked the lowering cloud race with blue light. At another point, blazing on an eminence, a geyser of flame wrapped itself in a thickly swirling mantle of brown smoke, a pall that spread upwards as slowly as porridge. Elsewhere, a pillar of white fire burnt without motion or smoke; it stood to the right of where Derek lay, like a floodlit sword in its perfection.

He nodded approval to himself. His drop had been successfully placed. This was the Region of Fire, where the Cliff lived.

To lie there was content enough, to gaze on a scene never closely viewed by man fulfilment enough—until he realized that a wide segment of landscape offered not the slightest glimmer of illumination. He looked into it with a keen warmsight, and found it was the Cliff.

The immense bulk of the thing blotted out all light from the ground and rose to eclipse the cloud over its crest.

At the mere sight of it, Derek's primary and secondary hearts began to beat out a hastening pulse of awe. Stretched flat on the ground, his paragravs keeping him level to 1G, he peered ahead at it; he swallowed to clear his choked throat; his eyes strained through the mosaic of dull light in an effort to define the Cliff.

One thing was sure: it was large! He cursed that although photosistors allowed him to use his warmsight on objects beyond the suit he wore, this sense was distorted by the eternal firework display. Then in a moment of good seeing he had an accurate fix: the Cliff was three-quarters of a mile away! From first observations, he had thought it to be no more than a hundred yards distant.

Now he knew how large it was. It was enormous!

Momentarily he gloated. The only sort of tasks worth being set were impossible ones. Star One's astrophysicists held the notion that the Cliff was in some sense aware; they required Derek to take them a pound of its flesh. How do you carve a being the size of a small moon?

All the time he lay there, the wind jarred along the veins and supporters of his suit. Gradually it occurred to Derek that the vibration he felt from this constant motion was changed. It carried a new note and a new strength. He looked about, placed his gloved hand outstretched on the ground.

The wind was no longer vibrating. It was the earth that shook, Festi itself that trembled. The Cliff was moving!

When he looked back up at it with both his senses, he saw which way it headed. Jarring steadily, it bore down on him.

"If it has intelligence, then it will reason—if it has detected me—that I am too small to offer it harm. So it will offer me none and I have nothing to fear," Derek told himself. The logic did not reassure him.

An absorbent pseudopod, activated by a simple humidity

gland in the brow of his helmet, slid across his forehead and removed the sweat that formed there.

Visibility fluttered like a rag in a cellar. The slow forward surge of the Cliff was still something Derek sensed rather than saw. Now the rolling mattresses of cloud blotted the thing's crest, as it in its turn eclipsed the fountains of fire. To the jar of its approach even the marrow of Derek's bones raised a response.

Something else also responded.

The legs of Derek's suit began to move. The arms moved. The body wriggled.

Puzzled, Derek stiffened his legs. Irresistibly, the knees of the suit hinged, forcing his own to do likewise. And not only his knees: his arms too, stiffly though he braced them on the ground before him, were made to bend to the whim of the suit. He could not keep still without breaking bones.

Thoroughly alarmed, he lay there, flexing contortedly to keep rhythm with his suit, performing the gestures of an idiot.

As if it had suddenly learnt to crawl, the suit began to move forward. It shuffled forward over the ground; Derek inside went willy-nilly with it.

One ironic thought struck him. Not only was the mountain coming to Mohammed; Mohammed was perforce going to the mountain. . . .

III

Nothing he could do checked his progress; he was no longer master of his movements; his will was useless. With the realization rode a sense of relief. His Mistress could hardly blame him for anything that happened now.

Through the darkness he went on hands and knees, blundering in the direction of the oncoming Cliff, prisoner in an animated prison.

The only constructive thought that came to him was that his suit had somehow become subject to the Cliff. How, he did not know or try to guess. He crawled. He was almost relaxed now, letting his limbs move limply with the suit movements.

Smoke furled him about. The vibrations ceased, telling him that the Cliff was stationary again. Raising his head, he could see nothing but smoke—produced perhaps by the Cliff's mass as it scraped over the ground. When the blur parted, he glimpsed only darkness. The thing was directly ahead!

He blundered on. Abruptly he began to climb, still involuntarily aping the movements of his suit.

Beneath him was a doughy substance, tough yet yielding. The suit worked its way heavily upwards at an angle of something like sixty-five degrees; the stiffeners creaked, the paragravs throbbed. He was ascending the Cliff.

By this time there was no doubt in Derek's mind that the thing possessed what might be termed volition, if not consciousness. It possessed too a power no man could claim: it could impart that volition to an inanimate object like his suit. Helpless inside it, he carried his considerations a stage further. This power to impart volition seemed to have a limited range: otherwise the Cliff would surely not have bothered to move its gigantic mass at all, but would have forced the suit to traverse all the distance between them. If this reasoning were sound, then the lightpusher was safe from capture in orbit.

The movement of his arms distracted him. His suit was tunnelling. Giving it no aid, he lay and let his hands make swimming motions. If it were going to bore into the Cliff, then he could only conclude he was about to be digested: yet he stilled his impulse to struggle, knowing that struggle was fruitless.

Thrusting against the doughy stuff, the suit burrowed into it and made a sibilant little world of movement and friction which stopped directly it stopped, leaving Derek embedded in the most solid kind of isolation.

To ward off growing claustrophobia, he attempted to switch on his headlight; his suit arms remained so stiff he could not bend them enough to reach the toggle. All he could do was lie there helplessly in his shell and stare into the featureless darkness of the Cliff.

But the darkness was not entirely featureless. His ears detected a constant *slither* along the outside surfaces of his suit. His warmsight discerned a meaningless pattern beyond his helmet. Though he focused his boscises, he could make no sense of the pattern; it had neither symmetry nor meaning for him. . . .

Yet for his body it seemed to have some meaning. Derek felt his limbs tremble, was aware of pulses and phantom impressions within himself that he had not known before. The realization percolated through to him that he was in touch with powers of which he had no cognizance—and, conversely, that something was in touch with him that had no cognizance of his powers.

An immense heaviness overcame him. The forces of life laboured within him. He sensed more vividly than before the vast bulk of the Cliff. Though it was dwarfed by the mass of Festi XV, it was as large as a good-sized asteroid. . . . He could picture an asteroid, formed from a jetting explosion of gas on the face of Festi the sun. Half-solid, half-molten, it swung about its parent on an eccentric orbit. Cooling under an interplay of pressures, its interior crystallized into an unique form. So, with its surface semi-plastic, it existed for many millions of years, gradually accumulating an electrostatic charge that poised . . . and waited . . . and brewed the life acids about its crystalline heart.

Festi was a stable system, but once in every so many thousands of millions of years, the giant first, second, and third planets achieved perihelion with the sun and with each other simultaneously. This happened coincidentally with the asteroid's nearest approach; it was wrenched from its orbit and all but grazed the three lined-up planets. Vast electrical and gravitational forces were unleashed. The asteroid glowed: and woke to consciousness. Life was not born on it: it was born to life, born in one cataclysmic clash!

Before it had more than mutely savoured the sad-sharp-sweet sensation of consciousness, it was in trouble. Plunging away from the sun on its new course, it found itself snared in the gravitational pull of the 4G planet, Festi XV. It knew no shaping force but gravity; gravity was to it all that oxygen was to cellular life on Earth; yet it had no wish to exchange its flight for captivity; yet it was too puny to resist. For the first time, the asteroid recognized that its consciousness had a use, in that it could to some extent control its environment outside itself. Rather than risk being broken up in Festi's orbit, it sped inwards, and by retarding its own fall performed its first act of volition, an act that brought it down shaken but entire on the surface of the planet.

For an immeasurable period, the asteroid—but now it was the Cliff—lay in the shallow crater formed by its impact, speculating without thought. It knew nothing except the inorganic scene about it, and could visualize nothing else, but that scene it knew well. Gradually it came to some kind of terms with the scene. Formed by gravity, it used gravity as thoughtlessly as a man uses breath; it began to move other things, and it began to move itself.

That it should be other than alone in the universe had never occurred to the Cliff. Now it knew there was other life, it accepted the fact. The other life was not as it was; that it accepted. The other life had its own requirements; that it accepted. Of questions, of doubt, it did not know. It had a need; so did the other life; they should both be accommodated, for accommodation was the adjustment to pressure, and that response it comprehended.

Derek Ende's suit began to move again under external volition. Carefully, it worked its way backwards. It was ejected from the Cliff. It lay still.

Derek himself lay still. He was barely conscious.

In a half-daze, he was piecing together what had happened.

The Cliff had communicated with him; if he ever doubted that, the evidence of it lay clutched in the crook of his left arm.

"Yet it did not—yet it could not communicate with me!" he murmured. But it had communicated: he was still faint with the burden of it.

The Cliff had nothing like a brain. It had not "recognized" Derek's brain. Instead, it had communicated with the only part of him it could recognize; it had communicated direct to his cell organization, and in particular probably to those cytoplasmic structures, the mitochondria, the power sources of the cell. His brain had been bypassed, his own cells had taken in the information offered.

He recognized his feeling of weakness. The Cliff had drained him of power. Even that could not drain his feeling of triumph. For the Cliff had taken information even as it gave it. The Cliff had learnt that other life existed in other parts of the universe.

Without hesitation, without debate, it had given a fragment of itself to be taken to those other parts of the universe. Derek's mission was completed.

In the Cliff's gesture, Derek read one of the deepest urges of living things: the urge to make an impression on another living thing. Smiling wryly, he pulled himself to his feet.

He was alone in the Region of Fire. The occasional mournful flame still confronted its surrounding dark, but the Cliff had disappeared; he had lain on the threshold of consciousness longer than he thought. He looked at his chronometer, to find it was high time he moved towards his rendezvous with the lightpusher. Stepping up his suit heating to combat the cold that began to seep through his bones, he revved up the paragrav unit and rose. The noisome clouds came down and engulfed him; Festi was lost to view. Soon he had risen beyond cloud and atmosphere.

Under Jon's direction, the space craft homed on to Derek's radio beacon. After a few tricky minutes, they matched velocities and Derek climbed aboard.

"Are you all right?" the partheno asked, as his master staggered into a flight seat.

"Fine—just weak. I'll tell you all about it as I do a report on spool for Pyrylyn. They're going to be pleased with us."

He produced a yellowy blob of matter that had expanded to the size of a large turkey and held it out to Jon.

"Don't touch this with your bare hands. Put it in one of the low-temperature lockers under 4Gs. It's a little souvenir from Festi XV."

IV

The Eyebright in Pynnati, one of Pyrylyn's capital cities, was where you went to enjoy yourself on the most lavish scale possible. This was where Derek Ende's hosts took him, with Jon in self-effacing attendance.

They lay in a nest of couches which slowly revolved, giving them a full view of other dance and couch parties. The room itself moved. Its walls were transparent; through them could be seen an ever-changing view as the room slid up and down and about the great metal framework of the Eyebright. First they were on the outside of the structure, with the bright night lights of Pynnati winking up at them as if intimately involved in their delight. Then they slipped inwards in the slow evagination of the building, to be surrounded by other pleasure rooms, their revellers clearly visible as they moved grandly up and down or along.

Uneasily, Derek lay on his couch. A vision of his mistress's face was before him; he could imagine how she would treat all this harmless festivity: with cool contempt. His own pleasure was consequently reduced to ashes.

"I suppose you'll be moving back to Earth as soon as possible?"

"Eh?" Derek grunted.

"I said, I suppose you would soon be going home again." The speaker was Belix Ix Sappose, Chief Administrator of High Gee Research at Star One; as Derek's host of the evening, he lay next to him.

"I'm sorry, Belix, yes—I shall have to head back for home soon."

"No 'have to' about it. You have discovered an entirely new life form; we can now attempt communication with the Festi XV entity, with goodness knows what extension of knowledge. The government can easily show its gratitude by awarding you any sort of post here you care to name; I am not without influence in that respect as you are aware. I don't imagine that Earth in its senescent stage has much to offer a man of your calibre."

Derek thought of what it had to offer. He was bound to it. These decadent people did not understand how anything could be binding.

"Well, what do you say, Ende? I'm not speaking idly." Belix Ix Sappose tapped his antler system impatiently.

"Er. . . . Oh, they will discover a great deal from the Cliff. That doesn't concern me. My part of the work is over. I'm just a field worker, not an intellectual."

"You don't reply to my suggestion."

He looked at Belix with only slight vexation. Belix was an unglaat, one of a species that had done as much as any to bring about the peaceful concourse of the galaxy. His backbone branched into an elaborate antler system, from which six sloe-dark eyes surveyed Derek with unblinking irritation. Other members of the party, including Jupkey, Belix's female, were also looking at him.

"I must get back to Earth soon," Derek said. What had Belix said? Offered some sort of post? Restlessly he shifted on his couch, under pressure as always when surrounded by people he knew none too well.

"You are bored, Mr. Ende."

"No, not at all. My apologies, Belix. I'm overcome as always by the luxury of Eyebright. I was watching the nude dancers."

"I fear you are bored."

"Not at all, I assure you."

"May I get you a woman?"

"No, thank you."

"A boy, perhaps?"

"No, thank you."

"Have you ever tried the flowering asexuals from the Cephids?"

"Not at present, thank you."

"Then perhaps you will excuse us if Jupkey and I remove our clothes and join the dance," Belix said stiffly.

As they moved out onto the dance floor to greet the strepent trumpets, Derek heard Jupkey say something of which he caught only the words "arrogant Earthborn." His eyes met Jon's; he saw that the partheno had overheard the phrase too.

In an instinctive gesture of his left hand, Derek revealed his mortification. He rose and began to pace round the room. Often he shouldered his way through a knot of naked dancers, ignoring their complaints.

At one of the doors, a staircase was floating by. He stepped onto it to escape from the crowds.

Four young women were passing down the stairs. They were gaily dressed, with sonant-stones pulsing on their costumes. In their faces youth kept its lantern, lighting them as they laughed and chattered. Derek stopped and beheld the girls. One of them he recognized. Instinctively he called her name: "Eva!"

She had already seen him. Waving her companions on, she came back to him, dancing up the intervening steps.

"So the brave Earthborn climbs once more the golden stairs of Pynnati! Well, Derek Ende, your eyes are as dark as ever, and your brow as high!"

As he looked at her, the wakeful trumpets were in tune for him for the first time that evening, and his delight rose up in his throat.

"Eva! . . . And your eyes as bright as ever. . . . And you have no man with you."

"The powers of coincidence work on your behalf." She laughed—yes, he remembered that sound!—and then said more seriously, "I heard you were here with Belix Sappose and his female; so I was making the grandly foolish gesture of coming to see you. You remember how devoted I am to grandly foolish gestures."

"So foolish?"

"Probably. You have less ability to change in you, Derek Ende, than has the core of Pyrylyn. To suppose otherwise is foolish, to know how unalterable you are and still to see you doubly foolish."

He took her hand, beginning to lead her up the staircase; the rooms moving by them on either side were blurs to his eyes.

"Must you still bring up that old charge, Eva?"

"It lies between us; I do not have to touch it. I fear your unchangeability because I am a butterfly against your grey castle."

"You are beautiful, Eva, so beautiful! And may a butterfly not rest unharmed on a castle wall?" He fitted into her allusive way of speech with difficulty.

"Walls! I cannot bear your walls, Derek! Am I a bulldozer that I should want to come up against walls? To be either inside or outside them is to be a prisoner."

"Let us not quarrel until we have found some point of agreement," he said. "Here are the stairs. Can't we agree about them?"

"If we are both indifferent to them," she said, looking out

and impudently winding his arm about her. The staircase
had reached the zenith of its travels and moved slowly sideways along the upper edge of Eyebright. They stood on the
top step with night flashing their images back at them from
the glass.

Eva Coll-Kennerly was a human, but not of Earthborn
stock. She was a velure, born on the y-cluster worlds of the
dense Third Arm of the galaxy, and her skin was richly covered with the brown fur of her kind. Her mercurial talents
were employed in the same research department that enjoyed
Belix Sappose's more sober ones; Derek had met her there on
an earlier visit to Pyrylyn. Their love had been an affair of
swords.

He looked at her now and touched her and could say not
one word for himself. When she flashed a liquid eye at him,
he assayed an awkward smile.

"Because I am oriented like a compass towards strong
men, my lavish offer to you still holds good. Is it not bait
enough?" she asked him.

"I don't think of you as a trap, Eva."

"Then for how many more centuries are you going to re-
frigerate your nature on Earth? You still remain faithful, if I
recall your euphemism for slavery, to your mistress, to her
cold lips and locked heart?"

"I have no choice!"

"Ah yes, my debate on that motion was defeated: and
more than once. Is she still pursuing her researches into the
transmutability of species?"

"Oh yes, indeed. The mediaeval idea that one species can
turn into another was foolish in the Middle Ages; now, with
the gradual accumulation of cosmic radiation in planetary
bodies and its effect on genetic stability, it is correct to a certain definable extent. She is endeavouring to show that cellular bondage can be——"

"Yes, yes, and this serious talk is an eyesore in Eyebright!
Must I hear of her when I want to talk of you? You are
locked away, Derek, doing your sterile deeds of heroism and
never entering the real world. If you imagine you can live
with her much longer and then come to me, you are mis-
taken. Your walls grow higher about your ears every century,
till I cannot—oh, it's the wrong metaphor!—cannot scale
you!"

Even in his pain, the texture of her fur was joy to his
warmsight. Helplessly he shook his head in an effort to shake
her clattering words away.

"Look at you being big and brave and silent even now!

You're so arrogant," she said—and then, without perceptible change of tone, "Because I still love the bit of you inside the castle, I'll make once more my monstrous and petty offer to you."

"No, please, Eva! . . ."

"But yes! Forget this tedious bondage of Earth, forget this ghastly matriarchy, live here with me. I don't want you for ever. You know I am a eudemonist and judge by standards of pleasure—our liaison need be only for a century or two. In that time I will deny you nothing your senses may require."

"Eva!"

"After that, our demands will be satisfied. You may then go back to the Lady Mother of Endehaaven for all I care."

"Eva, you know how I spurn this belief, this eudemonism."

"Forget your creed! I'm asking you nothing difficult. Who are you to haggle? Am I fish, to be bought by the kilo, this bit selected, this rejected?"

He was silent.

"*You* don't really need me," he said at last. "You have everything already: beauty, wit, sense, warmth, feeling, balance, comfort. *She* has nothing. She is shallow, haunted, cold —oh, she needs me, Eva. . . ."

"You are apologizing for yourself, not her."

She had already turned with the supple movement of a ve-lure and was running down the staircase. Lighted chambers drifted up about them like bubbles.

His laboured attempt to explain his heart turned to exasperation. He ran down after her, grasping her arm.

"Listen to me, will you, damn you!"

"Nobody in Pyrylyn would listen to such masochistic non-sense as yours! You are an arrogant fool, Derek, and I am a weak-willed one. Now release me!"

As the next room came up, she jumped through its entrance and disappeared into the crowd.

V

Not all the drifting chambers of Eyebright were lighted. Some pleasures come more delightfully with the dark, and these pleasures were coaxed and cosseted into fruition in shrouded halls where illumination cast only the gentlest ripple on the ceiling and the gloom was sensuous with ylang-ylang and other perfumes. Here Derek found a place to weep.

Sections of his life slid before him as if impelled by the same mechanisms that moved Eyebright. Always, one presence was there.

Angrily he related to himself how he always laboured to satisfy her—yes, in every sphere laboured to satisfy her! And how when that gratification was accorded him it came as though riven from her, as a spring sometimes trickles down the split face of a rock. Undeniably there was satisfaction for him in drinking from that cool source—but no, where was the satisfaction when pleasure depended on such extreme disciplining and subduing of himself?

Mistress, I love and hate your needs!

And the discipline had been such . . . so long, also . . . that now when he might enjoy himself far from her, he could scarcely strike a trickle from his own rock. He had walked here before, in this city where the hedonists and eudemonists reigned, walked among the scents of pleasure, walked among the ioblepharous women, the beautiful guests and celebrated beauties, with My Lady always in him, feeling that she showed even on his countenance. People spoke to him: somehow he replied. They manifested gaiety: he tried to do so. They opened to him: he attempted a response. All the time, he hoped they would understand that his arrogance masked only shyness—or did he hope that it was his shyness which masked arrogance? He did not know.

Who could presume to know? The one quality holds much of the other. Both refuse to come forward and share.

He roused from his meditation knowing that Eva Coll-Kennerley was again somewhere near. She had not left the building, then! She was seeking him out!

Derek half-rose from his position in a shrouded alcove. He was baffled to think how she could have traced him here. On entering Eyebright, visitors were given sonant-stones, by which they could be traced from room to room; but judging that nobody would wish to trace him, Derek had switched his stone off even before leaving Belix Sappose's party.

He heard Eva's voice, its unmistakable overtones not near, not far. . . .

"You find the most impenetrable bushels to hide your light under. . . ."

He caught no more. She had sunk down among tapestries with someone else. She was not after him at all! Waves of relief and regret rolled over him . . . and when he paid attention again, she was speaking his name.

With shame on him, like a wolf creeping towards a camp fire, he crouched forward to listen. At once his warmsight told him to whom Eva spoke. He recognized the pattern of the antlers; Belix was there, with Jupkey sprawled beside him on some elaborate kind of bed.

". . . useless to try again. Derek is far too entombed within himself," Eva said.

"Entombed rather within his conditioning," Belix said. "We found the same. It's conditioning, my dear."

"However he became entombed, I still admire him enough to want to understand him." Eva's voice was a note or two astray from its usual controlled timbre.

"Look at it scientifically," Belix said, with the weighty inflections of a man about to produce truth out of a hat. "Earth is the last bastion of a bankrupt culture. The Earthborns number less than a couple of millions now. They disdain social graces and occasions. They are served by parthenogenically bred slaves, all of which are built on the same controlled genetic formula. They are inbred. In consequence, they have become practically a species apart. You can see it all in friend Ende. As I say, he's entombed in his conditioning. A tragedy, Eva, but you must face up to it."

"You're probably right, you pontifical old pop," Jupkey said lazily. "Who but an Earthborn would do what Derek did on Festi?"

"No, no!" Eva said. "Derek's ruled by a woman, not by conditioning. He's——"

"In Ende's case they are one and the same thing, my dear, believe me. Consider Earth's social organization. The partheno slaves have replaced all but a comparative handful of true Earthborns. That handful has parcelled out Earth into great estates which it holds by a sinister matriarchalism."

"Yes, I know, but Derek——"

"Derek is caught in the system. The Earthborns have fallen into a mating pattern for which there is no precedent. The sons of a family marry their mothers, not only to perpetuate their line but because the productive Earthborn female is scarce now that Earth itself is senescent. This is what the Endes have done; this is what Derek Ende has done. His 'mistress' is both mother and wife to him. Given the factor of longevity as well—well, naturally, you ensure an excessive emotional rigidity that almost nothing can break. Not even you, my sweet-coated Eva!"

"He was on the point of breaking tonight!"

"I doubt it," Belix said. "Ende may want to get away from his claustrophobic home, but the same forces that drive him off will eventually lure him back."

"I tell you he was on the point of breaking—only I broke first."

"Well, as Teer Ruche said to me many centuries ago, only a pleasure-hater knows how to shape a pleasure-hater. I would say you were lucky he did not break; you would only have had a baby on your hands."

Her answering laugh did not ring true.

"My Lady of Endehaaven, then, must be the one to do it. I will never try again—though he seems under too much stress to stand for long. Oh, it's really immoral! He deserves better!"

"A moral judgement from you, Eva!" Jupkey exclaimed amusedly to the fragrant gloom.

"My advice to you, Eva, is to forget all about the poor fellow. Apart from anything else, he is scarcely articulate—which would not suit you for a season."

The unseen listener could bear no more. A sudden rage—as much against himself for hearing as against them for speaking—burst over him, freeing him to act. Straightening up, he seized the arm of the couch on which Belix and Jupkey nestled, wildly supposing he could tip them on to the floor.

Too late, his warmsight warned him of the real nature of the couch. Instead of tipping, it swivelled, sending a wave of liquid over him. The two unglaats were lying in a warm bath scented with ylang-ylang and other essences.

Jupkey squealed in anger and fright. Kicking out, she caught Derek on the shin with a hoof; he slipped in the oily liquid and fell. Belix, unaided by warmsight, jumped out of the bath, entangled himself with Derek's legs, and also fell.

Eva was shouting for lights. Other occupants of the hall cried back that darkness must prevail at all costs.

Picking himself up—leaving only his dignity behind—Derek ran for the exit, abandoning the confusion to sort itself out as it would.

Burningly, disgustedly, he made his way dripping from Eyebright. The hastening footsteps of Jon followed him like an echo all the way to the space field.

Soon he would be back at Endehaaven. Though he would always be a failure in his dealings with other humans, there at least he knew every inch of his bleak allotted territory.

ENVOI

Had there been a spell over all Endehaaven, it could have been no quieter when My Lord Derek Ende arrived home.

I informed My Lady of the moment when his lightpusher arrived and rode at orbit. In the receptor bowl I watched him and Jon come home, cutting north-west across the emaciated wilds of Europe, across Denmark, over the Shetlands, the

Faroes, the sea, alighting by the very edge of the islands, by the fjord with its silent waters.

All the while the wind lay low as if under some stunning malediction, and none of our tall trees stirred.

"Where is my Mistress, Hols?" Derek asked me, as I went to greet him and assist him out of his suit.

"She asked me to tell you that she is confined to her chambers and cannot see you, My Lord."

He looked me in the eyes as he did so rarely.

"Is she ill?"

"No. She simply said she would not see you."

Without waiting to remove his suit, he hurried on into the building.

Over the next two days, he was about but little, preferring to remain in his room while My Lady remained in hers. Once he wandered among the experimental tanks and cages. I saw him net a fish and toss it into the air, watching it while it struggled into new form and flew away until it was lost in a jumbled background of cumulus; but it was plain he was less interested in the riddles of stress and transmutation than in the symbolism of the carp's flight.

Mostly he sat compiling the spools on which he imposed the tale of his life. All but one wall was covered with files full of these spools: the arrested drumbeats of past centuries. From the later spools I have secretly compiled this record; for all his unspoken self-pity, he never knew the sickness of merely observing.

We parthenos will never understand the luxuries of a divided mind. Surely suffering as much as happiness is a kind of artistry?

On the day that he received a summons from Star One to go upon another quest for them, Derek met My Lady in the Blue Corridor.

"It is good to see you about again, Mistress," he said, kissing her cheek. "Staying confined in your room is bad for you."

She stroked his hair. On her nervous hand she wore one ring with an amber stone; her gown was of olive and umber.

"I was very upset to have you go away from me. The Earth is dying, Derek, and I fear its loneliness. You have left me alone too much. However, I have recovered myself and am glad to see you back."

"You know I am glad to see you. Smile for me and come outside for some fresh air. The sun is shining."

"It's so long since it shone. Do you remember how once it

always shone? I can't bear to quarrel any more. Take my arm and be kind to me."

"Mistress, I always wish to be kind to you. And I have all sorts of things to discuss with you. You'll want to hear what I have been doing, and——"

"You won't leave me alone any more?"

He felt her hand tighten on his arm. She spoke very loudly.

"That was one of the things I wished to discuss—later," he said. "First let me tell you about the wonderful life form with which I made contact on Festi."

As they left the corridor and descended the paragravity shaft, My Lady said wearily, "I suppose that's a polite way of telling me that you are bored here."

He clutched her hands as they floated down. Then he released them and clutched her face instead, cupping its melancholy oval between his palms.

"Understand this, Mistress mine, I love you and want to serve you. You are in my blood; wherever I go I never can forget you. My dearest wish is to make you happy—this you must know. But equally you must know that I have needs of my own."

Grumpily she said, withdrawing her face, "Oh, I know that all right. And I know those needs will always come first with you. Whatever you say or pretend, you don't care a rap about me. You make that all too clear."

She moved ahead of him, shaking off the hand he put on her arm. He had a vision of himself running down a golden staircase and stretching out that same detaining hand to another girl. The indignity of having to repeat oneself, century after century.

"You're lying! You're faking! You're being cruel!" he said.

Gleaming, she turned.

"Am I? Then answer me this—aren't you already planning to leave Endehaaven and me again soon?"

He smoke his forehead.

He said inarticulately, "Look, you must try to stop this recrimination. Yes, yes, it's true I am thinking. . . . But I have to—I reproach myself. I could be kinder. But you shut yourself away when I come back, you don't welcome me——"

"Trust you to find excuses rather than face up to your own nature!" she said contemptuously, walking briskly into the garden. Amber and olive and umber, and sable of hair, she walked down the path, her outlines sharp in the winter air; in the perspectives of his mind she did not dwindle.

For some minutes he stood in the threshold, immobilized by antagonistic emotions.

Finally he pushed himself out into the sunlight.

She was in her favourite spot by the fjord, feeding an old badger from her hand. Only her increased attention to the badger suggested that she heard him approach.

His boscises twitched as he said, "If you will forgive a cliché, I apologize."

"I don't mind what you do."

Walking backwards and forwards behind her, he said, "When I was away, I heard some people talking. On Pyrylyn this was. They were discussing the mores of our matrimonial system."

"It's no business of theirs."

"Perhaps not. But what they said suggested a new line of thought to me."

She put the old badger back in his cage without comment.

"Are you listening, Mistress?"

"Do go on."

"Try to listen sympathetically. Consider all the history of galactic exploration—or even before that, consider the explorers of Earth in the pre-space age, men like Shackleton and so on. They were brave men, of course, but wouldn't it be strange if most of them only ventured where they did because the struggle at home was too much for them?"

He stopped. She had turned to him; the half-smile was whipped off his face by her look of fury.

"And you're trying to tell me that that's how you see yourself—a martyr? Derek, how you must hate me! Not only do you secretly go away, you secretly blame me because you go away. It doesn't matter that I tell you a thousand times I want you here—no, it's all my fault! I drive you away! That's what you tell your charming friends on Pyrylyn, isn't it? Oh, how you must hate me!"

Savagely he grasped her wrists. She screamed to me for aid and struggled. I came near but halted, playing my usual impotent part. He swore at her, bellowed her for to be silent, whereupon she cried the louder, shaking furiously in his arms, both of them tumultuous in their emotions.

He struck her across the face.

At once she was quiet. Her eyes closed, almost it would seem in ecstasy. Standing there, she had the pose of a woman offering herself.

"Go on, hit me! You want to hit me!" she whispered.

With the words, with the look of her, he too was altered. As if realizing for the first time her true nature, he dropped

his fists and stepped back, staring at her sick-mouthed. His
heel met no resistance. He twisted suddenly, spread out his
arms as if to fly, and fell over the cliff edge.

Her scream pursued him down.

Even as his body hit the waters of the fjord, it began to
change. A flurry of foam marked some sort of painful struggle beneath the surface. Then a seal plunged into view, dived
below the next wave, and swam towards open sea over which
already a freshening breeze blew.

Man in His Time

His absence

JANET WESTERMARK SAT WATCHING THE THREE MEN IN THE
OFFICE: THE ADMINISTRATOR WHO WAS ABOUT TO GO OUT
of her life, the behaviourist who was about to come into it,
and the husband whose life ran parallel to but insulated from
her own.

She was not the only one playing a watching game. The
behaviourist, whose name was Clement Stackpole, sat
hunched in his chair with his ugly strong hands clasped
round his knee, thrusting his intelligent and simian face forward, the better to regard his new subject, Jack Westermark.

The administrator of the Mental Research Hospital spoke
in a lively and engaged way. Typically, it was only Jack Westermark who seemed absent from the scene.

Your particular problem, restless

His hands upon his lap lay still, but he himself was restless,
though the restlessness seemed directed. It was as if he were
in another room with other people, Janet thought. She saw
that he caught her eye when in fact she was not entirely looking at him, and by the time she returned the glance, he was
gone, withdrawn.

"Although Mr. Stackpole has not dealt before with your
particular problem," the administrator was saying, "he has
had plenty of field experience. I know——"

"I'm sure we won't," Westermark said, folding his hands
and nodding his head slightly.

Smoothly, the administrator made a pencilled note of the
remark, scribbled the precise time beside it, and continued, "I

know Mr. Stackpole is too modest to say this, but he is a great man for working in with people——"

"If you feel it's necessary," Westermark said. "Though I've seen enough of your equipment for a while."

The pencil moved, the smooth voice proceeded. "Good. A great man for working in with people, and I'm sure you and Mrs. Westermark will soon find you are glad to have him around. Remember, he's there to help both of you."

Janet smiled, and said from the island of her chair, trying to smile at him and Stackpole, "I'm sure that everything will work——" She was interrupted by her husband, who rose to his feet, letting his hands drop to his sides and saying, turning slightly to address thin air, "Do you mind if I say good-bye to Nurse Simmons?"

Her voice no longer wavered

"Everything will be all right, I'm sure," she said hastily. And Stackpole nodded at her, conspiratorially agreeing to see her point of view.

"We'll all get on fine, Janet," he said. She was in the swift process of digesting that unexpected use of her Christian name, and the administrator was also giving her the sort of encouraging smile so many people had fed her since Westermark was pulled out of the ocean off Casablanca, when her husband, still having his lonely conversation with the air, said, "Of course, I should have remembered."

His right hand went half way to his forehead—or his heart? Janet wondered—and then dropped, as he added, "Perhaps she'll come round and see us some time." Now he turned and was smiling faintly at another vacant space with just the faintest nod of his head, as if slightly cajoling. "You'd like that, wouldn't you, Janet?"

She moved her head, instinctively trying to bring her eyes into his gaze as she replied vaguely, "Of course, darling." Her voice no longer wavered when she addressed his absent attention.

There was sunlight through which they could see each other

There was sunlight in one corner of the room, coming through the windows of a bay angled towards the sun. For a moment she caught, as she rose to her feet, her husband's profile with the sunlight behind it. It was thin and withdrawn. Intelligent: she had always thought him over-burdened with his intelligence, but now there was a lost look there, and she thought of the words of a psychiatrist who had been called in on the case earlier: "You must understand that the waking brain is perpetually lapped by the unconscious."

Lapped by the unconscious

Fighting the words away, she said, addressing the smile of the administrator—that smile which must have advanced his career so much—"You've helped me a lot. I couldn't have got through these months without you. Now we'd better go."

She heard herself chopping her words, fearing Westermark would talk across them, as he did: "Thank you for your help. If you find anything . . ."

Stackpole walked modestly over to Janet as the administrator rose and said, "Well, don't either of you forget us if you're in any kind of trouble."

"I'm sure we won't."

"And, Jack, we'd like you to come back here to visit us once a month for a personal check-up. Don't want to waste all our expensive equipment, you know, and you are our star —er, patient." He smiled rather tightly as he said it, glancing at the paper on his desk to check Westermark's answer. Westermark's back was already turned on him, Westermark was already walking slowly to the door, Westermark had said his good-byes, perched out on the lonely eminence of his existence.

Janet looked helplessly, before she could guard against it, at the administrator and Stackpole. She hated it that they were too professional to take note of what seemed her husband's breach of conduct. Stackpole looked kindly in a monkey way and took her arm with one of his thick hands.

"Shall we be off then? My car's waiting outside."

Not saying anything, nodding, thinking, and consulting watches

She nodded, not saying anything, thinking only, without the need of the administrator's notes to think it, "Oh yes, this was when he said, 'Do you mind if I say good-bye to Nurse' —who's-it?—Simpson?'" She was learning to follow her husband's footprints across the broken path of conversation. He was now out in the corridor, the door swinging to behind him, and to empty air the administrator was saying, "It's her day off today."

"You're good on your cues," she said, feeling the hand tighten on her arm. She politely brushed his fingers away, horrid Stackpole, trying to recall what had gone only four minutes before. Jack had said something to her; she couldn't remember, didn't speak, avoided eyes, put out her hand and shook the administrator's firmly.

"Thanks," she said.

"Au revoir to both of you," he replied firmly, glancing swiftly: watch, notes, her, the door. "Of course," he said. "If we find anything at all. We are very hopeful. . . ."

He adjusted his tie, looking at the watch again.

"Your husband has gone now, Mrs. Westermark," he said, his manner softening. He walked towards the door with her and added, "You have been wonderfully brave, and I do realise—we all realise—that you will have to go on being wonderful. With time, it should be easier for you; doesn't Shakespeare say in Hamlet that 'Use almost can change the stamp of nature'? May I suggest that you follow Stackpole's and my example and keep a little notebook and a strict check on the time?"

They saw her tiny hesitation, stood about her, two men round a personable woman, not entirely innocent of relish. Stackpole cleared his throat, smiled, said, "He can so easily feel cut off you know. It's essential that you of all people answer his questions, or he will feel cut off."

Always a pace ahead

"The children?" she asked.

"Let's see you and Jack well settled in at home again, say for a fortnight or so," the administrator said, "before we think about having the children back to see him."

"That way's better for them and Jack *and* you, Janet," Stackpole said. "Don't be glib," she thought; "consolation I need, God knows, but that's too facile." She turned her face away, fearing it looked too vulnerable these days.

In the corridor, the administrator said, as valediction, "I'm sure Grandma's spoiling them terribly, Mrs. Westermark, but worrying won't mend it, as the old saw says."

She smiled at him and walked quickly away, a pace ahead of Stackpole.

Westermark sat in the back of the car outside the administrative block. She climbed in beside him. As she did so, he jerked violently back in his seat.

"Darling, what is it?" she asked. He said nothing.

Stackpole had not emerged from the building, evidently having a last word with the administrator. Janet took the moment to lean over and kiss her husband's cheek, aware as she did so that a phantom wife had already, from his viewpoint, done so. His response was a phantom to her.

"The countryside looks green," he said. His eyes were flickering over the grey concrete block opposite.

"Yes," she said.

Stackpole came bustling down the steps, apologising as he opened the car door, settled in. He let the clutch back too fast and they shot forward. Janet saw then the reason for Westermark's jerking backwards a short while before. Now the acceleration caught him again; his body was rolled helplessly back. As they drove along, he set one hand fiercely on the side grip, for his sway was not properly counterbalancing the movement of the car.

Once outside the grounds of the institute, they were in the country, still under a mid-August day.

His theories

Westermark, by concentrating, could bring himself to conform to some of the laws of the time continuum he had left. When the car he was in climbed up his drive (familiar, yet strange with the rhododendrons unclipped and no signs of children) and stopped by the front door, he sat in his seat for three and a half minutes before venturing to open his door. Then he climbed out and stood on the gravel, frowning down at it. Was it as real as ever, as material? Was there a slight glaze on it?—as if something shone through from the interior of the earth, shone through all things? Or was it that there was a screen between him and everything else? It was important to decide between the two theories, for he had to live under the discipline of one. What he hoped to prove was that the permeation theory was correct; that way he was merely one of the factors comprising the functioning universe, together with the rest of humanity. By the glaze theory, he was isolated not only from the rest of humanity but from the entire cosmos (except Mars?). It was early days yet; he had a deal of thinking to do, and new ideas would undoubtedly emerge after observation and cogitation. Emotion must not decide the issue; he must be detached. Revolutionary theories could well emerge from this—suffering.

He could see his wife by him, standing off in case they happened embarrassingly or painfully to collide. He smiled thinly at her through her glaze. He said, "I am, but I'd prefer not to talk." He stepped towards the house, noting the slippery feel of gravel that would not move under his tread until the world caught up. He said, "I've every respect for *The Guardian*, but I'd prefer not to talk at present."

Famous Astronaut Returns Home

As the party arrived, a man waited in the porch for them, ambushing Westermark's return home with a deprecatory smile. Hesitant but business-like, he came forward and looked interrogatively at the three people who had emerged from the car.

"Excuse me, you are Captain Jack Westermark, aren't you?"

He stood aside as Westermark seemed to make straight for him.

"I'm the psychology correspondent for *The Guardian*, if I might intrude for a moment."

Westermark's mother had opened the front door and stood there smiling welcome at him, one hand nervously up to her grey hair. Her son walked past her. The newspaper man stared after him.

Janet told him apologetically, "You'll have to excuse us. My husband did reply to you, but he's really not prepared to meet people yet."

"*When* did he reply, Mrs. Westermark? Before he heard what I had to say?"

"Well, naturally not—but his life stream. . . . I'm sorry, I can't explain."

"He really is living ahead of time, isn't he? Will you spare me a minute to tell me how you feel now the first shock is over?"

"You really must excuse me," Janet said, brushing past him. As she followed her husband into the house, she heard Stackpole say, "Actually, I read *The Guardian*, and perhaps I could help you. The Institute has given me the job of remaining with Captain Westermark. My name's Clement Stackpole —you may know my book, *Persistent Human Relations*, Methuen. But you must not say that Westermark is living ahead of time. That's quite incorrect. What you can say is that some of his psychological and physiological processes have somehow been transposed forward——"

"Ass!" she exclaimed to herself. She had paused by the threshold to catch some of his words. Now she whisked in.

Talk hanging in the air among the long watches of supper

Supper that evening had its discomforts, although Janet

Westermark and her mother-in-law achieved an air of melancholy gayety by bringing two Scandinavian candelabra, relics of a Copenhagen holiday, onto the table and surprising the two men with a gay-looking hors d'œvre. But the conversation was mainly like the hors d'œuvre, Janet thought: little tempting isolated bits of talk, not nourishing.

Mrs. Westermark senior had not yet got the hang of talking to her son, and confined her remarks to Janet, though she looked towards Jack often enough. "How are the children?" he asked her. Flustered by the knowledge that he was waiting a long while for her answer, she replied rather incoherently and dropped her knife.

To relieve the tension, Janet was cooking up a remark on the character of the administrator at the Mental Research Hospital, when Westermark said, "Then he is at once thoughtful and literate. Commendable and rare in men of his type. I got the impression, as you evidently did, that he was as interested in his job as in advancement. I suppose one might say one even *liked* him. But you know him better, Stackpole; what do you think of him?"

Crumbling bread to cover his ignorance of whom they were supposed to be conversing, Stackpole said, "Oh, I don't know; it's hard to say really," spinning out time, pretending not to squint at his watch.

"The administrator was quite a charmer, didn't you think, Jack?" Janet remarked—perhaps helping Stackpole as much as Jack.

"He looks as if he might make a slow bowler," Westermark said, with an intonation that suggested he was agreeing with something as yet unsaid.

"Oh, *him!*" Stackpole said. "Yes, he seems a satisfactory sort of chap on the whole."

"He quoted Shakespeare to me and thoughtfully told me where the quotation came from," Janet said.

"No thank you, Mother," Westermark said.

"I don't have much to do with him," Stackpole continued. "Though I have played cricket with him a time or two. He makes quite a good slow bowler."

"Are you really?" Westermark exclaimed.

That stopped them. Jack's mother looked helplessly about, caught her son's glazed eye, said, covering up, "Do have some more sauce, Jack, dear," recalled she had already had her answer, almost let her knife slide again, gave up trying to eat.

"I'm a batsman, myself," Stackpole said, as if bringing an old pneumatic drill to the new silence. When no answer

came, he doggedly went on, expounding on the game, the
pleasure of it. Janet sat and watched, a shade perplexed that
she was admiring Stackpole's performance and wondering at
her slight perplexity; then she decided that she had made up
her mind to dislike Stackpole, and immediately dissolved the
resolution. Was he not on their side? And even the strong
hairy hands became a little more acceptable when you
thought of them gripping the rubber of a bat handle; and the
broad shoulders swinging. . . . She closed her eyes momentarily, and tried to concentrate on what he was saying.

A batsman himself

Later, she met Stackpole on the upper landing. He had a
small cigar in his mouth, she had two pillows in her arms. He
stood in her way.

"Can I help at all, Janet?"

"I'm only making up a bed, Mr. Stackpole."

"Are you not sleeping in with your husband?"

"He would like to be on his own for a night or two, Mr.
Stackpole. I shall sleep in the children's room for the time
being."

"Then please permit me to carry the pillows for you. And
do please call me Clem. All my friends do."

Trying to be pleasanter, to unfreeze, to recall that Jack was
not moving her out of the bedroom permanently, she said,
"I'm sorry. It's just that we once had a terrier called Clem."
But it did not sound as she had wished it to do.

He put the pillows on Peter's blue bed, switched on the
bedside lamp, and sat on the edge of the bed, clutching his
cigar and puffing at it.

"This may be a bit embarrassing, but there's something I
feel I should say to you, Janet." He did not look at her. She
brought him an ashtray and stood by him.

"We feel your husband's mental health may be endan-
gered, although I hasten to assure you that he shows no signs
of losing his mental equilibrium beyond what we may call an
inordinate absorption in phenomena—and even there, we
cannot say, of course we can't, that his absorption is any
greater than one might expect. Except in the totally unprecedented circumstances, I mean. We must talk about this in the
next few days."

She waited for him to go on, not unamused by the play
with the cigar. Then he looked straight up at her and said,
"Frankly, Mrs. Westermark, we think it would help your husband if you could have sexual relations with him."

A little taken aback, she said, "Can you imagine——"
Correcting herself, she said, "That is for my husband to say.
I am not unapproachable."

She saw he had caught her slip. Playing a very straight bat,
he said, "I'm sure you're not, Mrs. Westermark."

With the light out, living, she lay in Peter's bed

She lay in Peter's bed with the light out. Certainly she
wanted him: pretty badly, now she allowed herself to dwell
on it. During the long months of the Mars expedition, while
she had stayed at home and he had got farther from home,
while he actually had existence on that other planet, she had
been chaste. She had looked after the children and driven
round the countryside and enjoyed writing those articles for
women's magazines and being interviewed on TV when the
ship was reported to have left Mars on its homeward journey.
She had been, in part, dormant.

Then came the news, kept from her at first, that there was
confusion in communicating with the returning ship. A sensational tabloid broke the secrecy by declaring that the nine-
man crew had all gone mad. And the ship had overshot its
landing area, crashing into the Atlantic. Her first reaction had
been a purely selfish one—no, not selfish, but from the self:
He'll never lie with me again. And infinite love and sorrow.

At his rescue, the only survivor, miraculously unmaimed,
her hope had revived. Since then, it had remained embalmed,
as he was embalmed in time. She tried to visualise love as it
would be now, with everything happening first to him, before
she had begun to—— With his movement of pleasure even
before she—— No, it wasn't possible! But of course it was, if
they worked it out first intellectually; then if she just lay flat.
. . . But what she was trying to visualise, all she could visualise, was no love-making, merely a formal prostration to the
exigencies of glands and time flow.

She sat up in bed, longing for movement, freedom. She
jumped out and opened the lower window; there was still a
tang of cigar smoke in the dark room.

If they worked it out intellectually

Within a couple of days, they had fallen into routine. It
was as if the calm weather, perpetuating mildness, aided
them. They had to be careful to move slowly through doors,
keeping to the left, so as not to bump into each other—a tray
of drinks was dropped before they agreed on that. They de-

vised simple knocking systems before using the bathroom. They conversed in bulletins that did not ask questions unless questions were necessary. They walked slightly apart. In short, they made detours round each other's lives.

"It's really quite easy as long as one is careful," Mrs. Westermark senior said to Janet. "And dear Jack is *so* patient!"

"I even get the feeling he likes the situation."

"Oh, my dear, how could he *like* such an unfortunate predicament?"

"Mother, you realise how we all exist together, don't you? No, it sounds too terrible—I daren't say it."

"Now don't you start getting silly ideas. You've been very brave, and this is not the time for us to be getting upset, just as things are going well. If you have any worries, you must tell Clem. That's what he's here for."

"I know."

"Well then."

She saw Jack walk in the garden. As she looked, he glanced up, smiled, said something to himself, stretched out a hand, withdrew it, and went, still smiling, to sit on one end of the seat on the lawn. Touched, Janet hurried over to the french windows, to go and join him.

She paused. Already, she saw ahead, saw her sequence of actions, for Jack had already sketched them into the future. She would go onto the lawn, call his name, smile, and walk over to him when he smiled back. Then they would stroll together to the seat and sit down, one at each end.

The knowledge drained all spontaneity from her. She might have been working a treadmill, for what she was about to do had already been done as far as Jack was concerned, with his head's start in time. Then if she did not go, if she mutinied, turned back to the discussion of the day's chores with her mother-in-law. . . . That left Jack mouthing like a fool on the lawn, indulging in a fantasy there was no penetrating. Let him do that, let Stackpole see; then they could drop this theory about Jack's being ahead of time and would have to treat him for a more normal sort of hallucinatory insanity. He would be safe in Clem's hands.

But Jack's actions proved that she would go out there. It was insane for her not to go out there. Insane? To disobey a law of the universe was impossible, not insane. Jack was not disobeying—he had simply tumbled over a law that nobody knew was there before the first expedition to Mars; certainly they had discovered something more momentous than anyone had expected, and more unforeseen. And she had lost——

No, she hadn't lost yet! She ran out onto the lawn, calling to him, letting the action quell the confusion in her mind.

And in the repeated event there was concealed a little freshness, for she remembered how his smile, glimpsed through the window, had held a special warmth, as if he sought to reassure her. What had he said? That was lost. She walked over to the seat and sat beside him.

He had been saving a remark for the statutory and unvarying time lapse.

"Don't worry, Janet," he said. "It could be worse."

"How?" she asked, but he was already answering: "We could be a day apart. 3.3077 minutes at least allows us a measure of communication."

"It's wonderful how philosophical you are about it," she said. She was alarmed at the sarcasm in her tone.

"Shall we have a talk together now?"

"Jack, I've been wanting to have a private talk with you for some time."

"I?"

The tall beeches that sheltered the garden on the north side were so still that she thought, "They will look exactly the same for him as for me."

He delivered a bulletin, looking at his watch. His wrists were thin. He appeared frailer than he had done when they left hospital. "I am aware, my darling, how painful this must be for you. We are both isolated from the other by this amazing shift of temporal function, but at least I have the consolation of experiencing the new phenomenon, whereas you——"

"I?"

Talking of interstellar distances

"I was going to say that you are stuck with the same old world all of mankind has always known, but I suppose you don't see it that way." Evidently a remark of hers had caught up with him, for he added inconsequentially, "I've wanted a private talk with you."

Janet bit off something she was going to say, for he raised a finger irritably and said, "Please time your statements, so that we do not talk at cross purposes. Confine what you have to say to essentials. Really, darling, I'm surprised you don't do as Clem suggests, and make notes of what is said at what time."

"That—I just wanted—we can't act as if we were a board meeting. I want to know your feelings, how you are, what you are thinking, so that I can help you, so that eventually you will be able to live a normal life again."

He was timing it so that he answered almost at once, "I am not suffering from any mental illness, and I have completely recovered my physical health after the crash. There is no reason to foresee that my perceptions will ever lapse back into phase with yours. They have remained an unfluctuating 3.3077 minutes ahead of terrestrial time ever since our ship left the surface of Mars."

He paused. She thought, "It is now about 11.03 by my watch, and there is so much I long to say. But it's 11.06 and a bit by *his* time, and he always knows I can't say anything. It's such an effort of endurance, talking across this three and a bit minutes; we might just as well be talking across an interstellar distance."

Evidently he too had lost the thread of the exercise, for he smiled and stretched out a hand, holding it in the air. Janet looked round. Clem Stackpole was coming out towards them with a tray full of drinks. He set it carefully down on the lawn, and picked up a martini, the stem of which he slipped between Jack's fingers.

"Cheers!" he said, smiling, and, "Here's your tipple," giving Janet her gin and tonic. He had brought himself a bottle of pale ale.

"Can you make my position clearer to Janet, Clem? She does *not* seem to understand it yet."

Angrily, she turned to the behaviourist. "This was meant to be a private talk, Mr. Stackpole, between my husband and myself."

"Sorry you're not getting on too well, then. Perhaps I can help sort you out a bit. It is difficult, I know."

3.3077

Powerfully, he wrenched the top off the beer bottle and poured the liquid into the glass. Sipping, he said, "We have always been used to the idea that everything moves forward in time at the same rate. We speak of the course of time, presuming it only has one rate of flow. We've assumed, too, that anything living on another planet in any other part of our universe might have the same rate of flow. In other words, although we've long been accustomed to some oddities of time, thanks to relativity theories, we have accustomed ourselves, perhaps, to certain errors of thinking. Now we're going to have to think differently. You follow me."

"Perfectly."

"The universe is by no means the simple box our predecessors imagined. It may be that each planet is encased in its own time field, just as it is in its own gravitational field. From the evidence, it seems that Mars's time field is 3.3077 minutes ahead of ours on Earth. We deduce this from the fact that your husband and the eight other men with him on Mars experienced no sensation of temporal difference among themselves, and were unaware that anything was untoward until they were away from Mars and attempted to get into communication again with Earth, when the temporal discrepancy at once showed up. Your husband is still living in Mars time. Unfortunately, the other members of the crew did not survive the crash; but we can be sure that if they did, they too would suffer from the same effect. That's clear, isn't it?"

"Entirely. But I still cannot see why this effect, if it is as you say——"

"It's not what *I* say, Janet, but the conclusion arrived at by much cleverer men than I." He smiled as he said that, adding parenthetically, "Not that we don't develop and even alter our conclusions every day."

"Then why was a similar effect not noticed when the Russians and Americans returned from the moon?"

"We don't know. There's so much we don't know. We *surmise* that because the moon is a satellite of Earth's, and thus within its gravitational field, there is no temporal discrepancy. But until we have more data, until we can explore further, we know so little, and can only speculate so much. It's like trying to estimate the runs of an entire inning when only one over has been bowled. After the expedition gets back from Venus, we shall be in a much better position to start theorising."

"*What* expedition to Venus?" she asked, shocked.

"It may not leave for a year yet, but they're speeding up the programme. That will bring us really invaluable data."

Future time with its uses and abuses

She started to say, "But after this surely they won't be fool enough——" Then she stopped. She knew they would be fool enough. She thought of Peter saying, "I'm going to be a spaceman too. *I* want to be the first man on Saturn!"

The men were looking at their watches. Westermark transferred his gaze to the gravel to say, "This figure of 3.3077 is surely not a universal constant. It may vary—I think it will vary—from planetary body to planetary body. My private opinion is that it is bound to be connected with solar activity in some way. If that is so, then we may find that the men returning from Venus will be perceiving on a continuum slightly in arrears of Earth time."

He stood up suddenly, looking dismayed, the absorption gone from his face.

"That's a point that hadn't occurred to me," Stackpole said, making a note. "If the expedition to Venus is primed with these points beforehand, we should have no trouble about organising their return. Ultimately, this confusion will be sorted out, and I've no doubt that it will eventually vastly enrich the culture of mankind. The possibilities are of such enormity that . . ."

"It's awful! You're all crazy!" Janet exclaimed. She jumped up and hurried off towards the house.

Or then again

Jack began to move after her towards the house. By his watch, which showed Earth time, it was 11.18 and twelve seconds; he thought, not for the first time, that he would invest in another watch, which would be strapped to his right wrist and show Martian time. No, the one on his left wrist should show Martian time, for that was the wrist he principally consulted and the time by which he lived, even when going through the business of communicating with the earth-bound human race.

He realized he was now moving ahead of Janet, by her reckoning. It would be interesting to have someone ahead of *him* in perception; then he would wish to converse, would want to go to the labour of it. Although it would rob him of the sensation that he was perpetually first in the universe, first everywhere, with everything dewy in that strange light— Marslight! He'd call it that, till he had it classified, the romantic vision preceding the scientific, with a touch of the grand permissible before the steadying discipline closed in. Or then again, suppose they were wrong in their theories, and the perceptual effect was some freak of the long space journey itself; supposing time were quantal. . . . Supposing *all* time were quantal. After all, ageing was a matter of steps, not a smooth progress, for much of the inorganic world as for the organic.

Now he was standing quite still on the lawn. The glaze was coming through the grass, making it look brittle, almost

tingeing each blade with a tiny spectrum of light. If his perceptual time were further ahead than it was now, would the
Marslight be stronger, the Earth more translucent? How
beautiful it would look! After a longer star journey one
would return to a cobweb of a world, centuries behind one in
perceptual time, a mere embodiment of light, a prism. Hun-
grily, he visualised it. But they needed more knowledge.

Suddenly he thought, "If I could get on the Venus expedition! If the Institute's right, I'd be perhaps six, say five and a
half—no, one can't say—but I'd be ahead of Venerean time.
I *must* go. I'd be valuable to them. I only have to volunteer,
surely."

He did not notice Stackpole touch his arm in cordial fashion and go past him into the house. He stood looking at the
ground and through it, to the stoney vales of Mars and the
unguessable landscapes of Venus.

The figures move

Janet had consented to ride into town with Stackpole. He
was collecting his cricket shoes, which had been restudded;
she thought she might buy a roll of film for her camera. The
children would like photos of her and Daddy together. Standing together.

As the car ran beside trees, their shadows flickered red and
green before her vision. Stackpole held the wheel very capa-
bly, whistling under his breath. Strangely, she did not resent a
habit she would normally have found irksome, taking it as a
sign that he was not entirely at his ease.

"I have an awful feeling you now understand my husband
better than I do," she said.

He did not deny it. "Why do you feel that?"

"I believe he does not mind the terrible isolation he must
be experiencing."

"He's a brave man."

Westermark had been home a week now. Janet saw that
each day they were more removed from each other, as he
spoke less and stood frequently as still as a statue, gazing at
the ground raptly. She thought of something she had once
been afraid to utter aloud to her mother-in-law; but with
Clem Stackpole she was safer.

"You know why we manage to exist in comparative
harmony," she said. He was slowing the car, half-looking at
her. "We only manage to exist by banishing all events from
our lives, all children, all seasons. Otherwise we'd be faced at

every moment with the knowledge of how much at odds we really are."

Catching the note in her voice, Stackpole said soothingly, "You are every bit as brave as he is, Janet."

"Damn being brave. What I can't bear is—nothing!"

Seeing the sign by the side of the road, Stackpole glanced into his driving mirror and changed gear. The road was deserted in front as well as behind. He whistled through his teeth again, and Janet felt compelled to go on talking.

"We've already interfered with time too much—all of us, I mean. Time is a European invention. Goodness knows how mixed up in it we are going to get if—well, if this goes on." She was irritated by the lack of her usual coherence.

As Stackpole spoke next, he was pulling the car into a layby, stopping it by overhanging bushes. He turned to her, smiling tolerantly. "Time was God's invention, if you believe in God, as I prefer to do. We observe it, tame it, exploit it where possible."

"Exploit it!"

"You mustn't think of the future as if we were all wading knee deep in treacle or something." He laughed briefly, resting his hands on the steering wheel. "What lovely weather it is! I was wondering—on Sunday I'm playing cricket over in the village. Would you like to come and watch the match? And perhaps we could have tea somewhere afterwards."

All events, all children, all seasons

She had a letter next morning from Jane, her five-year-old daughter, and it made her think. All the letter said was: "Dear Mummy, Thank you for the dollies. With love from Jane," but Janet knew the labour that had gone into the inch-high letters. How long could she bear to leave the children away from their home and her care?

As soon as the thought emerged, she recalled that during the previous evening she had told herself nebulously that if there was going to be "anything" with Stackpole, it was as well the children would be out of the way—purely, she now realised, for her convenience and for Stackpole's. She had not thought then about the children; she had thought about Stackpole who, despite the unexpected delicacy he had shown, was not a man she cared for.

"And another intolerably immoral thought," she muttered unhappily to the empty room, "what alternative have I to Stackpole?"

She knew Westermark was in his study. It was a cold day,

too cold and damp for him to make his daily parade round the garden. She knew he was sinking deeper into isolation, she longed to help, she feared to sacrifice herself to that isolation, longed to stay outside it, in life. Dropping the letter, she held her head in her hands, closing her eyes as in the curved bone of her skull she heard all her possible courses of action jar together, future lifelines that annihilated each other.

As Janet stood transfixed, Westermark's mother came into the room.

"I was looking for you," she said. "You're so unhappy, my dear, aren't you?"

"Mother, people always try and hide from others how they suffer. Does everyone do it?"

"You don't have to hide it from me—chiefly, I suppose, because you can't."

"But I don't know how much *you* suffer, and it ought to work both ways. Why do we do this awful covering up? What are we afraid of—pity or derision?"

"Help, perhaps."

"Help! Perhaps you're right. . . . That's a disconcerting thought."

They stood there staring at each other, until the older woman said, awkwardly, "We don't often talk like this, Janet."

"No." She wanted to say more. To a stranger in a train, perhaps she would have done; here, she could not deliver.

Seeing nothing more was to be said on that subject, Mrs. Westermark said, "I was going to tell you, Janet, that I thought perhaps it would be better if the children didn't come back here while things are as they are. If you want to go and see them and stay with them at your parents' house, I can look after Jack and Mr. Stackpole for a week. I don't think Jack wants to see them."

"That's very kind, Mother. I'll see. I promised Clem—well, I told Mr. Stackpole that perhaps I'd go and watch him play cricket tomorrow afternoon. It's not important, of course, but I did say—anyhow, I might drive over and see the children on Monday, if you could hold the fort."

"You've still plenty of time if you feel like going today. I'm sure Mr. Stackpole will understand your maternal feelings."

"I'd prefer to leave it till Monday," Janet said—a little distantly, for she suspected now the motive behind her mother-in-law's suggestion.

Where the Scientific American *did not reach*

Jack Westermark put down the *Scientific American* and stared at the table top. With his right hand, he felt the beat of his heart. In the magazine was an article about him, illustrated with photographs of him taken at the Research Hospital. This thoughtful article was far removed from the sensational pieces that had appeared elsewhere, the shallow things that referred to him as The Man That Has Done More Than Einstein To Wreck Our Cosmic Picture; and for that very reason it was the more startling, and presented some aspects of the matter that Westermark himself had not considered.

As he thought over its conclusions, he rested from the effort of reading terrestrial books, and Stackpole sat by the fire, smoking a cigar and waiting to take Westermark's dictation. Even reading a magazine represented a feat in space-time, a collaboration, a conspiracy. Stackpole turned the pages at timed intervals, Westermark read when they lay flat. He was unable to turn them when, in their own narrow continuum, they were not being turned; to his fingers, they lay under the jelly-like glaze, that visual hallucination that represented an unconquerable cosmic inertia.

The inertia gave a special shine to the surface of the table as he stared into it and probed into his own mind to determine the truths of the *Scientific American* article.

The writer of the article began by considering the facts and observing that they tended to point towards the existence of "local times" throughout the universe; and that if this were so, a new explanation might be forthcoming for the recession of the galaxies and different estimates arrived at for the age of the universe (and of course for its complexity). He then proceeded to deal with the problem that vexed other writers on the subject; namely, why, if Westermark lost Earth time on Mars, he had not reciprocally lost Mars time back on Earth. This, more than anything, pointed to the fact that "local times" were not purely mechanistic but to some extent at least a psycho-biological function.

In the table top, Westermark saw himself being asked to travel again to Mars, to take part in a second expedition to those continents of russet sand where the fabric of space-time was in some mysterious and insuperable fashion 3.3077 minutes ahead of Earth norm. Would his interior clock leap forward again? What then of the sheen on things earthly? And what would be the effect of gradually drawing away from the iron laws under which, since its scampering pleistocene infancy, humankind had lived?

Impatiently he thrust his mind forward to imagine the day when Earth harboured many local times, gleaned from voyages across the vacancies of space; those vacancies lay across time, too, and that little-understood concept (McTaggart had denied its external reality, hadn't he?) would come to lie within the grasp of man's understanding. Wasn't that the ultimate secret, to be able to understand the flux in which existence is staged, as a dream is staged in the primitive reaches of the mind?

And—— But—— Would not that day bring the annihilation of Earth's local time? That was what he had started. It could only mean that "local time" was not a product of planetary elements; there the writer of the *Scientific American* article had not dared to go far enough; local time was entirely a product of the psyche. That dark innermost thing that could keep accurate time even while a man lay unconscious was a mere provincial; but it could be educated to be a citizen of the universe. He saw that he was the first of a new race, unimaginable in the wildest mind a few months previously. He was independent of the enemy that, more than Death, menaced contemporary man: Time. Locked within him was an entirely new potential. Superman had arrived.

Painfully, Superman stirred in his seat. He sat so wrapt for so long that his limbs grew stiff and dead without his noticing it.

Universal thoughts may occur if one times carefully enough one's circumbendibus about a given table

"Dictation," he said, and waited impatiently until the command had penetrated backwards to the limbo by the fire where Stackpole sat. What he had to say was so terribly important—yet it had to wait on these people. . . .

As was his custom, he rose and began to walk round the table, speaking in phrases quickly delivered. This was to be the testament to the new way of life. . . .

"Consciousness is not expendable but concurrent. . . . There may have been many time nodes at the beginning of the human race. . . . The mentally deranged often revert to different time rates. For some, a day seems to stretch on for ever. . . . We know by experience that for children time is seen in the convex mirror of consciousness, enlarged and distorted beyond its focal point. . . ." He was momentarily irritated by the scared face of his wife appearing outside the study window, but he brushed it away and continued.

". . . its focal point. . . . Yet man in his ignorance has

persisted in pretending time was some sort of uni-directional flow, and homogenous at that . . . despite the evidence to the contrary. . . . Our conception of ourselves—no, this erroneous conception has become a basic life assumption. . . ."

Daughters of daughters

Westermark's mother was not given to metaphysical speculation, but as she was leaving the room, she turned and said to her daughter-in-law, "You know what I sometimes think? Jack is so strange, I wonder at nights if men and women aren't getting more and more apart in thought and in their ways with every generation—you know, almost like separate species. My generation made a great attempt to bring the two sexes together in equality and all the rest, but it seems to have come to nothing."

"Jack will get better." Janet could hear the lack of confidence in her own voice.

"I thought the same thing—about men and women getting wider apart I mean—when my husband was killed."

Suddenly all Janet's sympathy was gone. She had recognised a familiar topic drifting onto the scene, knew well the careful tone that ironed away all self-pity as her mother-in-law said, "Bob was dedicated to speed, you know. That was what killed him really, not the fool backing into the road in front of him."

"No blame was attached to your husband," Janet said. "You should try not to let it worry you still."

"You see the connection though. . . . This progress thing. Bob so crazy to get round the next bend first, and now Jack. . . . Oh well, there's nothing a woman can do."

She closed the door behind her. Absently, Janet picked up the message from the next generation of women: "Thank you for the dollies."

The resolves and the sudden risks involved

He was their father. Perhaps Jane and Peter should come back, despite the risks involved. Anxiously, Janet stood there, moving herself with a sudden resolve to tackle Jack straight away. He was so irritable, so unapproachable, but at least she could observe how busy he was before interrupting him.

As she slipped into the side hall and made for the back door, she heard her mother-in-law call her. "Just a minute!" she answered.

The sun had broken through, sucking moisture from the

damp garden. It was now unmistakably autumn. She rounded the corner of the house, stepped round the rose bed, and looked into her husband's study.

Shaken, she saw he leaned half over the table. His hands were over his face, blood ran between his fingers and dripped onto an open magazine on the table top. She was aware of Stackpole sitting indifferently beside the electric fire.

She gave a small cry and ran round the house again, to be met at the back door by Mrs. Westermark.

"Oh, I was just—— Janet, what is it?"

"Jack, Mother! He's had a stroke or something terrible!"

"But how do you know?"

"Quick, we must phone the hospital—I must go to him."

Mrs. Westermark took Janet's arm. "Perhaps we'd better leave it to Mr. Stackpole, hadn't we? I'm afraid——"

"Mother, we must do what we can. I know we're amateurs. Please let me go."

"No, Janet, we're—it's *their* world. I'm frightened. They'll come if they want us." She was gripping Janet in her fright. Their wild eyes stared momentarily at each other as if seeing something else, and then Janet snatched herself away. "I must go to him," she said.

She hurried down the hall and pushed open the study door. Her husband stood now at the far end of the room by the window, while blood streamed from his nose.

"Jack!" she exclaimed. As she ran towards him, a blow from the empty air struck her on the forehead, so that she staggered aside, falling against a bookcase. A shower of smaller volumes from the upper shelf fell on her and round her. Exclaiming, Stackpole dropped his notebook and ran round the table to her. Even as he went to her aid, he noted the time from his watch: 10.24.

Aid after 10.24 and the tidiness of bed

Westermark's mother appeared in the doorway.

"Stay where you are," Stackpole shouted, "or there will be more trouble! Janet, you see what you've done. Get out of here, will you? Jack, I'm right with you—God knows what you've felt, isolated without aid for three and a third minutes!" Angrily, he went across and stood within arm's length of his patient. He threw his handkerchief down onto the table.

"Mr. Stackpole——" Westermark's mother said tentatively from the door, an arm round Janet's waist.

He looked back over his shoulder only long enough to say,

"Get towels! Phone the Research Hospital for an ambulance and tell them to be here right away."

By midday, Westermark was tidily in bed upstairs and the ambulance staff, who had treated him for what after all was only nosebleed, had left. Stackpole, as he turned from closing the front door, eyed the two women.

"I feel it is my duty to warn you," he said heavily, "that another incident such as this might well prove fatal. This time we escaped very lightly. If anything else of this sort happens, I shall feel obliged to recommend to the board that Mr. Westermark is moved back to the hospital."

Current way to define accidents

"He wouldn't want to go," Janet said. "Besides, you are being absurd; it was entirely an accident. Now I wish to go upstairs and see how he is."

"Just before you go, may I point out that what happened was *not* an accident—or not as we generally define accidents, since you saw the results of your interference through the study window before you entered. Where you were to blame——"

"But that's absurd——" both women began at once. Janet went on to say, "I never would have rushed into the room as I did had I not seen through the window that he was in trouble."

"What you saw was the result on your husband of your later interference."

In something like a wail, Westermark's mother said, "I don't understand any of this. What did Janet bump into when she ran in?"

"She ran, Mrs. Westermark, into the spot where her husband had been standing 3.3077 minutes earlier. Surely by now you have grasped this elementary business of time inertia?"

When they both started speaking at once, he stared at them until they stopped and looked at him. Then he said, "We had better go into the living room. Speaking for myself, I would like a drink."

He helped himself, and not until his hand was round a glass of whisky did he say, "Now, without wishing to lecture to you ladies, I think it is high time you both realised that you are not living in the old safe world of classical mechanics ruled over by a god invented by eighteenth-century enlightenment. All that has happened here is perfectly rational, but if you are going to pretend it is beyond your female understandings——"

"Mr. Stackpole," Janet said sharply. "Can you please keep to the point without being insulting? Will you tell me why what happened was not an accident? I understand now that when I looked through the study window I saw my husband suffering from a collision that to him had happened three and something minutes before and to me would not happen for another three and something minutes, but at that moment I was so startled that I forgot——"

"No, no, your figures are wrong. The *total* time lapse is only 3.3077 minutes. When you saw your husband, he had been hit half that time—1.65385 minutes—ago, and there was another 1.65385 minutes to go before you completed the action by bursting into the room and striking him."

"But she *didn't* strike him!" the older woman cried.

Firmly, Stackpole diverted his attention long enough to reply. "She struck him at 10.24 Earthtime, which equals 10.20 plus about 36 seconds Mars or his time, which equals 9.59 or whatever Neptune time, which equals 156 and a half Sirius time. It's a big universe, Mrs. Westermark! You will remain confused as long as you continue to confuse event with time. May I suggest you sit down and have a drink?"

"Leaving aside the figures," Janet said, returning to the attack—loathsome opportunist the man was—"how can you say that what happened was no accident? You are not claiming I injured my husband deliberately, I hope? What you say suggests that I was powerless from the moment I saw him through the window."

" 'Leaving aside the figures . . .' " he quoted. "That's where your responsibility lies. What you saw through the window was the result of your act; it was by then inevitable that you should complete it, for it had already been completed."

Through the window, draughts of time blow

"I can't understand!" she clutched her forehead, gratefully accepting a cigarette from her mother-in-law, while shrugging off her consolatory "Don't try to understand, dear!" "Supposing when I had seen Jack's nose bleeding, I had looked at my watch and thought, 'It's 10.20 or whenever it was, and he may be suffering from my interference, so I'd better not go in,' and I *hadn't* gone in? Would his nose then miraculously have healed?"

"Of course not. You take such a mechanistic view of the universe. Cultivate a mental approach, try and live in your own century! You could not think what you suggest because that is not in your nature: just as it is not in your nature to consult your watch intelligently, just as you always 'leave aside the figures,' as you say. No, I'm not being personal; it's all very feminine and appealing in a way. What I'm saying is that if *before* you looked into the window you had been a person to think, 'However I see my husband now, I must recall he has the additional experience of the next 3.3077 minutes,' then you could have looked in and seen him unharmed, and you would not have come bursting in as you did."

She drew on her cigarette, baffled and hurt. "You're saying I'm a danger to my own husband."

"*You're* saying that."

"God, how I hate men!" she exclaimed. "You're so bloody logical, so bloody smug!"

He finished his whisky and set the glass down on a table beside her so that he leant close. "You're upset just now," he said.

"Of course I'm upset! What do you think?" She fought a desire to cry or slap his face. She turned to Jack's mother, who gently took her wrist.

"Why don't you go off straight away and stay with the children for the weekend, darling? Come back when you feel like it. Jack will be all right and I can look after him—as much as he wants looking after."

She glanced about the room.

"I will. I'll pack right away. They'll be glad to see me." As she passed Stackpole on the way out, she said bitterly, "At least *they* won't be worrying about the local time on Sirius!"

"They may," said Stackpole, imperturbably from the middle of the room, "have to one day."

All events, all children, all seasons

Other SIGNET Science Fiction
You Will Enjoy